The Dark One

BOOK I
THE LOST & CURSED

A NOVEL BY
RINA S. MAMOON

ISBN: 978-1-7752440-9-7

Author Website: rinasmamoon.ca

Acknowledgements

I like to thank my family and friends for their love and support. Especially Michael—I keep my ears open whenever you want to talk. Thanks for letting me share this four-year-old secret.

Thank you, Bret, for your guidance and understanding. I apologize that we could not continue working together on this. And I also wish to thank the anonymous editor for the excellent advice. If not for you, this project would not be where it is today.

And thank you, dear reader, for taking the time to read this book. I hope you enjoyed reading it as much as I enjoyed writing it.

Table of Contents

Chapter One

The Guide

A lone bell chimed within the darkness. The resonating sound echoed in her ears, pulling her from a deep sleep. Opening her eyes, she found her vision to be foggy at first. Her sight began to clear, but she did not recognize her surroundings. Only darkness and silence filled the old crypt. Where was she? More importantly, who was she? She could not find the answer within her hazy mind. Still groggy, she felt like going back to sleep.

"Mara, wake up."

A woman's voice jolted her awake. She shot up to a seated position and rubbed her eyes. The first thing she saw was a woman clad in armour. The dark silver metal clung tight to her body. Glowing blue gems and golden trimmings decorated her armour. Underneath the metal plating was a tight black suit. A red hood with gold hems adorned her head. The fabric cascaded down her back like a cape. The same red cloth covered the sides of her legs. Her face possessed seven blue eyes that glowed in the darkness. One of the eyes was larger and sat on her forehead. And no mouth could be seen on her face.

Now given a name, Mara rose to her feet. She glanced around, remaining befuddled. Her eyes finally fell onto the armoured creature.

"Your name is Mara," said the female creature.

The name seemed familiar. Mara opened her mouth to repeat it. "Mara..." It also felt like her first time speaking.

"You must come with me," the armoured woman told her. "We have very little time."

The creature walked into the darkness. Mara began to follow. After taking a few steps, she saw an object thrown towards her. Catching it, Mara obtained a gold-hemmed black hood and a mask. Pale fur lined the hood. Attached to it was a long black cape with holes and tears at the bottom.

"Go ahead. Put it on," the woman instructed.

Mara donned the hood and used the mask to cover her face.

The creature nodded. "Good, this is the first step."

Mara gawked at the strange woman in confusion.

"What is it?" After a moment of silence, the creature introduced herself. "I am the Watcher. I will be your guide to lead you out of the darkness. Once you leave this place, you must not show anyone your face."

Mara grew baffled. What sort of advice was that?

"I understand if you are confused," said the Watcher. "I am sorry you lost all of your memories." The guide turned and walked away. "Come, there is very little time remaining."

Mara followed her into the darkness, unsure where they were going or what was happening. The torches on the stone halls offered little light. The small flames were almost choked off by the dark. Mara still had no idea why she was down here, or how she ended up in this place.

"Please move quickly," the Watcher instructed. "We are not alone."

An echoing growl stopped Mara in her tracks. She looked behind but could see nothing in the darkness. The mysterious guide also stopped.

"Do not get caught," the guide recommended, and then moved forward.

Walking by some steel bars, Mara spotted a crouching figure. Careful observation revealed that it was inhuman. It watched Mara and made a guttural sound. Standing up, it sprinted away.

"Stay quiet," the Watcher said. "It has poor eyesight, but can hear you. I am speaking to you with telepathy. Only you can hear me."

Mara was unfamiliar with the word, telepathy, but it more or less explained how the guide could speak without a mouth.

The Watcher disappeared into the darkness, leaving Mara alone. She entered a room with three exits, not knowing which path to take. She glanced at the door on her right and entered. Hearing more growls, Mara froze. Her heart began to pound. She could feel something breathing down her neck. Her eyes widened. Turning around, Mara saw the deformed and grotesque face of a monster.

All she could do was run, her heart thumping. Mara gasped for air as she ran from her pursuer. She saw four bulging white eyes and a bird-like face. It had long black claws on slender fingers, and an emaciated body with skin stretched across its bones. It wore dirty and bloody brown rags, with a tattered cloth around its thin waist, and a hood on its head. After a moment, Mara stopped and looked behind. The creature stopped pursuing her.

This maze had many dead-ends, making Mara retrace her footsteps often. While wandering the labyrinth, she found a locked gate. Hearing the growls once more, she spun around and saw the creature approaching her. Mara froze and held her breath. The creature stopped. It glanced around, seemingly incapable of seeing her. Then it turned and walked away. A small brass key fell from its rags. She stared at the shiny object and remained still, waiting until the creature walked back into the darkness.

Mara dashed for the key, then ran back to the gate. While fumbling with the lock, she could hear the creature returning. Once the gate opened, she dashed through. The monster tried to grab her, but the gate slammed into its face. It cried out in pain. Mara stared at it briefly before fleeing.

Still hearing the creature's cries, Mara ran towards the light. Once she reached the end, she saw the Watcher again.

"Follow the path to Ozin Village," the guide instructed.

The armoured woman disappeared, leaving Mara to her own devices.

* * *

Mara meandered along a path down a mountain. She lifted her gaze to deciduous trees painted with golden colours. Dying leaves fell to the ground as a chill hung in the air. Birds sang from the bushes, dressed in grey with black caps. They spotted Mara, chirping to warn the others of her presence. The tiny birds all flitted away. Mara stopped at a signpost. The name, Ozin Village, was carved on a piece of wood. Walking further, she saw the village and stopped.

A low growl bellowed from her stomach. Mara could not recall the last time she ate. She spotted a nearby house. It seemed deserted. Approaching it, Mara discovered the door unlocked. Upon inviting herself, she found a cooking pot over a small hearth. Mara approached it and could smell something edible. She removed the lid and peered inside. While doing this, she was struck in the back of the head and knocked out cold.

* * *

"Hey, you awake yet?" asked a woman. "Wake up."

Mara opened her eyes to find herself bound to a chair, and her hands tied behind her back. She lifted her gaze to a group of people watching her apprehensively. Mara wore ratty clothes darkened by dirt and grime as dried blood stained her shirt and pants. Mara was unsure where the stains came from or if the blood belonged to her. She also wore mismatched gloves and dirty knee-high boots. And a worn leather belt wrapped around her hips. The hood cast a shadow over her face, as the mask concealed the rest from below the eyes.

A woman stepped forward from the crowd. "Ah, you woke up."

Mara lifted her gaze to her. The woman appeared to be in her thirties. Red braided hair went down to the middle of her back with some loose strands in the front. Her pale face was a little on the thin side with rosy cheeks and steel-blue eyes. Her nose was small but round at the nostrils. The red-haired woman also possessed thin lips.

Steel plating covered her left shoulder and both legs. She wore a tanned shirt with a brown open-bust leather cuirass. She had her dark brown sleeves rolled up above the elbows. Leather gloves covered her forearms with the left one adorned in steel. Black pants clung tightly to her figure. Tanned stockings rose past the knees, and she also wore brown leather knee-high boots. Strapped on her right hip was a large black book. The strong-looking woman was easy on the eyes.

"You're in Ozin Village," said the red-haired woman. "My name is Saskia. What's yours?"

"Mara," she responded.

The crowd murmured. The woman, named Saskia, lifted her right hand to silence them. She kept gazing at Mara.

"What brings you to our village? Why are you here?"

"I was told to come here."

More murmuring ensued. Saskia cleared her throat to silence the villagers. "Really?" Saskia questioned. "Who told you to come here?"

"A creature with seven eyes, wearing a red hood," Mara answered.

The villagers gave mixed reactions.

Saskia raised an eyebrow. "Okay, where did you come from?"

"I don't know."

"You don't know?" Saskia looked annoyed.

Mara shook her head. "I came from inside the mountain."

Saskia looked astounded, while the villagers gave a dubious expression. They did not hesitate to speak their minds.

"Unbelievable…"

"She came from that place?"

"She has to be lying!"

The astonished look melted from Saskia's face. "I believe her."

The villagers gawked at the red-haired woman.

A man stepped forward. "But, ma'am… She's—"

"She's lucky if she came from that place," Saskia interrupted him.

"Excuse me," Mara said quietly. "What day is it?"

The red-haired woman stared at her, becoming aware of Mara's amnesia. Taking pity on the poor girl, Saskia decided to answer her question. "It's November 5, 999ED. It is late autumn, and the first snow will fall soon."

Mara recalled the trees shedding their leaves and became a little familiar with the seasons, but remained very confused. How long did she stay in that mountain?

The red-haired woman studied her expression. "We live in the Era of Darkness, which began when the Golden Age came to an end a thousand years ago," Saskia explained. "Does any of this sound familiar to you?"

Mara responded with a vacant stare.

Saskia sighed, pressing her fingers to her forehead. She closed her eyes. "A monster scourge plagues the land of Ardana, and it grows worse every year."

The red-haired woman opened her eyes. She walked behind Mara to untie her restraints. The villagers became baffled by her actions.

Saskia walked in front of Mara and gazed at her. "You want to live in this village?"

4

The question surprised the villagers as well as Mara.

Mara shook her head. "No, but I do need help. I've no memory other than my name."

"Then your best bet is Mirahyll, the capital of Terra," Saskia suggested. "Their doctors could help, given you can afford their services."

Mara searched her pockets but had nary a piece of gold to her name. With no gold and her raggedy appearance, no doctor would touch her. She gazed back at Saskia, noticing her stare. Mara looked awful and was starving. She grew desperate.

"I don't have anything," Mara begged. "I need some gold."

Saskia raised an eyebrow while contemplating her options. "Okay, you can stay with me for now," she said, taking pity on the stranger. "Do some work around here, and I'll pay you. Before long, you'll earn enough gold to see a doctor."

Mara's eyes lit up, feeling grateful for the woman's heart of gold.

"What kind of work?" Mara asked.

Saskia folded her arms. "How about monster hunting? Pay is decent. There are always pests to deal with."

Mara frowned under her mask. "I've never done that before."

The red-haired woman grinned. "I'll teach you." She held out her hand. "Do we have a deal?"

Mara glanced up at Saskia, then her hand. She had no idea what she was getting herself into, but what were her choices? If she had to do this, so be it. Mara grabbed her hand.

Saskia nodded. "Good, let's get started."

She beckoned Mara to the training grounds and began with basic sword training.

* * *

The first thing Mara learned was how experienced Saskia was. Great to know she was to be trained by a very skillful swordsman. However, seconds into the training, the red-haired woman threw her to the ground. Mara's lack of experience was painfully obvious. She heard snickers and chuckles. Groaning, Mara sulked at a group of men who watched her train.

Saskia looked at her and smiled. "Come on. Get up."

Mara rose to her feet. The two sparred again.

"So, where do you call home?" Saskia asked.

"I don't know."

"Surely someone's looking for you?"

Mara shrugged. The red-haired woman raised an eyebrow.

"Well, someone might recognize you if you took off that hood. Why do you wear that thing?" As their wooden swords clashed, Saskia leaned in towards her ear. "I bet you're pretty underneath that hood," she whispered suggestively.

Mara's face heated up. Her grip on the training sword loosened. "Well, I... I..."

Saskia chuckled. "I am not that kind of person, but I must warn you."

With that, she knocked Mara down again. She hit the ground with a thud, causing the spectators to laugh once again. Saskia was nonchalant at first but soon began to grin.

"A beautiful woman can be the most dangerous thing in this land."

Mara gave a questioning glance. "What do you mean?"

"Know about the goddess, Kallisto?"

Mara shook her head. The red-haired woman grew annoyed and sighed.

"Kallisto is said to be so beautiful, she can bewitch any man who looks at her," Saskia said.

Mara was unfamiliar with such a goddess.

Then the red-haired woman warned, "But some creatures, like vampires, can appear beautiful to unsuspecting men."

The men stopped laughing as soon as Saskia mentioned this. They left the two women alone to train.

"Get up, training's not over yet," Saskia said.

Mara rose to her feet. They resumed their training. This time Mara blocked most of Saskia's swings. The red-haired woman nodded expectantly.

"You're getting good. Thought you said you had no experience?"

"I don't remember," Mara replied.

"It seems like you had some training before. Maybe it's coming back to you?"

The wooden sword was familiar to Mara. Looking up, she found herself in a clearing. Across from her was not Saskia, but an older dark-skinned man with greying hair. His face had a pronounced nose with high cheekbones. His dark eyes were almond-shaped. The man looked to be in his fifties, though in terrific shape. He had the kind of muscles that could let him carry two men. The older man appeared familiar, but she could not recognize him.

In her distraction, Mara got hit over the head by Saskia's training sword. A loud smack echoed through the village. Mara crumpled to the ground. She managed to recover and looked for the man again, but he vanished from her sight.

Saskia smirked. "I guess training's over."

Mara stared up at her in bewilderment before rising to her feet. "But I didn't learn anything!"

"Yes, you have. Just remember to keep your sword up and don't get hit." Then Saskia laughed.

Mara rubbed the top of her head.

Saskia looked at her sympathetically. "Hope I didn't hit you too hard. Or maybe I helped you remember?"

"Or cause me to lose more memories," Mara grumbled.

Saskia's smile faded. "You got distracted," she spoke sternly. Saskia waved her hand to the vast land outside the village. "Out there, you'd be dead."

Mara frowned underneath her mask.

The red-haired woman took notice and smiled again.

"Let's get dinner—you've earned that much at least. I'll even pay for your meal."

Mara perked up at the prospect of food. Saskia raised an eyebrow in amusement.

* * *

The two women entered the inn as the sun was setting. They arrived before the typical crowd, having the inn mostly to themselves. A barmaid guided them to a table at the far corner. As Mara sat down, Saskia made their request.

"We'll have some fried meat, vegetables, and some cow milk."

The barmaid nodded and left. A few minutes later, she returned with their meals. The smell filled Mara's nostrils, making her mouth water. Once the server walked away, she removed her mask to eat.

"Now I get to see your face," Saskia spoke, giving a wry smile.

Mara glanced up. She saw the smile fade from Saskia's face. The red-haired woman's expression changed to confusion before contorting in horror. Saskia opened her mouth, but her words got stuck in her throat.

Mara looked baffled. "Something wrong with my face?"

Saskia frowned. "You don't even know, do you?"

Mara shrugged in response.

The red-haired woman gaped at her. "You've never seen your face?"

"No, what's wrong with it?"

Saskia took a deep breath. "Well, I'll admit you look… very raggedy," she put it as gently as possible. "Not what I was expecting."

"I do?" Mara grew insecure. She searched for a reflection, but the dull dining utensils offered no help. Lifting her left hand, she immediately felt her sunken cheeks. Mara began to tremble. "I can't show my face."

Saskia looked confused. "What?"

"The Watcher told me."

"The Watcher?" Saskia reached for the black book strapped to her belt. The cover possessed some gold trimmings and a blue gem.

Mara eyed the book. "What is that?"

Saskia placed it on the table. "This is a bestiary."

"A beastly?"

"A bestiary!" Saskia corrected her, opening the book. "A monster index."

Mara saw the illustrations of monsters. Next to each picture was a description.

Saskia flipped through the pages. "These are all the creatures found in Ardana, other than the normal ones. Undead, vampires, werewolves, darklings, snow beasts, ghouls, and shadow beasts."

One of the drawings drew Mara's attention. She reached over to stop Saskia's hand.

"I've seen this one," Mara said.

Saskia stared at her. "You have?"

Mara glanced up at her and nodded.

Saskia looked down at the page. "The Dark Dweller: a deformed humanoid creature with a bird-like head. Despite having four eyes, it has limited sight, but remarkable hearing."

"The Watcher told me how to avoid it. If I remained still, it could not see me." Staring at the illustration, Mara recalled the creature's low guttural growls; it echoed in her mind.

The red-haired woman watched her, then looked down.

"Sounds like you had a very rough time," Saskia murmured, glancing up at Mara again. "I've been thinking about our encounter this morning. You said you came from the Dark Labyrinth."

"The Dark Labyrinth?" Mara looked back at her.

Saskia nodded. "It spans throughout Ardana. The closest entrance is on Golden Mountain, just outside this village. That area was once a mass grave," she explained. "Nowadays, the Faith of Kallikratés uses it to punish blasphemers." Saskia watched her. "So, what did you do?"

Mara was stunned. "I don't even know how I got there!"

Saskia watched her reaction and sighed. "I'm not judging you. Let's keep this between us. The Dark Labyrinth is home to many of these creatures." She turned the page. "No mentions of this Watcher. Must be new." Saskia turned the page again.

Mara noticed the new section. "What are these creatures?"

Saskia stopped. "The Undying. Cursed beings who cannot be killed by conventional means." She pointed to a creature. "This one plagues Ozin."

Mara saw the illustration of an undead woman in blood-soaked robes. Some branches sprouted from where her left arm used to be. Her midsection had rotted away with roots growing from within. Long white hair covered her face. An eerie glow from her eyes pierced the shadows.

"The White Lady," Mara read the title.

"She's been terrorizing this village, stealing children." Saskia frowned at the image. "She is the source of the Forgotten Ones. Last week, a young one went missing. We searched, but I fear she has taken him." Then she said, "Stories claim she was an expectant mother who was slain by her husband. She returned as a monster, trying to find her lost unborn child." Saskia took a deep breath. "Ozin used to sacrifice children to appease her. I put an end to them."

Saskia put the book away, then gestured to Mara's plate. "Eat your dinner before it turns cold."

Mara looked down at her plate and began to eat. Upon taking a bite, she noticed something unusual with her meal. The meat tasted fine, but the vegetables disagreed with her taste buds. Even the milk seemed bland. She glanced up at Saskia. The red-haired woman did not seem to notice anything wrong with her meal. Mara did her best to stomach her dinner. She did not want to come off as rude.

* * *

While dining, the two women heard a bell ringing. Mara glanced up. Saskia peered out the window with dread adorning her face. Mara also looked out. A thick fog rolled in.

"The warning bell," Saskia muttered.

Mara gazed back at her. Judging by the look on Saskia's face, she reckoned it meant trouble.

A group of men stormed the inn.

Saskia stood up and watched them. "What's going on?"

One of the men gazed back at her. "The Forgotten Ones are here!"

The red-haired woman sighed and looked at Mara. "Come on," she said. "We could use the help."

Mara hoped Saskia was kidding, but the red-haired woman's face indicated otherwise. She reluctantly rose from her seat. Putting her mask back on, Mara followed Saskia.

Exiting the inn, Mara discovered the fog enveloping the whole village. The sky was pitch black. The torches wielded by the villagers offered no solace. Mara stayed close to Saskia, following her to the guards' quarters. Soon, she saw the racks of weapons outside. While many adults took a sword, Saskia grabbed two of them.

"Here, this is for you." She handed one of them over to Mara. "Weapons forged with steel and silver are more effective on monsters."

Mara unsheathed the blade, revealing a straight sword with a leather grip and metal pommel. She looked up at Saskia.

"Follow me and stay close," the red-haired woman instructed.

Saskia entered the fog. Mara followed her as well as a group of men. She was frightened for she had never encountered a Forgotten One before. The group stopped, ready to face their foes. Mara was unable to see anything. After a few seconds, she saw a pair of glowing white orbs piercing the thick veil. A ghastly howl grew closer. The man to her right screamed. Mara turned her gaze onto him, but he vanished. Another was abducted, grabbing the group's attention.

One of the men stormed past Mara. "We're sitting ducks! We need to split up!"

Saskia glared at him. "No, that's what they want us to do!"

A loud gurgling sound drew their attention. Long skeletal fingers wrapped around another man's face. The monster sliced his throat with a sickle, butchering him like an animal. Saskia went to confront it, but it retreated into the fog. Then it grew quiet. Mara peered into the haze, trying to find the creatures.

"My children!" a woman's scream broke the silence. "They took my children!"

Chaos and panic ensued. The men fled, leaving Mara and Saskia behind. Mara glanced around frantically, holding the blade before her. She could not see the creatures for they moved swiftly, but could hear their ghastly howls flying past her ears. A hand grabbed her shoulder. Mara spun around to see Saskia glaring at her.

"We need to protect the children!" Saskia shouted.

The red-haired woman took off at a full sprint. Mara tried to catch up but lost sight of her. She kept running, hoping to find Saskia again. Her blind pursuit led her to a house where the front door was wide open. A child's whimper came from within the home. The fearful cries compelled Mara to enter.

A Forgotten One approached a mother and her frightened children. The hideous and lanky creature stood about a foot taller than a grown man. It wore filthy rags around its thin waist and bony shoulders. Mara took a step forward, causing the floorboards to creak. The mother noticed her. So did the Forgotten One, who gazed in Mara's direction. Glowing white eyes pierced through long dirty hair, paralyzing Mara in her tracks. The creature released a high-pitched scream, then dashed at her with a sickle in hand. It swung its weapon at her. Mara blocked its attack with her sword. The Forgotten One struck again while screaming at her.

Overwhelmed, Mara fell to the ground. Why did she attempt to fight this monster? Her mask fell off. Mara looked up to see the creature ready to strike. Squeezing her eyes shut, she waited for the end.

Upon hearing the sickle fall to the ground with a thud, Mara opened her eyes to see the Forgotten One falling to its knees. The long, bony fingers reached for her face. The cold claws touched her left cheek, making Mara shut her eyes tight.

"Mother…"

Mara opened her eyes and looked at the monster in confusion. Why did it call her mother? The creature trembled as tears spilled from its eyes.

"Mother… Moth—"

The creature stopped. Mara saw the tip of a spear emerge through the monster's chest. The Forgotten One died instantly as the glow in its eyes faded away. Mara was unable to register what had just happened. Overwhelmed by everything, she passed out.

"Are you okay? Can you hear me?" Saskia called out to her.

Unable to answer, Mara slipped away.

Chapter Two

The White Lady

The rising sun greeted Mara. Opening her eyes, she found herself lying in bed within a cramped room. Songbirds serenaded the day with their singing. Mara looked out the window, watching the tiny creatures flitting by.

"You awake yet?" Saskia called from beyond the door.

After rising out of bed, Mara left the tiny room. She entered a large room where the kitchen and the living room were one. Saskia sat at the table, eating some breakfast. The red-haired woman waved at Mara.

"I got breakfast," Saskia said. "Bread from the bakery in Mirahyll, some dried fruit from the Delta Farms, and cheese from the village goat."

Mara joined her at the table. She reached for her mask. She was about to pull it down until she noticed Saskia's apprehensive stare. The other woman had stopped eating, her appetite diminished.

"Sorry if I look revolting," Mara murmured.

"I understand," Saskia said. "Ending up in a dangerous place and with no memory... Talk about having your share of misfortunes. Speaking of which, have you been able to remember anything?"

Mara shook her head. Biting off a piece of cheese, she noticed the lack of taste again. Even the bread and dried fruit had no flavour. Mara's appetite began to vanish.

Saskia shrugged. "Well, that may be the least of your worries."

"You meant last night?" Mara questioned.

The red-haired woman sighed, "We lost ten villagers. The White Lady has returned. I guess it is time." Saskia glanced at Mara with intent in her eyes. "I have an idea. We'll find the White Lady and slay her ourselves."

Mara gaped at her. "But she can't be killed."

"It takes a decade before she regenerates," Saskia explained. "It may spare a generation."

Mara shook her head. "How can such a creature exist?"

"Magic infects this land," Saskia explained. "When it comes into contact with a living thing, it can change them. Cadavers rise as monsters. So, it is custom in Ardana to burn corpses soon after death." The red-haired woman gazed at her. "Well, what do you think?"

Mara looked at her, unsure of what to think.

Saskia sighed again. "Look, I know you're not crazy about this plan of mine, but I saw you last night. You were scared but showed some courage. I saw you run into that home to save those children. You're not the best swordsman, but you gave it your all, and that says a lot." The red-haired woman shook her head. "I know I shouldn't be asking you, but I have no choice. This village will go back to their old ways, thinking it's the safer route. But more innocent lives will be lost."

Mara was taken aback by her speech.

Saskia's frown became a look of determination. "I can see it in your eyes. You don't like seeing children get hurt. You have a conscience, which is something I haven't seen in a long time."

Mara kept watching her. The red-haired woman brought up some strong points.

"Fine, I'll help," Mara said.

Saskia appeared surprised yet elated. A small smile formed on the red-haired woman's face. "Good, I'm glad you feel the same."

"So, where do we find the White Lady?"

Saskia rose from her seat and approached the fireplace mantle. Then she returned with a large map depicting the land of Ardana. Saskia pointed to a spot west of Ozin.

"The White Lady resides deep within Misty Valley," Saskia explained, "beyond its village and waterfall. It should take about half an hour to get there." Saskia glanced at Mara with a solemn expression. "Be aware. The White Lady can drain the life force from her victims. But with the two of us, she shouldn't be a problem." She gave an optimistic look. "I will make sure you survive this. We'll celebrate. I will pay for your meal tonight—all you can eat."

Mara nodded in agreement. Saskia retrieved their swords.

"Here..." Saskia handed Mara one of the blades. "I don't think the guards will mind if we use these for one more hunt."

Mara strapped her sword onto her belt as Saskia led her out. They began their journey to Misty Valley.

* * *

As soon as the two left Saskia's home, a group of villagers confronted them. Leading the group was a tall man in his late fifties to sixties. Accompanying his silver hair was a growing beard and moustache. He wore a brown coat over a white dress shirt. He had matching brown pants and black shoes. The man glared at the two through round glasses. Mara did not know who he was, while Saskia sighed.

"Alderman Nigel," the red-haired woman greeted, "didn't expect to see you this morning."

The alderman scowled at her. "What is the meaning of this? Four children are missing! Six villagers are dead!"

"Yes, I'm aware of this," Saskia said calmly, "and we're going to Misty Valley to slay the monster."

"You'll do no such thing," Nigel barked. "We're going to talk about your incompetence!"

Mara was shocked. She stared at Nigel with wide eyes, then to Saskia. Even the red-haired woman was stunned. Saskia's jaw dropped.

"Incompetence?" Saskia sulked at him. "First, the White Lady has been inactive for almost a decade because of me. Second, your men died because they refused to listen. But I guess this is what happens when you train a bunch of ordinary folks rather than hire real professionals."

Everyone glared at the two women.

The sour expression remained on Nigel's face. "Well, I am sure you'll be pleased to know that for now on, we shall be using the Holy Blades instead of the Silver Thorns," he told Saskia. "You'll no longer have a place in our village!"

Mara could not believe her ears. She also wondered who the Holy Blades and the Silver Thorns were. She was unfamiliar with either group. Mara looked at Saskia's face. The red-haired woman looked as if she wanted to punch Nigel in the jaw.

Saskia turned her gaze onto Mara. "Go on without me. I'll meet you there." Then she warned, "Do not engage the monster alone."

Mara looked back at her. "Are you sure?"

Saskia glared back at Nigel. "I must speak with the alderman, to remind him who's been keeping his village safe."

Mara walked past them, still feeling the glares of the villagers.

* * *

Mara travelled west to Misty Valley, as pointed out by Saskia's map. As she drew closer to the village, the fog enshrouding it reached out towards her. It grew eerily quiet. Something fell from the sky. At first, she thought it was snow, but it did not feel cold. It was ash. The smell of smoke invaded her nostrils.

Within half an hour, Mara arrived at the entrance to Misty Valley.

"Oi! Wait up," a male voice called to her.

Mara looked behind to see a young man in hard leather armour running up to her. He held onto a spear and a great shield. After catching his breath, he lifted his dark grey eyes to her. His hair was short and black. A broad nose

13

sat on his round pale face. His thin lips formed a smile, revealing a gap in his front teeth.

"Ah, finally found you," he said.

"Who are you?"

He placed his spear in his left hand. With his right hand freed, he held it out for a handshake.

"The name's Boyd," he introduced himself. "I'm here to help you."

Mara hesitantly lifted her hand to shake his. "Where's Saskia?"

His smile faded. "Still talking to the alderman, so she sent me. A good thing as well—I saw you train with her yesterday. Ooh, it was shitty."

Mara grew apprehensive. Boyd noticed and scratched the back of his head.

"Well, you didn't do so great," he said quietly.

"I never used a sword before," she admitted, "but Saskia thinks I'm getting better."

"Still, you'll need my help," Boyd insisted. "You have little experience. Plus, I saved you last night!"

"That was you?"

She recalled a spear impaling a Forgotten One, killing it instantly. Mara looked at his weapon, recognizing the cutting edge. This man seemed trustworthy.

"Well, if Saskia said so…"

He grinned at her. "Great! Now, let's get going."

Upon entering Misty Valley, the two saw the ashen ground and smoky air. Boyd glanced around, his face contorted in fear.

Mara took notice. "Scared?"

Boyd frowned at her. "No! It's just…" He stopped. Boyd looked down at the ash-covered ground. "The curse spreads every day. Even Ozin will fall, as long as the White Lady remains."

Looking up at Mara, Boyd pointed past her. She turned around and observed her surroundings. Houses built with rotten wood stood before them. The smell of smoke grew more persistent as the ashes continued to fall. The two found a body clutching a worn sword. Someone tried to be a hero.

Going deeper, Mara saw more of the Forgotten Ones. The monsters seemed unaware of the two. They looked identical to the creature encountered last night. Another thing Mara had yet to notice was their rotten flesh. Flies laid eggs in open wounds and maggots squirmed beneath their skin. The sight made her stomach churn. Mara felt like vomiting.

"Hey, you heard of the White Lady?" Boyd asked in a low tone.

Mara glanced at him, ignoring her churning stomach. "Um… Yes, Saskia told me about her," she responded quietly.

Walking further into the village, she saw one of the Forgotten Ones holding what appeared to be a baby. The bundled creature had big glowing eyes in its chubby face. It was then Mara noticed the taller creature looking back at her. It lifted its head to release a high-pitched scream which echoed throughout the valley.

Boyd stepped forward and shouted, "Damn! They saw us!"

Four monsters approached them, each wielding a sickle. Boyd held his spear up. He glanced back at Mara, who remained frozen.

"We have to fight!"

Mara turned her gaze onto Boyd. He was right. She glanced down at her weapon, then up at the creatures. Gripping her sword tight, Mara gathered her courage. The two dashed at the monsters. Rushing them seemed to be an effective strategy. The Forgotten Ones were unable to retaliate. Even her sword-flailing skills overwhelmed them. Mara deflected one of the creature's attacks, cutting it down in a few hits. Another ran at her, but she countered. After Mara slew another Forgotten One, only two remained.

She saw Boyd kill one as well. The last one attacked him. He tried to block, but the curved blade bypassed his shield. It hit his arm, making Boyd drop his guard. The Forgotten One raised its sickle again. Mara dashed towards them. Thrusting her blade forward, she stabbed the creature in the back. The monster slumped to the ground. Mara gazed down at the blood-stained sword in her grasp. Then she saw Boyd gawking at her, appearing astonished that she defended him. Now they were even. Mara's eyes wandered to the nasty gash on his arm.

"Your arm's bleeding!" she cried.

Boyd held his wound. He tried to smile, though his face looked pained. "It's just a cut, nothing more."

"Do we need to go back?"

"I'm fine," Boyd reassured. "How about you go on ahead?" He gestured to his wound. "I need to fix this," he said softly. "Once you find the creature, return to me. We'll take her on together."

Mara nodded in agreement.

Venturing deeper, Mara found a river leading to a waterfall, where infant-sized bundles fell to the bottom. She peered over.

"She must be down there."

Then she felt a hand on her back, pushing her over the edge. Mara was helpless to stop it. As she fell, she saw Boyd's malicious smirk.

* * *

Mara awoke to find herself at the bottom of the waterfall. She glanced up at the cliff. She survived the fall, but her body was aching. Boyd was gone. Once the pain faded, Mara looked around. The fog grew heavier. More ashes fell from the sky. The smoke was overpowering. A smouldering house stood near the waterfall, only the charred frame remained. Within the haze, Mara saw a tall figure. They appeared to be holding something in their arms, facing away from her. Getting up, Mara spotted something in the water. A baby's skull peered up at her. She moved away in fright, only to see more tiny corpses. Her actions drew the attention of the figure, who turned around to greet her.

The White Lady perfectly matched the illustration in the bestiary. Roots grew from within her midsection. Rotting flesh hung from her ribs. Wasting muscles were wrapped around the spine. Decaying white skin stretched over her right arm, ending in razor-sharp claws. Tree branches and roots replaced her left arm, adorned with yellowish-green growths that glowed. Her long legs had roots growing under the skin. The tattered white hood cast a shadow over her face. A dress of bloodstained silk enveloped her body. Her dead eyes pierced the darkness with an eerie white glow. Long white hair cascaded over her face.

Mara was frozen. After her fear subsided, she reached for her sword. But it was not in its sheath. Her weapon embedded itself in a nearby bank. Mara ran to it, only to trip over something. Looking down, she saw the roots of the creature wrapped around her ankles. Mara could only watch as the White Lady pulled her in. Then the monster reached for Mara's neck and lifted her. Getting a closer look, Mara saw the monster's ghastly face, the rotted left side riddled with boils and warts. The White Lady opened her mouth, releasing a raspy sound. Mara suddenly grew weak and out of breath. Her body began to shut down. Unable to breathe, her vision went dark. Before slipping away, she saw a flash of silver.

Mara hit the ground with a thud. The feeling returned to her limbs, and she could breathe again. Mara opened her eyes to see severed roots writhing before her. She lifted her gaze and saw someone standing between her and the monster. Mara recognized the red hair, the leather armour, and steel plating.

Saskia glared back at her. "Get your sword! I'll hold her off!"

Mara scrambled to her feet. She ran to her sword while Saskia fought the White Lady. The creature released ghastly howls during the battle.

Reaching her sword, Mara pulled it out. The sounds of Saskia's screams spun her around. The creature grabbed the red-haired woman by the neck, threatening to drain her life. Mara had to save her friend. Dashing at the White Lady, she drove her sword forward.

Time stood still. The White Lady froze with the blade in her skull. The tip of the sword emerged through the left eye socket, destroying the eyeball. The monster opened her mouth as if to speak, but only gurgling sounds came out. She released Saskia, then fell to her knees. The sword slid out of her head, still held by Mara. Saskia moved away, transfixed by the White Lady. The undying stared back at her before falling face down. Her body convulsed for a few seconds, then went still. A pool of blood began to form around the creature's impaled skull. Mara gawked at the corpse. She slew the White Lady!

Mara looked at Saskia, who remained stunned. Eventually, the red-haired woman looked back at her, breathing heavily. That was one hell of a fight. Mara's heart pounded like a drum as the adrenaline rushed through her brain.

An orb of light emerged from the monster's corpse. It shone in the dark murk of the bog, grabbing their attention. Mara curiously reached out to touch it.

Saskia lifted her hand. "Wait!"

Before Mara could respond, the orb shot into her hand. A sudden jolt of pain surged throughout her body as if being set ablaze. The searing heat within her veins dropped her to the ground.

Chapter Three

Mara's Secret

Mara opened her eyes. She had no idea how long she was unconscious. Looking around, she found Saskia seated on a nearby tree stump. The red-haired woman was looking away. Mara attempted to rise, but her body felt stiff. Struggling to her feet, she noticed the area around them. The fog and smoke had lifted, and the ashes subsided.

"You're awake," Saskia began in a sombre tone. She turned her head to look at Mara.

Mara gazed at her in confusion. "What happened?"

"You passed out." Taking a deep breath, Saskia rose from her seat and approached Mara with a frown on her face. "We made it with our lives, but that was too close for comfort." She glared at Mara. "Why did you fight her alone?" Saskia demanded in a sharp tone. "You were supposed to wait for me!"

Taken aback by her words, Mara shook her head. "You sent him to help me."

"What are you talking about?" Now it was Saskia's turn to be confused.

"You sent Boyd because you were dealing with the alderman."

Saskia's jaw dropped. "What?" She furrowed her eyebrows. "I never sent him."

Mara gawked at her. "Who is he?"

The red-haired woman sighed and closed her eyes. All shock and anger faded from her face. "Boyd claims to be a travelling merchant, though how he gets his goods is questionable." She opened her eyes. "Well, I know now he's a scoundrel. While being forced to listen to Nigel, I saw him follow you to Misty Valley. Figured he was up to no good."

"And you saw him push me off the cliff?" Mara questioned.

Saskia nodded. "I did," she admitted. "Didn't think you would survive, but then I saw you stir. If I were a moment late…" Saskia sighed. "Look, I'm sorry. I never planned for this."

Mara sensed the red-haired woman was sincere. Then she noticed the White Lady's corpse. Walking past Saskia, Mara approached the creature's body. The White Lady appeared to be sleeping peacefully. All of her muscles were relaxed. The creature's elongated arm shrank down while the claws became fingernails. Her pale skin regained some colour as dark strands accompanied her white hair. Her face appeared more human. The creature's body sank into the swamp, leaving behind an item. Mara crouched down to reach for it.

Mara obtained a comb. Once made of silver, it became tarnished from a lack of proper care. Still, details and etchings of roses remained. While staring at it, a name surfaced in her mind.

"Evelyn," Mara uttered out.

"What did you say?"

Mara looked back to see Saskia approaching her. The red-haired woman appeared shocked. She saw the creature transform as well. Saskia's eyes wandered to the comb in her possession.

"Evelyn… the name just came to me." Mara glanced back at the spot while Saskia's gaze remained on the comb.

The red-haired woman folded her arms and shook her head, appearing distraught.

Mara took notice. "What's wrong?"

Saskia gazed back with tears welling up in her eyes. Her eyelids and nose turned red. "Look around. What do you see?"

Mara glanced around. "The fog is gone. So are the ashes." She sniffed the air. "I don't smell smoke anymore." She looked at Saskia. "This is what happens when you slay the White Lady, right?"

"No," Saskia answered, her voice breaking down. "The fog never lifted. The smoke lingered, and the ashes never stopped falling. For two hundred fifty years, this village was infected by her curse until today." She pointed at the burnt house. "That was her home. After her husband killed her, he set the house on fire, destroying everything she had. She believed no one cared, but she was wrong." The red-haired woman looked back at Mara with tears flowing down her face. "Her name was Evelyn. She was my friend." She pointed at the comb. "That comb belonged to her."

"What?" Mara's jaw dropped. She gawked at the comb before looking at Saskia.

Saskia wiped away her tears and regained her composure. "I'm not who you think I am." She approached Mara and noticed something. Saskia reached for her mask and pulled it down. She stared at Mara's face, her eyes wide with surprise. "And neither are you…"

"What do you mean?" Mara asked.

"Look at your face."

Mara's eyes wandered to the pool of water surrounding them. Crouching down, she gazed upon her reflection for the first time. No longer did her face appear rough or thin. Her face looked fuller with a healthy tan and was quite angular with a narrow chin. Her nose was slightly wider at the nostrils. Her lips were full yet proportioned to her face. She possessed light brown eyes that were doll-like. Her one odd feature was the faded blotches around her eyes and down the sides of her face. Even a layer of black painted her eyelids.

"My face..." Mara gazed at Saskia with a bewildered look. "How?"

The red-haired woman gave a sombre expression. She got on one knee to get a closer look. "You're easier on the eyes now, but there's only one explanation."

"What is it?"

The red-haired woman rose to her feet. "To slay an undying for good, another must absorb their soul."

Mara stared up at her in confusion. "What are you saying?"

"I need you to listen," Saskia hesitated softly. "You are one of the undying." She glanced at the spot where the creature was. "You killed the White Lady. And that orb you claimed was her soul." Saskia then looked back at Mara. "Probably the reason why you look human now."

Mara's mind began to reel. Her chest tightened. "I am one of them?"

Saskia frowned. "I'm afraid so, but it now makes sense. I knew you weren't human." She sighed. "Didn't want to scare you. I've been trying to figure out how to explain it."

"Is there a way to lift the curse?" Mara questioned, her voice growing tense.

The red-haired woman shook her head. "I know little about it, let alone remove it," Saskia explained. "There are others, but most succumb to their curse immediately, making them a threat." She watched Mara in curiosity. "Your humanity appears intact. You must have become one recently. Or it's your amnesia." She glanced back to the spot where the White Lady fell. "Either way, I've waited two hundred fifty years."

"What do you mean?" Mara questioned, rising to her feet. She began to catch on that Saskia was no ordinary individual either.

"I'll explain later, but I want to thank you," Saskia told her. "Evelyn can finally rest." She closed her eyes. A sad smile formed on her face. "As well as those wretches at Ozin."

With the comb in her hand, Mara held it out to Saskia as if to offer. Saskia opened her eyes and looked at the comb. She reached over but stopped. Pulling her hand back, she shook her head. "You keep it. I've no use for it."

"Okay," Mara said, putting it away in her pocket. "About that... I'm sorry."

Saskia gave a strange look. "Why are you apologizing?"

"You got kicked out of the village."

The red-haired woman nodded and sighed. "Yes, tonight is my last night. I will return to Greyward Hold, and I'd like you to accompany me."

Mara watched her in confusion, anticipating Saskia to elaborate.

"There may be someone who can help you."

Mara's eyes lit up. "Who?"

"The leader of the Silver Thorns, a guild that protects mankind from monsters," said the red-haired woman. "Master Harold has dedicated his whole life protecting Ardana from magic and the monsters born from it."

Mara gave a curious look. "Ozin's alderman mentioned the Silver Thorns. Are you one of them?"

"Yes, I am. I was stationed in Ozin to protect its people. But with my eviction and the curse lifted, it's almost a relief. Whatever befalls that village, it'll be someone else's problem."

"Can Master Harold help me?"

"I think he'll be more than willing. He's very knowledgeable about the undying." Saskia paused and looked at her attire. "And you could use a new change of clothes."

Mara glanced down at her clothing. "Well, they're not the greatest."

Saskia placed her hands on her hips. "You were ill-equipped, but I don't blame you. It's a miracle I persuaded the alderman to purchase weapons from our guild's blacksmith. When it comes to hunting monsters, being prepared is the difference between life and death. Much of my gear is in Greyward Hold. I'm sure there's something that will suit you far better." She beckoned Mara. "Our work here is done. Oh, and let's keep your situation a secret."

Mara nodded in agreement and pulled her mask back up. The two left Misty Valley.

* * *

The two women left Misty Valley the same way they entered. Much to Mara's surprise, they barely encountered any monsters but sensed their presence. The Forgotten Ones hid in rickety shacks, peering at them with glowing eyes.

"They're afraid of us," Mara commented.

"Probably because we murdered their mother," Saskia remarked. "With the curse lifting, they may be affected as well."

"Will they change back?"

"Hard to say," the Silver Thorn replied. "I've seen a human transform into a monster, not the other way around. By the way, ever find the missing kids?"

Mara shook her head.

The red-haired woman sighed, "Damn, probably ended up like the others."

"Maybe they'll change back," Mara said, feeling hopeful. "Hasn't been that long."

"I doubt the villagers will take them back, knowing how they treat the supernatural and outsiders."

RINA S. MAMOON

They finally reached the entrance. The return trip to Ozin would take half an hour. It was unusually quiet, so Saskia decided to talk about something else.

"Ever heard of the Dark One?"

Mara shook her head.

The Silver Thorn was mystified. "Really? Most people know."

"I have amnesia," Mara reminded her.

"Oh, that's right…" Saskia reached for the monster index. Opening the book, she flipped to a page that had an illustration of a massive dragon.

"Long ago, Kallisto and Kratés united the world, bringing peace and prosperity. However, the Dark One awakened, threatening this world. The Dark One is a creature of immeasurable power and the source of the magic blight. The Great Lord sacrificed himself to save the world. Thus, the Legend of Kratés was born. But much of Ardana was destroyed. Countless souls were lost. The Golden Age came to an end, and the Era of Darkness began. Today, seven seals keep the colossus from awakening again." Saskia closed the book as she gazed at Mara sombrely. "And I hope we never see the day it awakens."

"You think it will happen?"

The red-haired woman shrugged. "The Faith of Kallikratés believes it will. They're an ancient order prevalent in Ardana and the neighbouring countries, Corlin and Loris. They believe in a prophecy that tells of the Dark One's awakening when all the seals fail."

The conversation helped pass the time. The village drew closer.

* * *

Ozin was already in a festive mood. People were aware of the monster's demise, but Mara wondered how they knew. Of course, she remembered what happened. Boyd likely witnessed their victory and ran back to the village to tell what happened. Except he twisted the story. Now people praised him for slaying the monster they just killed. The two women remained silent while walking into the village. No one seemed to notice them.

"We should stay quiet," Saskia began in a low voice.

Mara looked at her with a questioning glance.

The Silver Thorn gestured to a group of knights in fluted armour. "The Guardsmen of Mirahyll are here. They may ask him to join."

"You don't think they should know the truth?" Mara questioned.

"He'll be exposed, but there's something about him I don't trust." Saskia glanced down to a pouch strapped to her belt and opened it. "Oh, I mustn't forget." The red-haired woman gave Mara some gold coins. "For your meal tonight." Saskia smiled. "Come to my house later. We'll leave first thing tomorrow morning."

Mara nodded. "Okay."

Saskia headed home, while Mara pocketed the gold coins and headed to the inn.

22

Walking into the inn, Mara saw some villagers surrounding Boyd as he spoke of his victory. Others had noticed her.

"You see that girl?" asked a male villager.

A woman questioned, "Didn't Boyd say she lost her life?"

Mara ignored them while watching Boyd. He had noticed her as well. The scoundrel shifted in discomfort as the villagers laughed and cheered and drank their ale. She went to the main table to get food and drink. After gathering her meal, Mara returned to the same corner table from last night. With her back to the crowd, she removed her mask. While eating, she heard someone approaching her.

"Hey there…"

Hearing a familiar voice, Mara snapped her gaze onto Boyd's smug little face.

"I see you're still alive," Boyd said, acting oblivious to his crime.

"Yeah, no thanks to you," Mara hissed in a low tone.

His eyes widened. "You ought to be more careful. I thought you died!" Boyd looked at her sympathetically. "Look, I'm very sorry. I'm glad you survived. Here, let me make it up to you." He presented a fancy steel sword. "The Guardsmen rewarded me for slaying the monster, but I think you deserve it. You can use it for practice."

"Oh, thanks," she said. "How nice of you… considering Saskia and I killed the monster."

"Keep your mouth shut!"

Mara saw the rage and fear that decorated Boyd's face. Then his tense expression lightened up. "The Guardsmen wish to add me to their ranks. The last thing I need is you blowing my cover. Then again, who will believe a mere girl who can't hold a sword in a fight?"

Mara's eyes flashed in anger, for Boyd had shown his true colours.

"Thanks, but you can keep the sword," she grumbled.

She turned her attention to the plate and ate her meal. Boyd left, taking the sword with him. Even though that man soured her dinner, Mara noticed a change within her meal. Everything had flavour. The vegetables and milk tasted better than before, not just the meat. Mara wondered why this was happening. At least she could enjoy her meal.

* * *

Night had fallen by the time Mara left the inn. She walked to a house with some bushes in front. Coming closer, Mara noticed that the Silver Thorn's home was dark inside. Reaching the front door, she decided to be polite and knocked on the door.

"Saskia, it's me."

Mara got no answer. She looked perplexed. Why was Saskia not answering?

She knocked again. "Hello?"

The door creaked open, yet Saskia never answered. Something was amiss. Guided by intuition, Mara entered the home and locked the door behind her.

Glancing around, Mara found the house ransacked. Some furniture looked out of place. Torn documents were scattered. It was then she found Saskia lying at the centre of the living room.

"Saskia?" Mara froze upon seeing a familiar sword sticking out of her friend's chest. The Silver Thorn's attire was already red. A pool of blood formed around Saskia. It slowly spread towards Mara. Her eyes wandered to the walls, decorated with red handprints. A struggle happened. Looking back at the red-haired woman, Mara noticed her heaving chest. Saskia remained alive.

"Saskia!" Mara dashed to the Silver Thorn's side while disregarding the blood. Coming closer, Mara found several smaller stab wounds on her friend's torso.

Saskia opened her eyes to see Mara kneeling before her. The red-haired woman slowly lifted her left arm and reached for her.

Mara's heart pounded like a drum while many thoughts raced through her mind. Here Saskia was—stabbed and impaled to the floor. "Who did this to you?"

"Go," Saskia whispered. The red liquid poured out of her mouth. She began to drown in blood. "Master Harold must know. Leave now…"

The light faded from Saskia's eyes as she slowly exhaled. Her arm fell onto her chest. Mara was unable to look away, for the sight burned in her memory.

Three loud knocks startled her. Before Mara could do anything, the door was kicked open. Two armoured men stormed into the house to see her hovering over Saskia's corpse. Instead of asking any questions, they apprehended her. Mara shouted in pain as they yanked her wrists to her back.

"Well, well, well… caught you in the act."

She heard a familiar voice and saw Boyd. He stood smugly with folded arms. He walked over to Saskia's corpse, then pulled the sword out. The guards hauled Mara out in silence. They dragged her before a group of villagers. Among them was the alderman.

Mara noticed the accusing glares on her. "I found her like that."

"How do you explain this?" Boyd asked, tossing the bloodied sword in front of her.

Mara gazed at the weapon, recognizing Boyd's so-called gift. She glanced up at the crowd. "Why would I kill her? She was kind to me."

"I don't know." Boyd approached her. "To hide your secret?"

Mara stared at him. He also knew!

Boyd looked back at the group. "This woman is an undying, just like the White Lady!"

Grabbing Mara's hood and mask, he yanked them off to reveal her face. The villagers gasped.

"She looks so human," said one of the villagers.

The barmaid from the inn stormed over and pointed at Mara. "That's not how her face looked before! She looked as if she rose from the grave. A living dead creature!"

A male villager stepped forward. "Probably devoured the souls of the missing young ones," he said to everyone. "That's how she's able to look like that!"

Madness ensued. People began to yell and scream at Mara.

"Murderer!"

"Monster!"

Her heart began to race. Mara shook her head, trying to fight back her tears. "No, I didn't kill them." But there was no reasoning with them.

The alderman glared at Mara. "Seize her! Don't let this vile revenant escape. Quickly! Before she takes more of our children."

Two guards grabbed her. She became numb as a black bag covered her head. She could see Boyd smirking at her through the black cloth while being taken to be executed.

"There's no need for a trial," Nigel declared. "A tree shall do."

* * *

Once the black bag came off, Mara saw the place of her execution—an old tree outside the village. Her executioners made her stand on a rickety chair. Another villager placed a noose around her neck. The moon illuminated the night sky. Mara gazed at the villagers. In the light of their torches, she saw the dark expressions painting their faces. Some children were also present, clinging to their parents' legs as they watched her. None encouraged the little ones to avert their eyes. Her heart was pounding. Her head was spinning. Mara felt sick.

Boyd approached her, still keeping that smug look. "Nothing personal…"

Mara snapped her gaze onto him.

"What chance did you have? You're nothing more than a monster." With that, Boyd kicked the chair out from under her feet.

Now dangling from her neck, Mara choked to death. She heard their screams and shouts.

"Her face is changing!"

"Her true form is exposed!"

The roars of the crowd bled together and grew distant. Everything went black.

Chapter Four

Journey to Greyward Hold

Mara's body remained hanging. The villagers had their fill of justice and went home. None remained this late, save for a large black bird who came to investigate. A raven perched on a nearby branch. The buzzard kept her company with its beak glistening in the moonlight. It cawed at her body. A gentle breeze passed by, making her sway. The rope creaked and strained under the weight of her body. The raven cawed one more time before spreading its black wings and flying away. A tingling sensation ran through her fingers, causing them to twitch. Soon, it became a burning sensation, rushing through her body, like fire through her veins.

Mara's body jolted in pain as she awoke. Her eyes flew open, revealing a pair of glowing yellow irises. She was alone. None stayed to witness her resurrection. Gasping for air, Mara reached for the rope that was strangling her again.

"Do not move," called a familiar female voice.

Mara became still. A creature with several eyes and a red hood walked before her.

The Watcher glanced up at her. "Please remain still. I will get you down."

In a blue flash, the guide released Mara from the tree. She coughed before looking at the creature.

"What are you?" Mara demanded.

The Watcher stared back at her, refusing to answer her question. Instead, she instructed, "You must tell Master Harold of Saskia's death. Return to her home and obtain the map, the bestiary, and her journal. Show him the murder weapon as well, to prove your innocence. It will be in the guards' quarters."

The Watcher disappeared into the darkness, vanishing from her sight. Mara looked back at Ozin Village. Returning to the village that just executed her was the last place she wanted to go, but she had little choice. All she could rely on was the advice of her guide.

* * *

At least it was easy to sneak around the village at night. With the White Lady gone, the Forgotten Ones barely posed a threat. Security was lighter, only two guards remained on duty. One patrolled the village while the other stood by the main entrance. Mara found Saskia's home, but a guard was approaching. She hid behind some bushes. The guard had helped himself to some leftover alcohol from the festivities. He stumbled past Saskia's home. Mara intended to wait until the coast was clear. The guard keeled over from his drunkenness—that also worked. She dashed to the front door, but it was locked.

"Damn it," Mara hissed to herself.

Looking around, she noticed a ring of keys shining on the unconscious guard's person. The key to Saskia's home might be among them. She approached the sleeping guard and lifted the keys off of him, taking care not to awaken him. The guard groaned as he rolled over and continued to sleep. Mara returned to the front door. After a few tries, she found the right key. She went inside and locked the door behind her.

The house remained the same. The only difference was the absence of Saskia's body. The massive bloodstain served as a reminder of where it was. Avoiding the blood, Mara searched the home. Walking by the kitchen table, she saw a large black book with several pages in it. Recognizing the gold trimmings and the blue gem, she found Saskia's bestiary. Mara reached over and touched the leather cover. Picking up the book, she opened it and flipped through the pages. She recalled Saskia showing it to her. It had a leather latch, allowing it to be attached to her belt. She equipped it, just like Saskia.

The map of Ardana sat above the fireplace. Mara spotted a marked location, which represented Greyward Hold. Its size made it too cumbersome to carry, even when folded. Mara found a travelling bag to use. She pulled the map off the wall and stuffed it away.

Mara entered Saskia's room. It had a single bed, a small dresser, and a washing tub. She found another travelling bag, hinting that Saskia had already packed her things. Mara walked up to the bed, where the journal sat.

While picking up the journal, something caught Mara's eye. A mirror sat on the dresser. She recalled the villagers claiming her face had changed while being executed. In curiosity, Mara pulled down her mask. Her reflection revealed a pale face with a tint of grey, riddled with black scars. Her cheeks were sunken and dark circles sat under her eyes. Her lips remained full, yet dark compared to her skin. Her face was gaunt. The markings around her eyes had blackened. Her eyes possessed dark scleras while the irises were bright yellow. Mara grew horrified. Her breathing became hitched as tears threatened to spill. She became a monster. The villagers were right about one thing, but she did not kill Saskia, and she would prove it. Mara pulled her mask up. Taking the journal, she placed it into the bag.

Before she left, Mara decided to enter the kitchen and search the pantry. All that remained was some dried fruit, bread, and a canister of water. She took them. Mara could use some provisions for her trip.

Now, she needed the murder weapon. Peeking her head outside, Mara left Saskia's house.

Around the corner, she heard two guards conversing with one another.

"Can't believe Saskia is dead."

"Yeah, it's too bad," the other replied.

"Well, at least they're happy."

Mara assumed they were talking about the villagers, recalling the looks on their faces and how they wanted her dead.

"But still… Everything was a set-up."

"Quiet! Don't blow our cover."

"Sorry! Do you have the weapon?"

"Yes, it's in the evidence storage at the guards' quarters."

"Good, the funeral will be tomorrow morning."

Mara sat in the darkness while the two guards walked by, unaware of her presence. She heard everything. As much as Mara wanted to know what was going on, there was no time to ask questions. The longer she remained here, the higher her chances were of being caught. She went to the guards' quarters.

The ring of keys allowed entry to the guards' quarters. Upon entering, she saw most of the guards asleep. Even the one guarding the evidence had already dozed off, sitting there with his arms folded. Across from him was a chest. Mara assumed this to be the murder weapon's location. She sneaked towards it while watching the guard cautiously. He was already fast asleep and snoring away. Mara raised an eyebrow before turning her gaze onto the chest.

'These guards sure do a great job.'

She tried to open the chest, but it was locked. Taking out the ring of keys, she hoped one of these worked. None of them fitted the lock. She sighed in defeat, then glanced back at the guard. He might have the key. She crept towards him.

Mara saw the key hanging from his pocket. She reached over to take it, but he began to shift and groan. Mara froze. He did not wake up, but no doubt her pick-pocketing might alert him. She tried again. After obtaining the key, she returned to the chest. Mara inserted the key into the lock. Upon turning it, she heard a light click. Opening the chest, she found the murder weapon. The sword remained coated in dried blood. Placing her hand on the hilt, she lifted the sword. Mara heard groaning. She snapped her head around, only to see the guard shifting in his sleep. She watched him while strapping the weapon to her belt.

'Keep up the good work.'

Mara left the guards' quarters in silence. She escaped the village without anyone noticing.

* * *

At dawn, Mara watched from a distance as the funeral pyre released smoke into the air. Saskia's body was burning. Only a few attended the funeral. Mara was not surprised by the lack of Nigel's attendance—the nerve of that jerk. He could not be bothered to show up, not after what he did to Saskia. After watching the flames engulf her friend, Mara turned around and left.

She travelled north throughout the day. Along the way, Mara spotted a large city. According to the map, this was the City of Mirahyll, the capital of Terra. Saskia had mentioned the city before. But based on her late friend's urging, Mara had to make haste to Greyward Hold. She wandered on the road through Terra, always checking her map. Greyward Hold was located on Grey Mountain, dividing the western regions of Terra and Hema. Mara gawked at the mountain. She had a feeling this would take at least a day to get there.

Only once did she stop to take a break. Mara reached into her bag to eat some bread and dried fruit. Immediately, she noticed the lack of taste from the small meal. Mara soon realized what had happened. Her sense of taste was more limited in her current form. Despite gaining insight into her predicament, her appetite faded fast. Sitting under the shade of a tree, she glanced around. The vast landscape before her was unfamiliar. No matter how hard she tried, Mara remembered very little. She had no idea how she became cursed. But meeting Master Harold gave her hope. After Mara finished her meal, she rose to her feet and continued her journey.

As Mara ascended the mountain, the weather grew harsh. The higher she went, the heavier the snow became. Ice formed on her tattered cape.

"Whose idea was it to have a guild so high atop a mountain?" Mara whined to herself. "Why can't this place be near the ground?"

Traversing the mountain path, Mara heard a growl in the wind. Looking up, she saw a strange creature peering at her from a rock wall. It had shaggy white fur. The skin and hooves were a dark shade of blue. The creature looked like a big cat mixed with a goat and owned a long bushy tail. Two pairs of curved blue horns protruded from its head. The monster watched her with amber coloured eyes. It leapt from the wall and landed before her.

The snow beast was very tall, as the bestiary depicted. The creature was at least twice Mara's height. It snarled at her while baring its teeth.

Mara had never seen a creature like this before in the flesh or at least recalled seeing one. With only the murder weapon, she drew the blade and got into a stance. A familiar feeling washed over her. She thought it was the training from Saskia. Regardless, Mara had to fight.

The creature gave a snarl before lunging at her. Mara dodged and countered. The attack connected, but barely made a dent in the creature's hide.

The sword seemed ineffective. Either way, she angered the snow beast. It swung its right hand at her. The force of the attack sent her flying into the rock wall. Mara released a pained cry while slumping to the ground. The impact disorientated her. She tried to get up, but every inch of her back throbbed in pain. Her strength was failing.

All of a sudden, two men dashed in front of her and confronted the snow beast. Underneath their dark grey capes, they wore tanned armour and steel plating, similar to what Saskia had. Wielding silver and steel swords, they dashed at the snow beast and attacked it. Their swords were more effective at penetrating the beast's hide. The creature roared and fought back. It swung at them, but they dodged. These men were far better fighters than Mara, fighting with style and finesse. Realizing that it was no match for these warriors and their blades, the snow beast fled. The creature leapt at a rock wall and scaled it. Mara saw the beast snarling at them before it disappeared from their sight. The two men panted as they stared up at the wall. Hopefully, that was the last they had seen of the creature. They turned around and looked at Mara.

She watched as the two men approached her. Their hoods obscured their faces. They had no distinguishable features to tell them apart.

"We are the Silver Thorns," said one of them. "We guard the mountain path to Greyward Hold."

The other folded his arms. "What's your business? Why did you come up here?"

Mara took a deep breath as she rose to her feet. The pain in her back began to fade. "I'm looking for Master Harold. Saskia sent me."

The two men exchanged glances. They seemed to know Saskia.

"Very well, we'll take you to Greyward Hold," the other man said.

The Silver Thorns escorted her the rest of the way. They thankfully did not have any more surprises.

* * *

Mara saw the frozen fort within half an hour. The large iron doors opened with their arrival. She stood in awe of the grand hall. Barrels and crates were stacked in the far corner, containing preserved food. She assumed their provisions were delivered. A roaring fire in the middle of the hall took the chill out of her body. As Mara began to thaw, the Silver Thorns took her to the infirmary. On the way, she spotted a blacksmith at a forge. An old muscular man hammered away at his creation as sparks flew from the heated metal. Mara watched him while being taken to the doctor.

The old doctor glanced at her with a raised eyebrow. "What do we have here?"

Mara gazed back at him. He seemed to have been here for quite a few decades, being the only doctor at Greyward Hold. She looked around the infirmary. There were also a few female nurses patching up the injuries of the Silver Thorns. Most of the guild members were male, save for two females. Mara wanted to say something, but the doctor began to examine her. Accompanying Mara were the two Silver Thorns who escorted her here.

"We found her travelling along the mountain path," one of the Silver Thorns answered. "Encountered a snow beast and got injured."

"Tried to fight it with a steel sword," the other man mumbled, folding his arms. "Those are useless on monsters."

Mara looked at the Silver Thorn in curiosity. Then she recalled Saskia telling her something similar before.

The doctor looked at her. Mara glanced back at him, noticing his intense gaze on her. The way he looked at her—it was as if he were aware of her inhuman status.

"She doesn't appear to be in any medical distress," said the doctor. Then he left to tend to another.

Mara wondered if he knew. His examination was very sparse. All he did was look at her.

The two Silver Thorns beckoned her. "Come, we'll take you to Master Harold."

They escorted her down the hall. Upon entering a room, Mara gazed up at a row of stairs. At the top, a mysterious man sat in a chair, adorned in dark grey robes with dull-gold trimmings. The shadows cast by his hood partially obscured his silver mask. In his black-gloved hands was a wooden staff with two silver stones. Mara assumed he was Master Harold.

"Come closer, child," he said in a deep elderly voice.

Mara gazed down at a sigil on the floor. Thinking this was something to stand on, she stepped onto it. It glowed in blue hues and created a field, trapping her inside. Silver Thorns flooded the room, holding up weapons and watching her with apprehension.

"Stand down," Harold ordered his warriors.

The Silver Thorns looked at their master and hesitantly lowered their weapons.

"But, sir... She's—"

"She is not human, nor does she appear hostile," Harold told them.

Mara gaped at the old master in bewilderment.

He glanced back at her and noted her reaction. "I suppose I owe you an explanation. The sigil produces an energy field when it comes into contact with supernatural beings."

Mara's shock faded away. "Oh, I see," she murmured, looking down at the sigil.

"You already know?"

She looked up at him and nodded.

"Those who die are reborn as creatures due to the magic poisoning this land," Harold explained. "But judging from your appearance..." He rose from his seat and descended the stairs. Harold walked up to her, gazing at her masked face and observing her demeanour. "You appear quite human. How peculiar..."

"I'm one of the undying," Mara replied.

"You are?" Master Harold asked, sounding intrigued. "How strange... Most undying succumb to their curse."

"Saskia also said that. She thought it's either my amnesia or I became one recently."

"You know her?" Harold asked. "Now, tell me. Why have you come?"

"Saskia sent me," Mara said.

He tilted his head to the right. "And just you?"

Mara opened her mouth to answer, but a Silver Thorn approached Harold with her bag. Another showed up with the murder weapon. They offered the items to their master.

"Sir, these were in her possession," said one of the Silver Thorns.

Harold reached inside the bag, retrieving Saskia's journal and the map. He studied them for a while, then glanced up at Mara. He also noticed the bestiary strapped to her belt.

"How did you get these?" Master Harold questioned. "She would never part with her belongings, unless..." Then, "Saskia is dead?"

Mara nodded in silence. Harold stood there, staring at her. The Silver Thorns expressed more surprise than their master.

Harold gazed at the blade. "Let me see the sword."

The other Silver Thorn gave the sword to Master Harold to examine. He placed the journal and map back into the bag before taking the weapon. The old guild master studied the sword in silence.

The two Silver Thorns looked at Mara. "What happened to Saskia?"

"Maybe she killed her?"

"No," Harold said, "she is not responsible."

The two men gazed at their master. "Sir, how can you know this?"

Harold studied the blade and then turned his gaze onto her. "If she is the killer, then she would not be standing before us."

"I was framed and executed for her death," Mara revealed. "Saskia was evicted from Ozin after an attack from the White Lady. She and I went to Misty Valley to slay the undying."

"You two killed the White Lady?"

Mara nodded. "That's when I found out. I absorbed her soul and killed her permanently." She pulled down her mask and revealed her face.

The Silver Thorns gawked at her undead visage. Master Harold watched her through his mask.

She then said, "I didn't always look like this, but upon killing the White Lady, I somehow changed. I looked more human. But thanks to that village..."

"I see," Harold said. "What else happened?"

"The plan was to leave in the morning. I went to the inn for dinner. When I returned, I found Saskia with that sword through her chest. She was also stabbed several times with..." She saw a dagger strapped to a Silver Thorns' belt, noting the width of the blade. Mara pointed at it. "With something like that."

The Silver Thorn glanced down at the dagger on his belt. Harold also looked at it before turning to her.

"She wanted me to find you," Mara continued, "but the villagers discovered my secret, and hanged me."

Harold gazed at her. "This is very troubling news."

He looked to a Silver Thorn and nodded. The guild member touched the sigil and deactivated it, freeing Mara.

"It saddens me to lose a dear friend," Harold spoke in a sombre tone. "Saskia was a valuable member of our guild."

Silence filled the room until Mara spoke. "Another reason why I came here to see you—Saskia believed you could help me."

The Silver Thorn master nodded. "I am willing. However, we must inform the others." He gestured to his warriors to get the envoys out.

The Silver Thorns nodded and left Mara and Harold alone. The old master looked at her. "Although I am curious—how did you meet Saskia?"

"I met her after escaping the Dark Labyrinth."

"The Dark Labyrinth?" Harold sounded intrigued. "May I ask what you were doing there?"

She shook her head. "I wish I knew, but I lost most of my memories."

"Oh, that is very unfortunate. I'm afraid I cannot help with your memory loss, but it may return on its own. The least I could do is help you with this curse," Harold said. "I assume Saskia told you about that area underneath Golden Mountain. Once a mass grave, it is now used by Kallikratés to punish blasphemers."

"Yes, but I don't know what I've done to end up there."

"Hmm, I see. Then I shall not press you further." He then beckoned her to discuss other things.

Chapter Five

The Meeting

On the day before the meeting, Harold led Mara to Saskia's former quarters. Being down a Silver Thorn, the guild master had decided to give the bed-chamber to her for now. Upon entering the room, Mara found three choices of attire.

"I encourage you to choose well," Master Harold advised. "We'll be receiving guests of the utmost importance." Then he walked away.

Mara took his advice to heart. She surveyed her choices.

The first looked identical to Saskia's attire. However, the steel plating felt heavy. The second was similar to the first but made with the pelt of a snow beast. It was very bulky to wear. The third looked like a modified version of the Silver Thorn armour, dyed black with the steel plating removed.

The black shirt had gold trimmings along the chest. A black lace criss-crossed over the open spot on the chest. The collar of a white tunic was visible underneath. The black sleeves appeared to be of a thicker material, rolled up above the elbows. The open-bust corset was held together by two brown belts and golden buckles. A third belt sat on the hips, containing two pouches, a flask holder, and a place to hold a sword. The long cloth also had gold hems and pale fur lining the bottom.

The black pants matched the shirt. The dark stockings rose past the knees, also lined with pale fur. They came with brown leather belts and golden buckles, adorned with feathers. Another belt wrapped around the left pant leg for additional items. Pale blue lace adorned the black knee-high boots. Navy blue gloves complemented the attire. They were lined with fur and feathers and held together with similar leather straps.

The black outfit stood out to Mara, so she chose that one to wear.

* * *

On November 11, Mara got dressed before the guests arrived. The garb fitted well and was very comfortable and warm. Mara also transferred all of her belongings to the pouches on the new belt. She also donned her hood and mask. Ready to go, Mara walked into the grand hall. As she made her appearance, the guests arrived for the afternoon meeting.

Master Harold approached her. "I see you have chosen that garb to wear."

Mara glanced down at her attire. "What's wrong with it?"

"On the contrary, I think it suits you," he said. "Saskia was never fond of the garb and thought it was too formal. She had it repurposed for monster hunting and combat."

The two watched as the guests arrived.

"Recognize any of these people?" Harold asked.

Mara shook her head. "No, I've never seen them before."

Harold gazed at the guests. "After the old kingdom had fallen, Ardana became two regions—Hema in the North and Terra in the South. Lady Isabella is Hema's current ruler, while Davis is Terra's chancellor."

Mara spotted Chancellor Davis, a middle-aged man dressed in a dark formal suit. He possessed pale skin and blue eyes. Greying facial hair partially hid his wrinkles.

Gazing at Lady Isabella, Mara could not look away. Hema's queen wore an ivory and purple dress made of expensive-looking silk and velvet. Amethyst gems and pearls decorated her dress. Adorning her long neck was a string of white pearls with silver. A crown of silver and jewels sat atop a head of long blonde hair. Her hourglass figure had pale skin. Her thin face had a narrow nose, thin lips, and a sharp jawline. Her cheeks were sunken, making her cheekbones more pronounced. Her most peculiar feature was the blood-red eyes.

"What is she?" Mara gawked at the strange woman.

"Lady Isabella is an eighteen-hundred-year-old vampire," Harold revealed. "She's been Hema's ruler for the past one thousand years."

Mara gaped at her. A real live vampire. She never recalled seeing one before, but the bestiary confirmed their existence. While looking on, three people approached Harold and Mara.

The first appeared to be a woman dressed in a white gown adorned with jewels. Matching gloves covered her arms, and a gauzy cloth obscured her face.

The second was a man who appeared to be in his sixties. He wore a clean dark suit, which hinted at his upper-class status. He had pure white hair with a matching moustache and beard. His eyes were bright blue. The plump and short man had a round face and a large nose.

The third was a much younger man. Appearing in his late twenties, he looked to be in top physical shape. His brown hair was semi-long in the front while short in the back. His narrow chin was graced with some stubble while a small tuft of hair sat below his bottom lip. He seemed to be meticulous with his appearance, judging by his well-groomed eyebrows. His pale skin was flawless. His vibrant green eyes demanded attention. The young man's face was somewhat slim, though he was not starving. His nose was proportioned. The upper lip was thinner than the bottom.

He wore a dark grey overcoat with gold engravings on the collar and coattails. Shiny golden plates adorned his left shoulder. On the right sat a brown leather shoulder pad holding a red cape. The cape was two pieces of fabric, one shorter than the other and covering only the right side. He wore a white shirt underneath. His pale blue scarf served as a neck guard, held with a gold chain and a ruby pendant. Covering his white pants were brown leather armour and matching knee-high boots. Golden plates adorned his knees. He stood proudly with his hands behind his back.

Of the three, the young man held Mara's attention. He looked like a prince. Her face grew warmer the longer she gazed at him. The young man became aware of her attraction to him. He did his best to ignore her.

Master Harold looked at them, speechless at first. Then he bowed in respect. "High Priestess Alena," he addressed the veiled woman. "I do not believe we sent an envoy to Kallikratés."

The young man walked up to him. "I was meeting with Chancellor Davis when the envoy arrived. We heard what happened."

Mara could not look away; this prince seemed too perfect. What was the catch? It was then she began to notice the faint smell of alcohol.

"Yes, Commander White," Master Harold addressed the young man. "This is very dire."

"You should have told us," Commander White spoke grimly. Then he looked at Mara. "Who is she?"

All three watched Mara, who took immediate notice of their stares. The older man gazed at her curiously while Commander White gave a hard look. Mara was unable to see the veiled woman's face but felt her strict gaze.

Mara's eyes wandered back onto Commander White and the well-crafted sword in his possession. Half the grip was black. The other half was deep red, wrapped in thin strips of gold crossing over each other. The golden pommel had a ruby in it. The gold and silver cross-guard was curved towards the blade and decorated with a ruby gem. The black sheath had similar decorations. The sword looked very stunning; no mere blacksmith could have forged it.

Her gawking grabbed the attention of its owner. She glanced up and got caught by his scowl. Commander White gazed at her from head to toe and grimaced. His critical stare made her feel uncomfortable.

"This is Mara," Harold explained. "She came to us with the news of Saskia's death."

The commander gazed at Harold. "Is that so?" He looked back at Mara. "I've heard of Saskia's murder."

She wanted to reply, but her words got stuck in her throat.

"Yes," Harold responded, gesturing to Mara. "And she was caught up in all of this."

The Silver Thorn master nodded to her. Mara pulled down her mask to reveal her undead visage. The commander's face twisted in disgust. The older man looked horrified but showed pity. The priestess did not react and was unmoved by Mara's plight. Mara pulled her mask back up. She had shown enough already.

Master Harold looked back at the three. "She risked everything to come here. Even crossing paths with a snow beast. If we had not found her, then this meeting wouldn't have happened."

Alena remained quiet. She kept her gaze on Mara for a while before walking away. The two accompanying the priestess followed suit.

"Please take your seats," Master Harold announced. "The sooner everyone is seated, the sooner we can get to the pressing matters at hand."

Mara and the others took their seats. Even the uninvited guests made themselves comfortable. The others watched the three, some expressing disappointment in seeing them. The three seemed aware that they were unwanted but never cared. Mara gazed back at Master Harold, watching him sigh. Then he rose to his feet.

"Thank you for coming," Harold began. "It is with sadness I announce the death of Saskia."

Some expressed surprise while others looked at Harold with dread. A tall and muscular man shot up to his feet. He had tanned skin and short silver hair. A scarred nose sat on his muscular yet clean-shaven face. The silver-haired man also wore heavy leather armour with metal plates and a wolf's pelt. His wide dark eyes watched Harold.

"How could this be?"

"Yes, Heru," Harold responded, "this is quite troubling."

Chancellor Davis rose from his seat while Heru sat down. Sitting next to him was a middle-aged man with wrinkles and greying blonde hair. His blue eyes remained bright and vibrant behind round glasses. The white outfit he wore made him look like a doctor or scientist. The other man was young with short black hair and a smug look. Recognizing Boyd, Mara glared at him.

"I've heard of this terrible news, but is that not the killer standing next to you?" The chancellor pointed at Mara.

"No, Chancellor Davis," Harold said, shaking his head, "she did not kill Saskia."

"How would you know?" Davis questioned.

Boyd rose to his feet, smirking at them. "We know she killed Saskia and those four children. She's an undying, a soul-devouring demon!"

The guests looked at Boyd, then to Mara. She felt humiliated, knowing she never did those things. Mara would give anything to wipe the smirk off his face.

The Silver Thorn master turned his gaze to Boyd. "What proof do you have?" Then Harold glanced back at Davis. "I've heard her side of the story. Saskia was still alive when she found her, telling her to find me." He gestured to Mara. "She was executed with no proof or evidence."

"Is that so?" Davis asked.

"Yes," Mara replied, "I've no reason to kill Saskia, but they never gave me a chance to defend myself. And after I rescued two of their children."

People murmured to each other, unsure of what to believe.

The older man with glasses stood up and gazed at Harold and Mara. "We can find out right here, right now, if she's the killer," he suggested.

The chancellor looked at him, his face contorted in fear. He grabbed his sleeve and frowned at him. "Dr. Moen!" Davis cried. "You brought that thing here?"

"Of course," Dr. Moen chimed, smiling back at him.

Boyd raised an eyebrow. "Well, that explained why you asked for a private carriage."

Davis looked at the new guardsman before gazing at the doctor. The chancellor eventually released his sleeve.

"I think she can help." The doctor looked at Master Harold. "If that's all right with you?"

The Silver Thorn master nodded. "Very well, you may bring her in."

The doors opened to reveal a woman in form-fitting armour with a skin-tight suit underneath. Glowing crystals with gold trimmings adorned the dark metal. The red fabric forming her hood flowed behind her in an ethereal manner. She moved with fluid and grace. Mara gawked at her face, recognizing her guide. Now that they met face-to-face, Mara could see her details more clearly. The creature's face was a mask.

"This is the Watcher," the doctor introduced. "My finest creation, she's a powerful psychic who can read minds."

The Watcher approached Mara with glowing eyes. Mara felt a strange sensation in her head. She rubbed her eyes, trying to break contact with the creature's gaze.

A big smile formed on Dr. Moen's face. "Ah, she's using her powers now."

"What?" Mara looked at him, feeling nervous that this creature could read her mind.

"Relax, it won't take long," the doctor reassured. "She will determine if you're telling the truth. We'll get this straightened out."

Mara followed his instructions and gazed at the Watcher. The doctor approached the two.

"Watcher, did she kill Saskia?" Dr. Moen asked.

"No, she did not," the creature spoke in a monotone voice.

Gasps and murmurs filled the room.

Boyd glared at them. "This is bullshit!" All eyes fell on him. "I don't believe in all this psychic crap. The creature is fake!"

The Watcher turned her glowing gaze onto Boyd. "However, she did kill the White Lady permanently with Saskia's aid, for only an undying can kill an undying."

Both the chancellor and the doctor directed their questioning glances to Boyd. No one expected the Watcher to say that. Boyd's jaw dropped as he stared at the doctor's creation. He shook his head as if to deny her claims.

"He pushed her off a cliff, hoping the fall would kill her," said the Watcher. "He intended to sell every item from her corpse. But Saskia came to her aid. They killed the undying together. He saw this and ran back to the village. He lied about killing the White Lady. Everyone believed him. Word reached Mirahyll, who sent the guardsmen to congratulate and ask him to join. He accepted. After all, who would believe that a mere girl—who couldn't hold a sword in a fight—killed the White Lady?"

Mara gawked at the Watcher. "That's what he said to me!" She glared at Boyd.

Everyone stared at Mara and the Watcher, and then finally to Boyd. The new guardsman gawked at the Watcher, who had exposed him. He sat back down and stared at her with apprehension. Davis gazed at Boyd, unsure what to think.

The chancellor looked at Dr. Moen. "Doctor, this creature—is it true?"

Dr. Moen nodded, but before he could answer, he was interrupted.

"Do not rely on such a creature," High Priestess Alena warned, her voice sounding hoarse. Rising to her feet, the priestess pointed at the Watcher. "Its powers are fake. Its existence goes against the will of the gods."

Dr. Moen sulked at the priestess and her disciples. "Her powers are more real than your gods," he hissed. He pointed at Commander White. "Why don't you ask him? He's seen her powers."

Commander White silently glared at Dr. Moen. He wanted no involvement in this drama.

"Speaking of unnatural existences," Lady Isabella began. She gazed at the followers of Kallikratés with a dismissive air. "I find it hypocritical you criticize her of being unnatural while some of us are inhuman."

"Ah, yes… I haven't forgotten you, horrible creatures!" Alena spoke harshly. "All of you are a blight upon humanity!"

"Such compliments," said another veiled woman. A dark purple bustle dress adorned her voluptuous figure. Black gloves covered her arms. The shadow of her hood obscured much of her face, save for a pair of smiling full lips.

"Indeed, Morgan," Isabella addressed the dark veiled woman. Then she eyed Kallikratés' followers. "Besides, isn't your church dedicated to a pair of power-hungry warmongers?"

Commander White rose to his feet. He was about to say something, but Alena placed a hand on his arm and stopped him. He glanced at her and sat down. Mara watched the spectacle unfold. Once again, her gaze fell on the commander. He took notice and glared at her. She turned away, knowing she got caught ogling him.

"How dare you speak of the gods in such vulgarity?" Alena bellowed. "They gave us the Golden Age, leading us to prosperity! Where were you when the Great Lord made his sacrifice?"

"And where was he when millions of souls were lost?" Morgan asked. "On another note, the cataclysm long ago was small compared to the bloody crusade that birthed the Golden Age." She looked at Commander White. "And I've heard so much about you and your dedication to Kallisto."

Commander White frowned back at the mysterious woman. He looked disturbed to have her eyes on him as if his composure was about to falter. The commander shook his head and kept a strong face. "I must serve. It is my duty."

Morgan smiled. "You are willing to serve a goddess who never cared for this world?"

The commander remained quiet, but it was clear he couldn't stand to look at her any longer. Mara watched in silence.

A loud thud echoed throughout the room, Harold struck the ground with his staff. Everyone looked at him.

"May we have silence," Harold called. He looked at the Watcher. "I believe the doctor's creation. Everything she said matched what I heard." He gestured to Mara. "And I have proof of this one's innocence."

Master Harold glanced at a Silver Thorn and beckoned him with a hand. The Silver Thorn nodded and left. He then returned with a sword.

Everyone, except Mara, froze upon seeing the sword. What made it so special? She gazed at the weapon, seeing a katana-like blade in a black and gold sheath. The most notable feature was a blue gemstone mounted in the black and gold hilt. Everyone watched the Silver Thorn place the sheathed weapon before Master Harold.

"Lord Slayer Godstruck."

Mara glanced at Heru, hearing him utter out the name of the sword. She looked around and saw everyone's similar reactions. Even the three uninvited guests gawked at it. She saw dread and apprehension in the faces of the commander and the older man. The priestess was as still as a statue. Her face might be unreadable, but she had an adverse reaction to seeing the blade.

Master Harold watched Godstruck before gazing at his guests. "Saskia's life was bound to a spell meant to protect this blade. The spell was created by the very magic flowing through Ardana, allowing her to live for a thousand years."

Only Chancellor Davis and Mara expressed surprise. Saskia had hinted about her inhuman status, but this revelation was unexpected. Mara saw Davis staring at Boyd once more. Boyd's face turned pale as his lies unravelled.

"Saskia was the guardian of Godstruck, the sword that can slay anything," Harold explained. "She would never grow old as long as the spell was intact. And Godstruck was safely hidden." He glanced down at the sword. "A weapon with the ability to absorb magic or the sword's destruction were her weaknesses. Saskia's death broke the spell. Godstruck is now vulnerable." He pointed at Mara. "Smaller stab wounds had been found on Saskia's body. I believe she was killed by a magic siphoning weapon, like a moonstone-enchanted dagger."

Davis gaped at Harold and Mara. "I don't know what to say," he murmured.

The doctor glanced at the chancellor. "The Watcher was right."

Mara looked at Boyd, who was as pale as a ghost. His lies were exposed, but the knowledge of Saskia's murderer remained a mystery.

"Whoever killed Saskia knew her weaknesses," Harold said, "and they might be among us, here in this room."

Everyone gazed at Harold. Some expressed astonishment.

"You can't be serious," Heru said.

"I'm afraid so." Master Harold looked at Hema's ruler. "Lady Isabella, you and Saskia became enemies after she played a role in the slaughtering of your kin. You also blamed her for losing many of your human subjects."

Isabella gaped at him, looking hurt and offended. "Master Harold, how could I raise a hand to another possessor of the seals?"

Mara looked puzzled. "Possessor of the seals?"

Harold gazed at her. "After the Dark One's defeat, seven seals were created to imprison it. The seals siphon its power, keeping it weakened. If all the seals fail, the Dark One will awaken."

"Saskia told me, but the seals are…?"

"Yes, that is correct," Harold said. "The remaining are bound to Lady Isabella, Heru, Morgan, Anna, Khan, and myself. If one of us dies, then our seal will break. Khan is missing, while Anna remains sealed within the Black Tower. Now Saskia is gone. We may be the only ones left."

It was no wonder that Harold called for this urgent meeting.

"As for the other suspects." Harold cast his gaze onto High Priestess Alena and her two disciples. "Saskia was also an enemy of the Faith."

Everyone looked at the three uninvited guests. Alena shook her head while the commander stood up in defence.

"How dare you accuse us?" Commander White snarled, glaring at Harold.

"We committed no such crime," Alena hissed. "You have overstepped your boundaries."

Mara watched the priestess in silence. The way she presented herself—this woman saw herself superior to others.

"Does Kallikratés not seek the destruction of Godstruck?" Harold questioned. "As far as I'm concerned, you're also familiar with magic siphoning weapons."

"Your logic is flawed." Commander White shook his head. "The heretics of the Outer Frontier should be suspected as well, for they also possess such knowledge. Their ancestors forged that weapon." He glared at the blade.

Mara noticed his stare and glanced back at Godstruck.

"Why would they seek Saskia's death?" Harold questioned. "She is not their enemy."

"We did not kill her," the priestess insisted. "We have sought that sword's destruction for a while because of how dangerous it is. However, we also knew her true role."

Mara glanced at Harold, then to the three members of the Faith.

"How does killing her benefit us?" Commander White questioned. He sat down and folded his arms. The commander shot a glare at Lady Isabella. "She would have more reason to want her dead."

The vampire chuckled. "Oh yes, blame me when all evidence points at you!"

Harold sighed.

Davis gazed at the Silver Thorn master. "Maybe we need more time to deliberate on this matter. No need to jump to conclusions."

"Very well, at least we can clear the name of an innocent." Harold gazed at Mara. "I apologize for your misfortune—to be hung while the true murderer walks free. We shall seek justice." He then beckoned a Silver Thorn to take Godstruck.

Eyeing the weapon, the commander stood up. "The sword should be handed over to Kallikratés."

Heru gazed at him with curiosity. "Why should they hand it over to you?"

The young commander looked at him indifferently, holding his hands behind his back. "It's existence is an affront to the gods." He scowled at Heru. "But what would an uneducated mutt know?"

Heru's face darkened as he released a low growl.

Commander White looked at Master Harold. "That sword is dangerous and should be destroyed."

Harold stood silent for a brief moment as if to contemplate. "We shall do no such thing."

The commander's face darkened. "You dare offend the gods?"

"What if the Dark One awakens, and the gods do not return?" Master Harold gestured to the sword. "With Godstruck, we have a glimmer of hope."

Chancellor Davis nodded. "Yes, I agree." He looked to the three members of Kallikratés. "This sword may benefit Ardana if that day ever comes."

The commander glared at the chancellor. "I see," he addressed Davis in a cold tone, "and I thought Mirahyll was an ally to Kallikratés."

The meeting ended. The Silver Thorn took the blade away where it would remain hidden. The priestess and her two disciples were the first to leave. The chancellor and his two companions walked behind them, followed by the possessors of the remaining seals. As Mara followed them, she noticed the chancellor looking at her and talking to Boyd. It escalated to an altercation, leading to Boyd getting left behind. Walking out, Mara stopped and stared. She felt relieved from clearing her name.

Master Harold approached her. "I'll let you stay here for now." He changed the subject. "I now seek the true killer. Your assistance may prove useful. In exchange, I shall assist you with your curse."

After hearing his offer, Mara sighed. She figured his help was not for free. "I suppose I can help."

"Any information found, you'll report to me. I shall also send a group to Ozin to investigate, and Misty Valley to confirm the White Lady's death." He then nodded, "Good luck."

She gazed at him while he walked away.

Mara entered the main hall. The other guests were preparing to leave. Lady Isabella and Morgan approached her.

"So, you're now one of us?" Isabella asked in a snobbish tone.

Mara glanced at her. "What?"

"You don't know?" Isabella became annoyed.

"We've heard of your misfortune," Morgan said, "that you are cursed?"

Mara nodded. "I killed the White Lady and absorbed her soul. I became human again, but not anymore…"

Isabella and Morgan exchanged glances before turning their astonished gazes on her.

Morgan smiled. "Very unfortunate, though some of your humanity remains. How unusual…"

The two women turned around and left. Mara watched them walk away.

Another person approached her—the doctor from earlier. He walked up to her with a big grin on his face. "Hey, you're the girl that got accused and all."

"Yes, I—"

"Why do you wear that mask and hood?" he interrupted.

"To hide my face. I was able to restore my humanity, but…"

"Ah, no worries. You look like the Watcher." The doctor held out his hand and smiled. "My name's Doctor Moen. Nice to meet you."

She lifted her hand to shake it. "My name is—"

The doctor glanced over her shoulder. "Oh, I have to go. See you later." With that, he left.

She gawked in disbelief as he strode away to join the chancellor. For his age, he was very energetic and kind. He did put a smile on her face, although no one could see it.

"I also wondered why you conceal your face," a male voice addressed her.

Mara turned around and saw Commander White, who watched her in scrutiny.

"But now I know," he said coldly.

"Well, I… I…" Her stammering seemed to annoy him. Mara could not understand his hostility. The faint scent of alcohol was noticeable again.

"So, what else do they call you?" Commander White asked, looking at her with disdain. "The Raggedy One? How about hideous and ugly?" He turned around. "I think that is more accurate." Then he left, holding his hands behind his back.

Mara felt hurt—he was no Prince Charming anymore. She did look bad, but it did not give him the right to treat her like garbage.

Another man approached her. He was the older man accompanying the commander and the priestess.

"Miss, I must apologize." He held out his hand for a handshake. While shaking hands, he introduced himself. "My name is Arthur White, but you may call me Mr. White. My son, Karl, is not a bad person. His role as Commander of the Holy Blades often gets to him, as well as other things. Please, forgive us."

Mara was surprised, for Mr. White looked nothing like his son. If he had never mentioned this, she would be none the wiser. At least the older man seemed kinder.

"Fine, I forgive," Mara sighed, pulling her hand away.

"Thank you!" He grabbed her hand and shook it again. Then he let go after realizing they shook hands before. He was a very awkward man. Mr. White cleared his throat. "I see you're with the Silver Thorns."

"I'm just helping Master Harold find Saskia's killer," she explained.

"I hope you find the fiend. I'm sure you'll be very reliable. Very good. Very good, indeed!"

With that, Mr. White left.

Mara watched him rejoin High Priestess Alena and Commander White. She then glanced down at her hand, which was shaken by Mr. White.

"What have I got myself into?"

Chapter Six

An Invitation to Hema

Greyward Hold became Mara's home as she helped search for Saskia's murderer. Despite knowing two possible suspects, she had no clue who was responsible. Mara's search began in Saskia's former bedchambers, now belonging to her.

Standing before the mirror, Mara pulled down her mask. She sighed while gazing at her undead reflection. She needed to find another way to restore herself. Not wanting to see her face anymore, Mara placed her mask back on.

She drew her attention onto her travelling bag. Rummaging through it, she spotted Saskia's journal and picked it up. Mara reckoned it might be useful—a good thing she listened to the Watcher. Sitting on the bed, she opened the journal and began to read.

"August 5, 749ED," Mara read out loud. "Found Evelyn dead, her home set ablaze. She later resurrected. Kept asking for her husband. She claimed he stabbed her in the abdomen with a double-edge long sword. The unborn is gone. Evelyn lost it and transformed into a monster. I had no choice but to end her. I buried the dead fetus near his mother. Hope Evelyn found peace."

Mara stared at the entry briefly before turning the page.

"August 6, 759ED... I think I've made a botch of things. Evelyn returned, seeking her lost child. Now she seeks other children. If only I had not removed the fetus. People of Ozin call her the White Lady. Took to sacrificing children, believing it will keep them safe. It's my fault this is happening."

She turned the page again and found the following entry, written two days later.

"Damn those Holy Blades to hell! Must they ruin everything? I pacified Evelyn by reuniting her with her lost child. But those bastards attacked her by setting her ablaze. Evelyn died again, but not before taking a few Holy Blades with her. The rest fled like cowards."

The entries further proved Saskia's inhuman status, as well as revealing her strong opinion towards Kallikratés and the Holy Blades. Turning the page, Mara found the final entry.

"Mara is one of the undying. I know how she ended up in that place. I must take her to Master Harold. It's not safe—"

The rest of the entry was missing. Mara figured Saskia wrote it during the attack. She flipped through the pages and spotted another clue.

"Did you find anything?" Harold asked.

Mara snapped her gaze onto him. She never saw or heard the Silver Thorn master approaching her. After getting over her surprise, she glanced down at the journal.

"Saskia knew what I am," Mara answered. "And she suspected how I ended up in the Dark Labyrinth. She wanted to bring me here, and felt the village wasn't safe."

Harold glanced down at the floor. "Hmm, it doesn't give us much to go on."

"What about Boyd?" Mara questioned. "He also knew. Saskia was suspicious of him, and the alleged murder weapon was the same sword he offered me earlier."

"The Silver Thorns will also search for him," Harold said. "If you were human, you would have been taken to Mirahyll for judgment. Not many places will tolerate non-humans. Speaking of which, I'd keep a distance from Ozin, if possible." Then, "Anything else?"

Mara looked down at the journal. "Saskia suspected Kallikratés responsible for Khan's disappearance. She was investigating them in secret." She glanced up at him again.

"It is true," he said, nodding his head. "We've been searching for the wandering monk. Despite not being able to find Khan, we know he is alive."

She shook her head. "I don't understand."

"Know the difference between knowing where one is and finding them."

Mara looked puzzled. "You know where he is?"

"We possessors can sense each other and when a seal fails," Harold explained. "I admit I was aware before you arrived, but did not think it would be Saskia though." He shook his head. "A thousand years ago, just before the cataclysm, Khan lost a loved one. He blamed the gods and their followers for his loss and the cataclysm. He went to confront them after sealing the Dark One, but this was the last we saw of him." Harold took a step towards her. "Kallikratés does not take well to those critical of them or the gods. Becoming their enemy will be a grave mistake."

"Am I not already an enemy?" Mara reached for her mask and pulled it down.

"All supernatural are enemies of the Faith. Cross paths with the Holy Blades and they'll show no mercy." He paused briefly. "However, if you appeared human, they may be none the wiser. Are you familiar with moonstone?"

Mara shook her head.

"Long ago, ancient warriors and sages used moonstone to neutralize the Dark One's magic," he told her. "They come in many forms, but a Healing Stone may prove useful. Filled with purified magic, it may ease your troubled spirit should you find yourself at an impasse."

"Where do I find one?"

"Monsters tend to possess them, possibly to ease their minds. They possess a milky white colour. However, they are rare. They are also fragile and crumble away upon use."

Harold turned around and walked away. Mara watched him leave, contemplating his advice. She pulled up her mask and continued onto other businesses.

* * *

Staying with the Silver Thorns was okay—Mara got to train with some of the guild members. Her skills improved beyond the simple sword-flailing, but she did notice a decline in numbers. Harold assigned a group to investigate Misty Valley and Ozin Village. Despite sending a small group, it made Greyward Hold quieter. Even with their return, the guild grew more deserted.

By November 14, around eight Silver Thorns left to pursue a better life elsewhere. Master Harold did not object to their departure. Living on Grey Mountain was anything but pleasant.

Still, the blacksmith remained in Greyward Hold. The old blacksmith forged weapons for the shrinking guild, as well as enhancing and repairing equipment.

Mara walked by him, grabbing his attention.

"Hey," he began with a gruff voice.

She looked at him.

"Yes, you," he continued. "Come over here..."

Mara was unsure what to think of him, being rough around the edges. Shrugging it off, she approached him.

"Yes, what is it?" Mara asked, stopping before him.

For an older man, he remained very muscular and in terrific shape. He owned a long greying beard and a matching moustache. His long grey hair was tied back. The wrinkles on his face were hidden well by his bushy facial hair. The old blacksmith hammered away at his newest sword before looking up at her.

He took note of her attire. "Ah, this garb found a new owner?"

She glanced down at her Silver Thorn armour, and then back at him.

The old blacksmith gazed at her with dark eyes. "I remember Saskia bringing that to me long ago to modify it," he told her. "But she never got to wear it."

Mara gazed at her outfit again. "Oh," she murmured.

"At least it's being put to use." He introduced himself. "The name is Talon. I've been in Greyward Hold for the past two decades. I can forge your weapons. Without the services of a decent blacksmith, you won't last long." He laughed briefly. Then he reached for a wrapped object. "Master requested this for you. It'll be more useful than that steel sword you brought." He handed her the gift.

She unwrapped it, revealing a Silver Thorn straight sword. Mara unsheathed it and saw a basic steel and silver sword. A part of the blade, closer to the hilt, was darker than the rest of the metal.

"What do you think, lass?" Talon asked.

She stared at the blade. "It's nice."

The plain-looking sword looked well-crafted, and she got it for free.

The blacksmith watched her briefly before returning to work.

A thought crossed Mara's mind while sheathing her blade. "The people from Kallikratés—I saw the commander's sword."

Talon gazed back at her with brightened eyes. "Aye, I saw that too. That caught your fancy? I believe that's the Hand of Kratés—reforged from the Great Lord's blade in the battle against the Dark One. Commander White travels to Corlin to see a master blacksmith, which is odd..." Talon paused. "Old Edwin is a master blacksmith—the best in all of Ardana, given one can afford his services. He even puts my skills to shame. However, there was another who could rival him, but is no longer around."

"What happened?" Mara asked.

"He vanished about thirty years ago," he answered, then went back to work.

Mara watched as he struck the heated metal with his hammer. The sound was familiar, but she could not remember where. After staring at the embers, Mara headed to the training grounds to practice on a dummy with her new sword.

* * *

Mara rested in her bedchambers later that evening. The pale moonlight filled the room. Hearing a wolf howl over the distance, she opened her eyes and glanced at the window. She got up and looked out. The snow was falling lightly. Hearing a knock on the door, she went to answer it. Opening the door, she saw Master Harold and bowed in respect.

"It's an honour to see you, sir," she greeted. "Is there anything you need?"

"I have some news," Harold began. "The group I sent a few days ago returned with more findings, concerning Saskia's murder and the state of Misty Valley."

"Is the White Lady gone for good?"

"Yes, they found her corpse and confirmed everything you told us," Harold said. "Misty Valley is reverting to normal, albeit slowly. Then again, a cursed area cannot recover overnight. The Forgotten Ones are less hostile. They now resort to hiding and show signs of fear if approached. I guess it is natural, for they are still children."

Mara felt her stomach twist in guilt. She recalled killing a few Forgotten Ones when they showed hostility towards her.

"The missing children were found alive and unharmed," Harold added.

Mara's eyes lit up. "They were?"

"They lived in the nearby woods, living off wild berries. Ozin refuses to take them back, so they shall go to the orphanage in Mirahyll."

"Oh," Mara murmured, glancing down. "Saskia said the village wouldn't take them back."

"They are in better hands," he reassured her. "Mirahyll is safer."

Mara looked up at Harold and asked, "What of Saskia's murder?"

Harold looked down at the floor. "We have discovered that someone had bribed the village, possibly to divert attention from the true killer. The village guards confessed. However, the alderman denied any wrongdoing."

"Did they find Boyd?" Mara asked.

"We could not find him. Regrettably, the Holy Blades have begun their investigation, barring us from continuing." He gazed up at her. "It is also possible that the Blackthorn Guild may be responsible."

"The Blackthorn Guild?"

"Yes, I know them quite well," Harold replied. "The guild's founder is Theo Blackthorn, the most wanted man in Ardana. While they tend to terrorize people travelling on the roads alone or at night, they do accept the occasional assassination job. Lady Isabella or the Faith could have hired them to avoid suspicion. Regardless, they remain prime suspects, which leads to another thing…"

"What is it?"

"I've been invited to Hema. Lady Isabella wishes to plead her case and clear her name. She has also invited the Faith, although High Priestess Alena will not be there. Two representatives will attend on her behalf. We are to meet in Hema's capital, Hemal."

"Okay, so what's the problem?" Mara asked.

"If two possessors meet, it may spell disaster, especially if someone seeks to kill us. It is a risk I am unwilling to take. So, you shall go in my stead. Come, a carriage is waiting."

Taking her sword, Mara followed the Silver Thorn master. She had the bestiary strapped to her belt.

"I'll go," Mara agreed, "but I've noticed they don't see eye to eye."

"Ah, yes… It is probably because of the treaty," Harold spoke. "Once finalized, Kallikratés will have a presence in Hema for the first time in a thousand years. Lady Isabella is less than keen about it."

Approaching the main entrance, Mara watched the large iron doors open. On the other side was a black carriage pulled by two black horses. In the driver's seat sat a veiled rider.

Harold looked at her. "I'm sure Lady Isabella will explain the treaty, but please find evidence. And keep your sword ready."

Mara glanced at her sword before looking at Harold.

"Hema can be very dangerous," he continued. "Be safe."

Mara nodded, then left Greyward Hold. Once she entered the transport, the carriage began to move.

* * *

The horses galloped down Grey Mountain. The ride felt bumpy. Mara wondered if this was safe. The recent snowfall made the path slick, but the rider did not seem to care. Never once did he adjust his speed.

Looking out the window, she saw the moon lighting up the night sky. Mara could also see Ghost Mountain to the East, covered in mist. Some snow beasts scaled the higher elevations. Thankfully, she was going the other way. The carriage reached the main road to Hema, passing in between the two mountains. The rider picked up speed. Soon she saw the city of Hemal.

The carriage stopped upon reaching the entrance to Hema's capital. Mara watched the door open. Realizing she had to leave, she sighed and got out.

"Is this it?" Mara glanced at the rider.

The rider left in silence.

She watched the carriage travel to the castle beyond Hemal. She sighed again and walked into the city.

The falling snow sparkled under lit lamp posts. Walking past gothic buildings and townhouses, Mara found not a soul around. It was unusually quiet at the moment. The light of the full moon broke through heavy clouds. All of a sudden, she heard a crash and a scream. Gripping her sword, Mara went to investigate.

She found many dead, slaughtered as if by an animal. Mara stood frozen before the massacre until she spotted a victim who remained alive. A young girl held her wounded neck in a vain attempt to stop the bleeding. Mara approached her, taking note of the massive injury. The bite tore through vital arteries. The girl would be lucky to have a minute to live with the amount of blood she was losing. She opened her mouth to utter one word.

"Werewolf…" she spoke barely above a whisper.

Mara gaped at her—a werewolf in Hemal. She never signed up for this! Soon, the girl stopped moving. Mara stared at her body, then closed her eyes. This girl was the second person to die in front of her. Mara's eyes snapped open upon hearing another loud crash. She looked up and followed the source of the sound. The creature even killed the guards. People screamed as they fled into their homes. They shut their doors tight, waiting for the madness to end. Mara was stunned with all the chaos and death caused by this monster. She, too, sought a hiding place. Being outside was not safe. Mara knocked on several doors, hoping to find sanctuary. But none offered their homes out of fear. Growing desperate, she found an abandoned house and entered.

She soon regretted her choice upon discovering a slaughtered family, their bodies torn to pieces. Blood painted the walls. The stench invaded her nostrils. It was more overpowering compared to the gruesome encounter at Saskia's home. Mara identified a father, a mother, and two small daughters.

Mara heard a crash from the next room. Raising her sword with a shaky hand, she went to investigate. Opening the door, she found the beast—a werewolf with light brown fur, sitting in the centre of the room. The monster's body looked human at one point, but now it was twisted and deformed by unknown forces. The creature's back was turned to Mara, unaware of her presence. Mara grew terrified, as it was her first time seeing a live werewolf. It looked bigger than her, though the snow beast was much larger, and she had the Silver Thorns' aid. Alone, she stood no chance. Mara snuck out of the room, but the sounds of her footsteps alerted it. The creature turned around and snarled at her. Mara saw glowing yellow eyes and sharp bloodied fangs. Standing on all fours, it lifted its head and roared. She turned and ran, and the creature gave chase.

She ran to the door, but the creature was much faster and blocked her exit. Mara had to fight. Holding her sword, she stood her ground. The werewolf charged at her. She swung her sword, but the beast repelled her attack. Mara froze as her weapon flew out of her grasp. The creature pounced on her, knocking her to the floor. Massive claws pinned her wrists. Mara had no idea why she decided to fight this monster. Her heart thumped, ready to leap out of her throat. The werewolf sank its fangs into her. Mara screamed while the creature chewed on the left side of her neck and shoulder. Her heart was pounding. The intense pain put her into a state of shock. Before slipping away, she saw the creature snarling at her. The moon glowed red. Her vision blurred. Everything went black.

* * *

Mara awoke with blurry vision. Within the haze, she saw a man approaching her.

"Ah, you're awake," he began.

"What happened?" Mara asked in a coarse voice. Her throat was stinging.

Looking around, she found herself in an unfamiliar place. No longer was she in the home of the slaughtered family.

After blinking a few times, Mara's eyesight became clear, allowing a better glimpse at the middle-aged man. He wore a black dress shirt underneath a grey vest, a pair of black pants, and matching shoes. A prominent nose sat on his thin, pale face as bushy eyebrows sat above his dark eyes. He possessed thinning dark hair, while silver strands graced the sides of his head. A monocle adorned his left eye.

A frown graced his thin lips. "I am Doctor Simon of Hemal Clinic," he explained. "I hear you had an unfortunate encounter."

Mara reached for her neck and felt a burning sensation.

The clinic doctor noticed the bite wound. "Do you feel inflammation?"

She looked back at him and nodded.

The doctor sighed, "I'm afraid it's lycanthropy. You will become a werewolf."

Mara's ears perked up. "What?"

It was not as painful to speak this time, but she was better off letting her wounds heal. Mara recalled the terrible attack. Even though she survived, Mara was unsure about being lucky. Now she had lycanthropy on top of memory loss and a curse.

"Fortunately, you'll have time to cure it." He stepped forward and passed her a sealed letter. "Lady Isabella requests your presence."

Opening the letter, Mara began to read. "I have received word of your plight. As soon as you recover, come to Bartharoy Castle. I wish to cure you, as well as compensate. I recommend you make haste. Lady Isabella Bartharoy…"

Mara looked up, feeling relieved to know there was a cure. She looked back at Dr. Simon and reckoned she owed him for treating her injuries.

"Do not worry," Dr. Simon said. "Lady Isabella requested your treatment. I suspect she'll request a favour from you."

Mara nodded. She turned and left the clinic.

* * *

The sun broke through the heavy clouds. Morning arrived. Mara looked to the castle beyond Hemal. Walking down the streets, she saw the chaos and carnage left by the werewolf. It was a mess that had to be cleaned up by Hemal's inhabitants. Some of these victims had family and friends. Some lost their fathers, while others lost their mothers. There were even children—brothers, sisters, sons, and daughters.

People mourned the dead. Mothers and children cried. The men tried to keep a brave face, but none could hide the devastation of last night.

As Mara watched them haul the dead away, a thought crept into her mind. Such a creature should not be allowed to live. She reckoned a bounty would be declared. Mara glanced at her sword, still in her possession. Whoever brought her to the clinic also retrieved her weapon. She hoped not to encounter that creature again. Mara made her way to the castle.

Walking by an inn, she noticed some men in golden armour, wielding gold and silver swords. Mara reckoned they were the Holy Blades, who accompanied the two representatives from Kallikratés. Much to her surprise, they appeared fine and unharmed. They could have helped last night. There could have been more survivors.

Approaching the castle gate, she found a huddled figure pleading to the guards.

"Please, I must see her," begged an older man. "Only she can save him." Sensing Mara's presence, he turned around. Upon seeing her, his blue eyes grew wide. "You!" He scrambled to his feet, grabbed her hand, and shook it. All of a sudden, the old gentleman was in a cheery mood. "We meet again. What a coincidence!"

Mara watched him in confusion. "Do I know you?"

"Of course you do. My name is Mr. White. We met a few days ago."

She recalled the older man apologizing for his rude son. His snow-white hair reminded her.

"What are you doing here?" Mara asked.

His smile faded as he released her hand. "I'm one of the two representatives sent by the Faith." Then he grew silent for a brief moment. "Did you see that dreadful creature last night?"

"Yes, and it bit me," she replied.

Mr. White noted her bloodstained clothes. "I'm very sorry," he murmured, glancing down. "You see, I'm trying to request an audience with Lady Isabella, but she does not think highly of the Faith." He gazed at her. "Maybe you can help me? If you're here, then you must have received an invitation."

Mara tilted her head in curiosity. "Okay, with what?"

He cleared his throat. "I must save that creature."

"Why do you want to do that?"

"The beast from last night was… Karl."

Mara gaped at him. She froze, processing the words spoken to her. The man she first saw as Prince Charming turned out to be quite a monster. Now he was a werewolf, the same creature that attacked her last night. Perfect.

The castle gates opened. Mara and Mr. White saw a well-dressed man walking towards them. He wore a suit of black, red, and gold. His skin was pale, contrasting with his short dark hair. He owned a pair of pale blue eyes. The young man had much of his colour drained.

"Welcome," greeted the young man. "I am Evan, the steward of Bartharoy Castle. Milady has been expecting you." The steward beckoned Mara to come inside.

Mr. White was about to follow, but the guards stopped him. Mara noticed and looked at Evan with a questioning glance.

"Lady Isabella only invited you," Evan explained to Mara.

"I don't understand," Mara said. "I thought she invited Kallikratés as well."

"For a different matter," he answered, turning around. "However, given the circumstances, all discussions are now delayed."

Mara closed her eyes and sighed. "Maybe you can make an exception." She opened her eyes and gestured to Mr. White. "Commander White is the beast from last night. His father needs Lady Isabella's help to cure him."

Evan and the guards glanced at her, and then to Mr. White. The old gentleman shifted around nervously, seeing all those eyes on him.

After watching him for a while, the steward nodded. "Very well. I shall grant you both an audience." Evan beckoned them to follow.

* * *

They walked past dead gardens, withered and frozen. Evan guided them to a pair of large bronze doors, which opened upon their approach. They entered a grand foyer. Mara noticed how cold and dark it was. The many burning candles offered little warmth. Dark blue wallpaper decorated the walls. Tall pillars had the same shade with some gold adorning them. A grand staircase with golden rails led either to the left or right. Mara spotted a couple of servants, as they cleaned the floors and furniture. She and Mr. White followed Evan up the stairs. They went left, passing through the grand dining hall. Mara spotted a long table with several candles burning on top.

"Thank you," Mr. White told her. "If not for you, I'd never get into the castle."

Mara looked back at him and nodded. Evan brought them to an anteroom.

"Please wait here until Lady Isabella is ready to see you," said the steward. "Oh, and I must warn you—uttering the names of the gods before Her Majesty is strictly forbidden."

"What?" Mr. White cried. "That's sacrilege!"

Mara was perplexed, yet she never questioned it. After a few moments, the steward led them into a very fancy room with elegant furniture and dark red walls. Heavy curtains blocked the sunlight. Lady Isabella sat on a golden chair, while a servant poured a thick red liquid into her crystal goblet. The ruler of Hema saw Mara and smiled.

"Welcome to my home," she greeted in a pleasant voice. "I will admit I was surprised Master Harold sent you in his stead. But considering last night, it was fortunate that he was not in your place." Lady Isabella noticed Mr. White and her smile dropped. Hema's queen glared at Evan.

"What is he doing here?" Isabella demanded in a sharp tone.

"Milady," Evan addressed his queen. He carefully made sure not to provoke more of her ire. "The young woman requested to bring him. He wished to speak with you."

Lady Isabella watched Evan before gazing at the two. "I'm afraid there are more serious matters at hand," she said, gesturing to another guest.

Mara saw a tall and muscular man with silver hair, tanned skin, and wearing leather armour. Heru stood up, staring at her with dark eyes.

"You've been bit," he murmured.

Isabella mockingly gazed at Heru. "Ah, so you've noticed?" She looked at Mara. "Since Heru has not the heart to slay his kind, I'll cure and pay you for the rogue's head."

Mara's jaw dropped. Despite having some training, she was no professional hunter. She never stood a chance against the werewolf last night. Heru growled at Isabella, looking angry. Mara also heard the older man release a stuttering gasp. She glanced at Mr. White, noticing his horror.

Isabella ignored them and glared back at Heru. "What is your problem? You made that rogue and unleashed it onto my city!"

Mara looked back to see Heru glowering at Isabella.

"It was never my intention," he said in a low voice.

"Yet, here it is… running amok in my kingdom," Isabella retorted.

"We have rules, yes?" Heru asked. "We have laws that we follow."

"What is your point exactly?" Isabella asked dismissively, folding her arms.

"My home, the Old Hunting Ground, is a haven for my clan," he explained. "Humans are not allowed to step foot there. Anyone who defies these rules are warned at first, and then hunted and killed. Yesterday, a young man reeking of alcohol trespassed into my domain and goaded me into biting him."

Mara glanced at Mr. White with a raised eyebrow. The older man looked humiliated, knowing his son became inebriated and got bitten. No one else seemed to notice. She looked back at Heru, seeing his eyes on her.

"I bit him on the neck, thinking it would kill him," Heru explained softly. "But things turned out different." He frowned at her and scratched the back of his head. "I'm sorry this happened."

Mara watched Heru, then gazed at Isabella. "I'm afraid I can't take this task."

Isabella scowled at her. "Why is that? You're with the Silver Thorns, are you not?"

"I'm helping Master Harold find Saskia's killer. And in exchange, he'll help me with my curse." Mara looked at Mr. White. "Besides, he wants to save the creature."

Everyone watched the old gentleman, some appearing curious.

Mr. White's eyes shifted around before addressing Lady Isabella. "Please, that is my son, Karl White, Commander of the Holy Blades. Losing him will be catastrophic and not just to me."

Lady Isabella's red eyes lit up. "Commander White is your son?" She smiled. "You raised a very handsome young man. It'll be a pity if he is lost."

"So, you'll spare him?" Mr. White asked.

"I am aware of his importance to the Faith. If he dies, no doubt Kallikratés will blame me." Hema's ruler looked at Mara. "I shall modify the deal. For curing the commander, not only will I cure you, but I'll also reward you in kind. Do we have an agreement?"

Mara frowned at her. "Why ask me?"

Isabella's smile faded away. "You are cursed with immortality. Such an ability is valuable since I cannot afford to lose more of my loyal knights."

"Fine, what do I have to do?" Mara inquired.

Isabella reached for a bell on a table. After ringing it a few times, a servant entered with a golden box. He stopped before Mara and opened it. Within the box, she found a large syringe filled with red liquid. She reached in and picked it up. Mara glanced at Lady Isabella with curiosity.

"That is the cure to Lycanthropy. Use it to save the commander." Isabella glanced at her sword. "But silver is fatal to a werewolf. Using your sword is out of the question."

Mara gaped at Isabella, hoping she was kidding. However, the ruler of Hema wanted this dealt with as soon as possible. There was no time to waste.

* * *

Within fifteen minutes, Mara returned to the city with Mr. White following her.

"What a relief," Mr. White said optimistically. "I will have my son back."

Mara felt conflicted. Her new task was curing the one responsible for last night's massacre. At least she would be rewarded. They approached an inn, where they parted ways for now.

Mr. White stopped and looked at her. "I hope Karl will be fine."

Mara glanced at the cure in her hand. "According to Lady Isabella, this should work."

"Yes, I'm sure it will, but will he be okay?"

"I'm sure he'll be fine." As Mara turned away, she felt a grip on her arm. Looking back, she saw the pleading eyes of Mr. White.

"Please, bring him back," he pleaded. "Make sure he returns, safe and sound."

Knowing this was a very concerned father, Mara searched for Commander White.

* * *

Mara stood alone in a clearing, just outside the city and near the border to the Old Hunting Ground. Two men with a horse and wagon stood far away. They guided her to this spot, believing she would encounter him here. She found a tree stump and sat down. Mara released a sigh, rested her head on her left hand, and closed her eyes. After a few moments, she heard a snarl. She opened her eyes and saw a large hairy creature approaching her on all fours. It was the werewolf from last night. Mara rose from the stump, holding the cure in her right hand.

The werewolf dashed at her, snarling and gnashing his jaws. Mara stood her ground, gripping the cure. It was now or never. The beast knocked her down, ready to kill her. He snarled for a while, then stopped. While he lunged at her, Mara stabbed the needle into his abdomen and administered the cure. The creature pulled the empty needle out in curiosity. Studying the empty syringe, his hand began to tremble. Mara took notice and was not staying close to see what happened next. She shoved him off balance and moved away. The werewolf was unhappy and roared.

However, he could not move another step. He fell to the ground and began convulsing. The creature made a series of strange growls. Then he straightened out and released a bloodcurdling scream of intense pain. The sound was horrifying enough to silence the wilderness. His body began to twist, as his bones made a series of cracking sounds.

Commander White's trembling form eventually emerged. His puzzled face still held traits of the werewolf. Mara saw his yellow eyes. Even his fangs remained until they shrank. The yellow hues in his irises faded to green. He remained on the ground with moulting skin covering his nakedness. His hair was messy. The commander opened his mouth to speak, but a red liquid spewed forth. He threw his head forward, vomiting blood onto the ground. Mara grimaced, watching him heave and cough.

The two men in the distance approached them.

"The cure worked," said one of them.

Mara raised an eyebrow. "Really? It doesn't look like it."

"Lycanthropy is an infection of the blood," the other man explained. "The cure forces the infected blood out."

The two men approached Commander White with a blanket. They wrapped it around him while helping him to his feet. As the men escorted the commander, Mara saw his pale face. In spite of his blood loss, he still had the strength to glare at her. She was baffled as to why he gave such a look. She just saved him! After the two men assisted him onto the cart, they rode back to the city.

* * *

Mara followed the wagon as they enter Hemal. Several people watched them. Among them stood Mr. White and Evan.

The older man stared at Commander White in concern, as if he never saw his son so pale and sick before. He gazed at Mara. "What happened to him?"

"The cure worked as it should," Evan said, taking a step forward. He looked at the old gentleman. "Your son will need a blood transfusion."

The men helped the commander off the wagon, then escorted him to the clinic.

Mr. White gazed at the steward. "What do you mean?"

"Since being forced to vomit the infected blood, he will need a transfusion to compensate for the blood loss. I assure you he will be fine." The steward glanced at Mara. "Lady Isabella expresses her gratitude. Please, come with me to the castle."

A carriage appeared. As Mara and the steward entered it, she noticed Mr. White not accompanying them. She looked back at him, seeing him shake his head.

"I wish to stay with Karl," Mr. White said, "until he recovers."

Evan nodded. "Very well. Another carriage will be available for you. Lady Isabella has decided to welcome you both."

The carriage took off.

The ride to Bartharoy Castle was uneventful and silent. Once the carriage reached the castle, the two got out and approached the gate.

"Hema owes you much gratitude," Evan said. "Please, come inside. Milady offers her grand hospitality to you."

Mara followed him into the castle, through the frigid gardens, past the large doors, and into the cold and dark foyer. Evan walked ahead of her.

"This way," he beckoned.

She followed him up the main stairs and turned right. He took her to an arranged guest room. The room was much larger than her quarters at Greyward Hold. Even the bed looked more comfortable and luxurious.

"Dinner will be in a few hours," Evan said. "Make yourself comfortable for the time being."

Evan left Mara to her own devices. Lying on the bed, she thought about the cure and its extremes. Commander White vomiting out his blood was burned deep into her mind.

The bed helped relax her weary bones. Dozing off to sleep, Mara hoped she would not suffer a similar fate when she received the cure.

Chapter Seven

The Cure

Two hours later, Mara awoke to three knocks on the door. Getting up, she left her room. Entering the dining hall, the undying found the others. The commander and his father sat at one end of the table while Heru sat on the other end. Lady Isabella was seated at the centre.

Hema's queen beamed at Commander White. "I see you are doing well. You look better already," she told him. "I hear you recovered within two hours as if yesterday never happened."

The commander stood still with folded arms and closed eyes. A frown was stuck on his face.

"I am," he began. "No thanks to him."

Heru kept his cool and watched him with a forced smile. "None of this would have happened if you hadn't trespassed into my domain."

Commander White shook his head. "You gave no warning and attacked me," he hissed.

Mara's eyes drifted onto the commander's outfit. He donned a dark grey vest with golden buttons over his white dress shirt. From the top button to the left breast pocket was a golden chain. She also saw black dress pants with matching shoes. His father probably retrieved a new change of clothes for him. A glass sat next to him with a small trace of wine remaining.

Opening his eyes, the commander saw Mara. She also drew the others' attention.

"So nice of you to join us," Lady Isabella addressed her.

Coming closer to the dinner table, Mara spotted a vacant chair opposite to Hema's ruler and Kallikratés' disciples. She sat down and removed her mask, giving everyone a view of her scar-riddled visage.

"Thanks for ruining my appetite," Commander White said, directing his hostility onto her.

Mara looked up at the commander, seeing him grimace at the sight of her face.

"Oh my," Mr. White uttered, dropping his jaw.

Even Heru and Lady Isabella looked astonished.

After seeing everyone's reactions, Mara wanted to run back to her room.

Lady Isabella rose from her seat. "I figure now is the time to reward you."

She reached for a bell and rang it a few times. An audible chime echoed in the dining hall.

A servant arrived with a golden box. He placed it before Mara, then left the dining room.

Mara opened the box, revealing a bag worth five hundred gold, a glowing white stone, and a vial filled with a red liquid. Drawn to the shining gem, Mara reached for it. She lifted the stone for everyone to see.

"This is…" Mara stopped, for the stone began to crumble. It shattered into fine dust, releasing the magic within. The magic flowed into her arm, then her whole body. After the light faded, Mara noticed the commander rising to his feet.

Commander White stared at her in astonishment.

"Her face," Mr. White spoke, his eyes growing wide with shock. "She looks so human!"

Hearing his words, Mara reached for a spoon. She saw her reflection and was stunned. Mara no longer looked like an undead creature, but a human woman. With a free hand, she reached for her face. Mara felt like crying out of joy. She lowered her hood to reveal long dark hair tied in a loose messy braid.

"What was that?" Commander White demanded. "How did she change?"

"That was a healing stone," Mara said. She looked away from her reflection and glanced up at the commander, who was studying her face. Mara turned away from his scrutinizing gaze and looked at Lady Isabella. "Master Harold mentioned them earlier."

"I kept it for a while, but have no use for it," Isabella said. "Since you are undying, I figured you would benefit more from it. But be warned—the stones are fragile and rare. Try not to die often."

Mara nodded.

Mr. White gazed at Lady Isabella. "She's one of the undying?"

"Wasn't the curse cast only once?" Heru inquired.

Heru's question made Mara curious. "What is the Curse of the Undying?" she asked, directing her question to anyone.

"The curse was cast upon an individual long ago," according to Hema's ruler. "The woman, whose name is only known to a few, sought to break the curse no matter the cost. But the curse was rooted deep within her soul. Thus, she broke her soul in two. One half remained with her while the other half created a reincarnation. Unfortunately, the reincarnation also inherited the curse. Upon death, the soul breaks in half, repeating the cycle." Looking at her guests, Lady Isabella gestured to Mara. "I believe that she's one of the unfortunate inheritors. Lost and cursed—a true immortal who will never know the peace of death."

Heru and Mr. White watched Mara in wonder. Commander White's face remained stuck in a frown as he kept his judgmental gaze on her. The tale Lady Isabella shared seemed unbelievable and almost insane. A broken soul scattered across time, and Mara was one of them. If this was true, what about the White Lady? Mara wasn't one to think of such possibilities. Then again, she had another dilemma on her hands—her amnesia.

Mara gawked at Hema's queen. "How do you know this?"

Isabella gave a smug smile. "If you live as long as we have, you are bound to learn many things. I learned about the Curse of the Undying from Morgan of Désir, who is originally from Thoron." She glanced at the two disciples. "Some of us have lived longer than the gods."

Mr. White looked dumbfounded. Commander White scowled at the vampire. The ruler of Hema smiled back, not caring if she offended.

"Do you know how to remove it?" Mara asked.

Isabella looked at her dismissively. "I do not possess such knowledge. Master Harold would know more about your predicament."

Glancing back into the box, Mara noticed the vial filled with red liquid. "The cure?"

"Yes," Isabella answered. "It'll rid you of the putrid essence of the mongrel. Such an unfortunate creature, like you, has had your fill of bad luck. And the last thing you need is to become a beast. I hope you take it."

Mara took the vial out of the box. With her free hand, she reached for the crystal stopper that sealed the potion within.

"Wait," called a male voice.

Mara stopped and looked at Heru. He had risen from his seat with an arm raised towards her.

"Are you sure you want to take the cure?" Heru asked, lowering his arm.

She stared at him. "I need it."

As Mara reached for the lid again, Heru began to move towards her.

"It's not as bad as you think," he told her.

She stopped and glanced back at him. "But I was turned against my will."

"I'm sorry, but it's not so bad to be a werewolf."

Isabella laughed. "What makes you think she wants to stay as a mongrel?"

Heru kept watching Mara. "I'll take care of you and give you the best life I could ever offer."

Everyone stared at Heru. Mara was stunned and speechless.

Even Mr. White expressed surprise. "Sounds like you want to marry her."

Heru gazed back at him. "Oh, I didn't realize you had a problem. Maybe you are interested in her?" He gestured to the commander. "You want her to marry your son?"

"What are you talking about?" Commander White demanded, snapping his glare onto Heru. "You seriously think I'm interested in her?" He sulked at Mara.

Mara looked back at him in discouragement. Tensions began to flare.

"Oh, dinner is here," Lady Isabella said.

Servants entered the dining hall, serving each guest with a plate of roast beef. The sight and smell took Mara's eyes off of the commander.

"Even though this is an improvement," the commander said in a calmer tone, "she's not much to look at."

Mara looked back at Commander White, knowing he was talking about her.

"Karl!" Flustered, Mr. White refused to tolerate this behaviour any longer, even if his son was Commander of the Holy Blades. "How rude! Apologize to her."

The commander frowned at Mr. White, surprised that his father demanded an apology.

Mara shook her head. "It's okay. I'll take it as a compliment."

"Well, I'm sorry," the older gentleman told Mara. "He says that about every other woman."

Heru snorted. "Well, he'll never get married at this rate."

Even Lady Isabella smiled at the remark.

Mara could see the humiliation on Commander White's face. He kept glaring at his father until the aroma of the meal before him drew his gaze to his plate. He became transfixed by the medium-rare meat as everyone else began to eat.

Using his utensils, the commander sliced into his feast with trembling hands. He stabbed the meat, then raised a piece to his lips. He shuddered upon taking the first bite. After pulling the fork out, Commander White put it down. He did the same with his knife, but it hit the edge of the plate with a clang. It drew his father's attention.

"Karl?" Mr. White called.

He ignored his father, his eyes hypnotically drawn to the red meat. He lifted his hands and reached for it. Picking up the meat with his bare hands, he lifted the slice to his mouth and bit into it. Juices leaked from the meat and filled his mouth, and a trickle descended his chin.

Mara had also witnessed his strange behaviour.

"What are you doing?" Mr. White asked, expressing more concern.

Lost in his hunger, Commander White bit deeper into the meat. He shook his head, tearing off a piece and swallowing.

Mara glanced at Lady Isabella and Heru with concern, but they ate their meals as if nothing was happening. The commander's odd display was abnormal as if he remained a werewolf. While wolfing down his meal, he stopped and stared off into space. The look in his eyes was unreadable. Something inside of him was taking over.

"You must stop," Mr. White said with a stern voice. "This isn't like you."

The father reached for his son's hands, attempting to take the meat away. The commander began to growl. No one was taking his meal away. Rising from his seat, he lashed out at his old man with an inhuman expression. His chair was knocked over, finally grabbing everyone's attention.

Mr. White shrank away in fear. "Karl!"

The commander's face had finally softened as his father's voice reached him. Confusion took over. He glanced at the meat with horror. Evan approached to set his chair back up to its proper position. Sitting back down, the commander lowered his meal to the plate with shaky hands.

"What's happening to me?" Commander White asked.

Evan stood by his left side. "Sir, you are experiencing the after-effects of lycanthropy."

He looked at Evan in bewilderment. "What? Is this permanent?"

"No," Evan answered, "it will fade over time."

The commander stared at his dinner plate for a few seconds. He rose from his chair again and stormed away from the table.

Mr. White looked concerned. "Where are you going?"

"I'm going to my room. I'm not hungry."

Once the commander disappeared, Heru gave a mocking grunt. "You can take the man out of the beast, but you cannot take the beast out of the man."

Isabella remained silent for a brief moment. "If you wish, I can help the commander," said Hema's queen, turning her gaze onto Mr. White.

The older man watched her with curiosity. "How?"

"I can use my glamour."

Mara looked confused. "Glamour?"

Lady Isabella glanced back at her. "It is a form of hypnosis." She turned her gaze onto Mr. White. "I can help your son overcome this problem."

Mr. White pondered her offer. "Okay, I'll allow it, as long as Karl agrees. Thank you."

After a very awkward dinner, Mara retired to her room. She felt Heru's eyes on her while leaving.

* * *

Mara heard three knocks on her door.

"It's me, Mr. White," called a voice from the other side.

Mara answered the door, allowing Mr. White entry.

"What is it?" Mara asked.

He looked at her with a frown. "I wish to apologize for my son's behaviour."

Mara looked at him strangely. Why was he apologizing again? He already did that. She sighed, "Fine, I forgive you." A question crossed her mind. "I don't mean to pry, but does he drink?"

His eyes widened. "How did you know?"

"Could smell it on him at the meeting."

Mr. White grew silent for a moment. "He's been struggling with it," the older man confessed, "since the death of his wife."

"Oh, he was married?" Mara grew curious about the commander's former wife. But she was a stranger to the father and son. It was not in her place to know. "Sorry to hear that."

"I know, but let's not end on a sad note." Then, "I also want to address Heru."

"Oh, that…"

"Are you going to do it?"

She shook her head. "I wish I said no, but didn't know how he would react."

Mr. White nodded. "Make your own decisions. Don't let anyone else decide for you."

With that, he bid her goodnight.

They were to settle the murder of Saskia in the morning. Mara was unsure how the opposing parties would do this as they blamed each other. Still, any evidence or information was helpful. After the discussions, she would take the cure. Knowing tomorrow was going to be a big day, Mara turned in for the night. She closed her eyes and fell asleep.

* * *

Mara opened her eyes to unfamiliar surroundings. No longer was she in the guest room, but a cave filled with scattered bones of animals and humans.

"Where…?"

The howls of wolves cut her off. Flashes of last night's events came to her mind. She remembered being carried by a werewolf with white fur. She was surrounded by sniffing and whining wolves. Mara was no longer in Isabella's castle, but the Old Hunting Ground. Heru abducted her, promising to care for her.

All Mara could do was hold her head and sigh in distress. For some reason, Heru assumed she wanted to be with him. Mara decided to wait for his return and tell him this was all a big misunderstanding. She made up her mind and planned to take the cure.

Morning passed. Heru had yet to return.

While waiting, she began to wonder about the cure. Did she have it?

After rummaging through her belongings, Mara found the small phial. She took the cure out. Mara glanced up at the cave entrance before removing her mask. She wondered what will happen when she took it. She recalled Commander White nearly vomiting out all of his blood. But his transformation required a larger dosage.

After opening the bottle, Mara tilted her head back and drank the whole concoction. The cure tasted a little sweet and was thick. Placing the vial on the ground, she waited for the cure's effects. Glancing down at a smooth stone, Mara saw a drop of black blood fall onto it. She stared at the blood with curiosity and lifted her hand to her nose. Mara saw blood on her fingers; her nose was bleeding. Her body began to shake. Her throat burned, making her cough and wheeze.

She felt like throwing up. Mara tried to stand, only to fall to her knees. She threw her head forward and vomited out a large quantity of blood. The choking sounds alerted the wolves, who entered the cave and growled at her. Mara gazed up to see Heru standing among them. Black liquid seeped from her eyes and ears. Despite losing a lot of blood, she began to feel better already. But Mara was now in trouble.

Heru frowned at her, and then looked down. His eyes began to glow yellow when he glanced up at her again. He released a roar as his skin split open. Heru tore at his flesh, allowing white fur to take its place. Mara stood back, watching the beast emerge. He was very impressive. His head resembled a wolf's while the rest of his body appeared human. He had large hands with sharp claws. His legs resembled a wolf's hind-quarters. And he owned a bushy tail. He still kept his brown slacks, although more torn from his transformation. Mara stared in awe until she noticed his angry face. He bared his razor-sharp fangs as he roared.

She dashed from Heru. He gave chase. The rough trail was seldom touched by humans, making it easy to lose one's footing. She had to be careful lest she stumbled and fell. Mara looked back while running from the creature. Heru snarled and gnashed his jaws as he ran on all fours. Witnessing her consumption of the cure angered Heru, now he wanted to end her life. The beast leapt into the air and lunged at her. She ducked underneath a thick tree branch, but Heru went right through it. It did not slow him down.

As she ran, Mara recognized the place where she cured Commander White. Hemal was close. She kept running until she reached a dead end. Turning around, she saw the beast approaching her. Heru bared his teeth and snarled.

"Heru, please listen to me," Mara pleaded.

There was no reasoning with him. Heru kept snarling as he came closer.

Mara's eyes began to glow. Holding her hands behind her back, she pulled out a small silver dagger from her left glove. If there was one thing she learned from the Silver Thorns, it was to have a secret weapon. Her eyes continued to glow yellow while staring back at her attacker. Heru lunged at her. A powerful force knocked the air out of her lungs. A loud screech rang in her ears, followed by a weak growl. She slipped away into the darkness.

* * *

Mara awoke to find herself underneath Heru. He remained in his beast form. She shoved him to the side and moved away from him. Standing up, she realized he was unmoving. Turning him over, she knew why. Her silver dagger was embedded deep in his chest. Blood seeped from the wound and his mouth. She recalled Lady Isabella's warning about silver being lethal to a werewolf. But what were her choices?

She nudged him to see if he remained alive. He did not stir. Staring at the dagger, Mara reached over and pulled it out. A hand suddenly grabbed her wrist and held on tight, startling her. Still alive, Heru changed back. She gazed at his pale and near lifeless face. He looked up at her with glowing eyes.

"Why... did you do this?" Heru asked weakly.

"You tried to kill me," Mara explained.

"I thought you wanted to be... in the pack..."

"What?"

"That letter you gave me..." He coughed up some blood. "You told me you wanted to stay as a werewolf."

Mara grew confused. "What letter?"

After retrieving an item from his torn trousers, Heru passed it to her with shaky hands. Upon seeing the letter, Mara's eyes widened. It was addressed to Heru and signed in her name.

"I want to remain as a werewolf. Have no desire to be cured. Meet me in my bedchambers. We'll leave in the middle of the night." She looked up from the letter, her mind reeling.

"You wrote this... you didn't want the cure."

Mara looked at Heru. "I didn't write this."

Heru stared at her in bewilderment. He started heaving, drawing closer to his last breath.

"Who gave you this?" Mara asked.

"That man..." Heru exhaled slowly. His body became still as the glow faded from his eyes.

Mara then looked back at the letter. She knew she didn't write it; this was not even her handwriting. Gazing back at Heru's corpse, Mara realized this looked bad for she slew a guardian of a seal to the Dark One. Mara heard howls in the distance. She had no choice but to remove the dagger and leave his body behind.

Chapter Eight

Choosing Sides

Mara reached Hemal by the afternoon. Returning from the Old Hunting Ground, her mind still reeled. Her heart was pounding as she tried to understand what happened. Her bloodstained attire grabbed the attention of bystanders. She ignored them while approaching Bartharoy Castle. She wanted to run but did not have enough energy. Eventually, she reached the castle gate. Mara looked at the guards who refused to budge.

"Please, I need to talk to Lady Isabella," she requested.

After a moment, the castle gates opened.

Evan greeted her with indifference. "Hello. How may we help you?"

Mara noticed his cold demeanour. He acted like they never met.

"I need to speak with Lady Isabella," she told him.

Evan watched her. "For what reason do you seek an audience with Milady?"

Mara grew silent, sensing that none welcomed her here. Was it because of what happened last night? She intended to correct this misunderstanding.

"Heru is dead."

Evan and the knights froze, for they never expected such news. The guards glanced at each other, then to Evan for further instruction. Gaping at her, the steward beckoned her in.

"Please, do come in! Milady must know about this."

He led Mara to Isabella's main chambers.

Lady Isabella sat at her favourite chair with a glass of blood. Mr. White drank a cup of tea while the commander indulged in a glass of brandy. The three took notice as Mara entered the chambers. Isabella and Mr. White stood up.

The older man approached her, looking confused. "What are you doing here?"

"Yes, that is a question I would like to know as well," Lady Isabella said, folding her arms. She looked displeased to see Mara. "I thought you wanted to spend the rest of your life as a beast." After watching Mara for a while, the ruler's dismissive gaze began to change. "The infection in your blood—I no longer sense it. You took the cure?"

Mara nodded.

"And what of Heru?" Isabella questioned.

Mara tried to think of an answer, but only one surfaced in her mind. "He's dead."

She saw wide eyes and open mouths. Mara suspected they were horrified, considering Heru was bound to a seal. However, Hema's ruler looked amused.

"Is that so?" Lady Isabella asked with a hint of excitement. "How did he meet his end?"

Mara took a deep breath. "I killed him."

Everyone stared at her in silence.

Lady Isabella smirked. "Oh, you did?"

"It was in self-defence!" Mara exclaimed. "He abducted me. I only had the cure and a silver dagger. He saw me take the cure and tried to kill me. I thought the dagger would incapacitate him..." She watched every one of them, anticipating a response.

The vampire's surprise faded. "I should have warned you about taking the cure in front of him," she said softly. "Heru was known to care for those bound to turn, hence why he showed compassion towards you. It was in his nature to care for them as if they were his children, but there was only so much he could do to keep them in check. He sometimes created a rogue that went out of control. These rogues often wandered near human settlements and caused problems." Isabella turned away. "Long ago, one wandered into Marrow and slaughtered everyone. It drove me to find a cure. I hired many doctors and scientists to create it. It took a while to perfect it, but now I can prevent such tragedy from ever happening again. I even offered to cure Heru, but he refused." She looked at Mara. "He took great pride in being a werewolf."

Mara gazed at her. While feeling guilty about killing Heru, she had not forgotten the details of the incident. "He thought I wanted to stay as a were-wolf."

"And did you?" Mr. White questioned.

Mara shook her head. "We spoke last night. You knew I intended to take the cure."

Isabella folded her arms. "Possibly a set-up."

The commander began to approach them. He was glaring at Mara the whole time ever since she returned from the Old Hunting Ground. Mara noticed his hateful stare, as well as the empty glass in his hand.

"Likely story," he spoke in a cold tone.

Everyone watched him.

Mr. White looked at his son with caution. "What do you mean?"

"You don't believe me?" Mara asked, frowning at him.

Commander White shook his head. "No, I do not," he replied. He turned his attention to his father. "This is another possessor to die around her." He glanced back at her. "I believe she's the Cursed Herald from the prophecy."

"Prophecy? Cursed Herald?" Mara questioned.

Isabella rolled her eyes. "Great, you're now going to spill that drivel?"

Mara looked at her. "What is it?"

"The Prophecy of Kallikratés foretells the return of the Dark One," Lady Isabella explained. "An entity, known as the Cursed Herald, will break all the seals and awaken the great beast. However, the Great Lord shall return. Reborn as a human, he will reunite with his goddess. And they shall defeat the Dark One, reviving the Golden Age."

While listening to Isabella, Mara could sense the disdain in her voice. Hema's ruler was never fond of the gods or the Faith. Even the two disciples had noticed. Ignoring her tone, Mr. White approached Mara with a meek expression on his face.

"Ardana will be the first to face its wrath, then the rest of the world," the older man added.

The commander rolled his eyes. "I don't think it is mere coincidence. You are the Cursed Herald. I am sure of it." He stared her in the eye. "You killed Heru. You broke a seal to the Dark One. Now I'm beginning to believe that you killed Saskia as well!"

Mara began to tremble. What nerve he had—accusing her of Saskia's murder. There was more evidence on Lady Isabella and the Faith, and Mara was proven innocent. Now it seemed Commander White was shifting all the blame back onto her. She never heard of this Cursed Herald before. It sounded like he made this up on the fly.

Speaking of evidence and proof, Mara recalled the letter from Heru. She reached into her satchel and retrieved it.

"What is that?" Mr. White asked, looking at the letter.

"Heru had this," Mara explained. "It was addressed to him and signed in my name, but I didn't write this."

"Then who did?" Isabella questioned.

"Before Heru died, he said a man gave him this last night," Mara replied. "Whoever did this must be responsible."

"Then the culprit must be within these castle walls," Hema's queen responded.

The father continued to gaze at the letter. "May I see it?"

Mara glanced back at the older man and offered it to him.

After studying it for a few seconds, Mr. White's eyes began to widen. "It can't be."

Mara looked at him with a questioning glance. "What is it?"

"I recognize this writing," Mr. White replied grimly, then he looked at his son. "It's yours!"

The commander gaped at his father in confusion, then snatched the letter from the older man's hands. He furrowed his brow while studying it. Mara watched in surprise, as Lady Isabella folded her arms in amusement.

"Seems we've caught the true culprit!" Lady Isabella gave a smug smile.

Commander White gave Hema's ruler a death glare. "I didn't write this letter, nor did I give this to Heru!"

"But Karl," Mr. White said, "this handwriting is yours. Even I recognize it."

The commander glowered at his father. "This is a mistake," he began to shout. "I didn't write this letter!"

Evan came forward. "My apologies, but I saw you deliver a letter to Master Heru last night."

Mara gazed at Evan. Everything fell into place. She looked back at Commander White, who had turned his glare onto the steward. Even Evan was not safe from his furious scowl.

"No, I didn't give him this letter," Commander White maintained, but his composure began to falter. "I... I... don't remember."

Mara remained silent, unaware of the older man's gaze on her.

"What do you think?" Mr. White addressed her.

She glanced at him, then noticed everyone looking at her. Even the commander's fiery gaze fell on her.

"Yes, my dear," Lady Isabella said. "What do you think?"

Mara folded her arms and pondered the evidence. "It's obvious. He did it."

A powerful force threw her off balance. Mara was on the ground in an instant with distorted vision. A stinging sensation began to spread from the left side of her face. Eventually, she came to terms with what happened. Mara glanced up to see the culprit responsible for striking her. Commander White glared down at her with a dark and angry expression. His rage-filled face made him appear demonic.

"How dare you make such accusations?" Commander White raged. "What do you know? Nothing!" He threw his glass down, shattering it into several shards.

Mara winced in response. She hoped not to get any glass in her eyes.

Taking the letter, the commander ripped it up. Everyone looked on in shock as he destroyed a crucial piece of evidence before their eyes. Even Mr. White was stunned at his son's behaviour. He stepped in between the two.

"Please, let's calm down." The older man gazed at Mara. "This is all a misunderstanding."

Evan approached Mara and helped her to her feet. She looked down at the ground, unwilling to look at anyone, especially the commander.

"Hitting a woman," Lady Isabella said, folding her arms. "Thought you followers of the Faith possessed a shred of decency, but it seems I was proven wrong... again." She gazed at Evan. "Take her to her room. Tend to her injuries."

Evan bowed and then escorted Mara to her room. She could still sense the commander's hateful glare on her.

"It seems I may have to reconsider our treaty," Isabella said.

Mara heard no more of their conversation. Evan escorted her to her room, where she was to rest for the next couple of hours.

* * *

Mara sat on the edge of her bed, feeling the left side of her face. It still stung from the hit.

"Are you okay?"

She looked up and saw Isabella in the doorway. Standing up, Mara shook her head.

"I'd be lying if I said I was," Mara grumbled.

Isabella folded her arms and gazed down at the floor. "Unbelievable," the ruler muttered. "He would stoop so low to hit a girl, human or not."

"It's okay," Mara said. "I know he's drunk."

"His behaviour is unsuitable for the Commander of the Holy Blades," Lady Isabella spoke. "Such a man would never become captain of my knights."

Mara shook her head. "He's been struggling since the death of his wife. His father told me."

Isabella tilted her head to the right. "Perhaps I should have helped him overcome these issues as well?"

"I guess…" Mara changed the subject. "You think he orchestrated Heru's death?"

Isabella gazed back at her. "Is it not human nature to get defensive when caught? Besides, they are followers of Kallikratés. I do not trust them."

"Why would they do it?" Mara asked.

"Heru was critical of Kallikratés. Long ago, he was a loyal general to the gods. But he was assassinated over a rumour."

"What was the rumour?"

"He was conspiring to murder the Great Lord and take his place," Lady Isabella explained. "The King found out and ordered his assassination. Since then, he never trusted them."

Mara began to wonder if the deaths of Saskia and Heru were Kallikratés' doing. Master Harold mentioned their notorious reputation of being intolerant. And considering the commander's recent actions, her thoughts and views began to align with those of Hema's queen.

"Saskia suspected Kallikratés' involvement in Khan's disappearance," Mara revealed.

"Is that so?" Isabella turned away. "Khan was also very critical of them. The gods and their followers were responsible for the loss of his daughter." She gazed back at her. "Have you shared this knowledge with Master Harold?"

"Yes, and he warned me about Kallikratés."

Isabella smiled. "Not crossing the Faith is smart." She beckoned her. "We shall have dinner soon. Come, join us."

Mara joined Isabella. They both walked to the dining hall.

"Now we need to solve the murders of Saskia and Heru," Mara muttered.

"And finalize the treaty, which is why Commander White and his father are here."

"Master Harold mentioned this," Mara said. "And before I left, I heard you talking about it."

"According to Kallikratés, my outlawing of the Faith is an attack on religion," Lady Isabella revealed. A frown formed on her face. "But I believe they are corrupt and power-hungry, as they have been since the gods came into existence. After the fall of the old kingdom, the Faith has dwindled in Ardana. Now they target my kingdom to hold onto whatever power they have left. That old priestess threatened war if I don't accept the terms."

Mara gaped at Isabella. "She threatened war?"

The ruler's face turned grimmer. "The Holy Blades outnumber my knights. The Faith controls Mirahyll, while Davis serves as their puppet. The Silver Thorns prefer neutrality, and their numbers are dwindling. I do not have many options."

Mara looked away. "If you don't mind me asking, why did you outlaw the Faith?"

"Kallikratés and their gods murdered my family."

Mara was surprised to hear this.

"Yes, I remember it as if it were yesterday," Isabella began her tale. "While their empire grew, many kingdoms fell. But my family, the proud Bartharoy Royal Family, stood in their way. We wielded a great army, leading us into a stalemate. To prevent further bloodshed, we agreed on a peaceful truce. We were to be a vassal state—allowed to keep our kingdom and rule as long as we worshipped the gods. However, they betrayed us."

"What happened?"

"Kallisto had her followers poison my family. Kratés rallied his armies and decimated our military, destroyed defenceless villages, and slaughtered several innocents. I believe they did this to keep Hema weak, and to send an example should anyone rise against them."

Mara frowned. "I'm sorry for your loss."

Isabella gave a sympathetic smile. "My family may be gone, but I remain. The strange magic of this land allowed me to return. I was fortunate to witness the fall of that kingdom. It was a delight to see the Dark One emerge and raze their palace to the ground."

Mara looked disturbed. "So many people died."

Isabella gazed at her. "It is true. I remember the day Master Harold approached me, asking me to join him and five others to seal the Dark One away. In exchange, I requested two things: to be reinstated as the rightful ruler of Hema and demand the Faith to answer for their crimes. Unfortunately, the Faith refused to acknowledge my request. So, I took my land back and outlawed the worship of Kallikratés as long as I remain ruler."

Mara was quite impressed with Isabella's story. Despite hearing much praise for the gods, not a peep of their misdeeds ever arose. Not many were willing to talk about peace and prosperity at the cost of several lives. One side would say that it was justified, but what about the other side? Lady Isabella was a victim of their cruelty, someone on the other side.

"Very sorry to hear that, but can't you use recent events as leverage?" Mara asked.

"Ah, yes, the attack on Hemal," said Hema's queen. "Under normal circumstances, justice would have been served. But you chose to spare the commander."

Mara shook her head. "You can't persecute him?"

"The Faith will come to his aid. I'll be on the losing side."

"So, he's untouchable?"

"I'm afraid so," Isabella replied. "The Faith will never let anything happen to him."

"Why is he so special?" Mara asked.

Isabella smiled. "You seem so curious about him—do you care for Commander White?"

Mara's face heated up. "No! Not after what he did."

"You sure? I've seen your eyes upon him at the meeting. He would have been a true prince had he not done or said those things to you."

Mara's face grew hotter. Her infatuation towards him was all plain to see. Who else knew about her attraction to the commander? She felt embarrassed, knowing her gawking had drawn the attention of others.

"You poor thing," Isabella cooed. "Your affection is in vain."

"I..." Mara didn't want to admit to being in love, but she would be lying to herself.

"I can help you," Isabella offered.

Mara looked back at her in confusion. "How?"

Reaching out with her cold hands, Isabella took Mara's face. The vampire guided the undying's gaze to her glowing red eyes. Mara grew paralyzed while staring into her lustrous eyes.

"Turn off your humanity," Isabella ordered.

"What?" This confused Mara. She didn't know what Isabella was doing to her.

"Humans fear us, but they commit more crimes to their own."

"But... I..." Mara's words became slow. So hard to think when looking into Isabella's eyes.

"You are one of us. Now, turn it off."

A part of her faded away. Like being stranded in a vast ocean, she sank deeper into the darkness. She heard a distant voice, telling her it was okay. Mara felt as if a weight had lifted from her shoulders. She no longer had a care in the world. All the terrible things she endured became a distant memory.

"That must feel better," Isabella said, releasing Mara's face. "It is good for you to cast aside your silly human emotions."

She blinked at Isabella with faded eyes. Mara remained silent, while the ruler of Hema smiled at her.

"Let us go to dinner. Our guests are waiting for us." Isabella walked ahead of her.

Mara's motions were slow and robotic, trailing behind Hema's queen.

* * *

The two finally reached the dinner table. Commander White and his father were already seated. They noticed the stiff movements of Mara but remained quiet. She turned to stare at the commander with cold eyes. He glared at her, still mad about her accusation. He should get over it. She ignored his fiery gaze and sat down. Mr. White watched her, appearing more concerned.

"I apologize," said Lady Isabella. She gestured to Mara. "We were having a conversation."

The father and son exchanged glances. They looked at Mara for confirmation. After a few seconds, Mr. White gazed at Isabella while Commander White kept his eyes on Mara.

"That is fine," Mr. White said.

Commander White watched Mara with folded arms. "What did you two talk about?"

Mara gave a cold stare while removing her mask.

"None of your business," she replied in a cold tone. Mara gazed down at her plate and began to eat, ignoring the commander's angry expression.

"Excuse me?" Commander White hissed.

Even Mr. White looked surprised. "Oh my… How rude!"

Isabella smiled at her. "There is no need for hostility." She looked at the two men. "I would be glad to talk about our conversation."

Armoured guards filled the room. The two men looked around, stunned by the number of knights surrounding them. All the exits were blocked. Mr. White looked frightened while the commander scowled at Isabella.

"What is the meaning of this?" Commander White questioned. He gazed at Mara, who was still eating.

Mara did not acknowledge the guards' presence. Even the commander was taken aback by her lack of response. He looked back at Isabella.

The ruler of Hema took a sip from her wine glass. She pulled away and gazed at her guests. "I think you already know," she said dismissively. "Perhaps now you want to confess?"

The commander rose from his seat, glaring at Isabella. His father joined him.

"That accusation is ridiculous!" Commander White exclaimed. "Even you know that!"

"Why would we kill them?" Mr. White cried. "Chances are, it was you!"

"Once again, you blame me." Isabella rolled her eyes. "Yet you have no evidence. The Faith had more reason to kill Saskia and Heru than I do. And I'm going to get the truth out of you, one way or another."

The guards closed in around them. The commander and his father looked around, but escape was impossible. Commander White glanced back at Mara, noticing no change. Even the older gentleman gazed at her.

"Please, you must help us," Mr. White pleaded, but his cries fell on deaf ears.

Commander White stared at her in anger. "How can you sit there and eat? Don't you see what is going on?"

Mara did not respond. She could care less about what was happening to them. Angered, he slammed his hands on the table, causing everything to jump.

"Answer me, goddammit! What the hell is wrong with you?" Commander White shouted, his eyes burned with hatred.

Mara froze for a moment.

"Not my problem," she said in a singsong voice as if to taunt him.

He glared at her in bewilderment. The guards grabbed them. Mara watched as they shouted and screamed, yet nothing would make her move.

Isabella smiled at her. "You are welcome to join us later."

Mara watched Lady Isabella leave. The guards hauled Commander White and his father to who-knows-where. They yelled and shouted, demanding to be released. Eventually, the dining hall grew silent.

Evan approached to serve her. She gazed at him and pointed to her plate.

"Can I please have more gravy?"

Chapter Nine

Change of Heart

After finishing her dinner, Mara pulled her mask back up. Evan guided her to another location. While being led down the hallway, she wondered what Isabella had planned for the father and son. How would Hema's ruler obtain a confession? Mara's stiff muscles began to relax, allowing her to move freely.

Mara looked at Evan. "Where are we going?"

The steward guided her to a room at the end of the hallway. It looked like an ordinary room until Evan approached the fireplace. Pushing on a fake wall, it opened up to reveal a corridor.

"This way," Evan beckoned.

Mara followed him into an old brick pathway lit by torches. Despite its age, the corridor was still in use. As Mara walked further, she could hear the pleading cries of Mr. White.

Once Evan opened the door, Mara spotted the old gentleman inside a cell. Then her attention fell onto some servants surrounding a strange contraption. They forced Commander White onto a chair. He struggled against them, but it was futile. Upon strapping him in, the servants inserted needles into his arms and legs. Each needle was attached to a thin pipe that stretched to a tank behind the chair. Once a lever was pulled, the tubes filled with red liquid. The commander grew pale as he watched his blood drain away.

Mr. White saw Mara. "Please, you must help!"

She stared back at him. "Why?"

Mr. White watched her in disbelief.

"A wise choice," Isabella said, appearing in the doorway. She floated over to Mara and stood beside her.

She looked at Isabella. "What is this?"

"A blood-draining machine," Isabella replied. "To curb the issue of ghouls, I was encouraged to use this. The ghoul is a result of a vampire draining a human of all their blood. I prefer the traditional method, but this machine has benefits. It is efficient in harvesting large quantities in a short amount of time. I have one set up in Hemal's clinic. This one is for interrogations."

Mara gazed at Commander White, seeing his scowl.

"Please, you must help us," Mr. White pleaded again.

"Don't bother, old man," said the commander. "She won't help us."

Isabella leered at him. "Why do you think she would help you? You should be helping yourself."

Commander White glanced at the ruler of Hema. "What do you want?"

Isabella walked to the back of the tank, watching the blood flow into it. "If you value your lives, you shall confess to the murders. And renounce the treaty."

"So, that's it? Your petty disagreement with Kallikratés?" Commander White stared ahead, not bothering to look at anyone. "Confess the crimes and renounce the treaty, and you won't kill us. Is that your plan?"

Hema's ruler smiled. "You possess a very high position in the Faith. Endangering your life may persuade that priestess."

"It won't work," the commander argued. "You will bring war upon yourself."

"You don't think the Faith will be devastated if I kill the Commander of the Holy Blades?"

Mara looked at Isabella. Even without her humanity, she knew this was not part of the plan. They were only seeking a confession. No one was supposed to die.

The vampire's face darkened. "Answer my question! Is it not true the Faith's presence has strengthened in Ozin after Saskia's departure?"

"We are protecting them," the commander answered. "Ozin chose to use our services before she died. We have a contract with them."

Mr. White nodded in agreement. "Yes, we're helping them, as the teachings have taught us. To hold on to hope in these dark times. And bring peace and prosperity of the Golden Age, lost long ago."

Isabella gazed at Mr. White in annoyance. "Peace? Prosperity? Hope? Do not make me laugh." She walked in front of Commander White. "The gods declared war upon the world, destroying millions of lives!"

Silence filled the room except for the machine's hum. About half a litre of blood filled the tank, yet Commander White showed no signs of fatigue. He glared back at Isabella and said, "Those who died chose to do so. They could live in a world given to them by the gods, or die in their world. So, such was their fate."

Mr. White's eyes widened. "That is from the Book of Kallikratés," the older man murmured.

Isabella glowered at the commander. "So, you believe all those people deserved to die because they refuse to obey?"

Commander White nodded. "Yes," he replied.

Isabella's eyes glowed in anger. She growled at the commander, but kept her cool and walked to the back of the tank. Grabbing another lever, she pulled on it. Commander White shuddered. His eyes rolled into the back of his head as more of his blood drained away. The tank began to fill much faster. Isabella gazed at him.

"You have just proven that humans commit more atrocities to their own, yet we are the monsters!" Isabella looked at Mara. "You have heard it yourself. Now you must be grateful that I shut your humanity off!"

Both men stared at Mara. Mr. White seemed horrified, while the commander appeared more surprised.

"No wonder why she's acting this way," Mr. White murmured.

"Glamoured?" Commander White questioned. At least a litre of his blood had filled the tank. Growing weaker, he closed his eyes and fell unconscious. His body went limp, for he no longer had the strength to stay awake. He was as pale as a ghost while his blood was draining away.

Mr. White saw this and cried, "Karl!"

Mara stared at the commander. He seemed so peaceful, his face relaxed and looking angelic.

Mr. White glanced back at Mara with begging eyes.

"Please help us," he pleaded, gripping the bars.

Mara looked back at the older man.

"Why should she help you?" Isabella hissed. "For all we know, the Faith murdered Saskia and Heru. And you intended to blame her!"

The father ignored Hema's ruler and looked at Mara. "Please, hear me out," he persisted.

"Do not listen to him!" Isabella bellowed. "He'll do anything to save himself!"

Mara might have fallen victim to Isabella's glamour, but it only shut off her humanity. She remembered Mr. White's advice.

"Make your own decisions," she recalled the nobleman's words. "Don't let anyone else decide for you."

With the conversation resonating in her mind, Mara looked at Mr. White.

"Go on," Mara spoke quietly. "I'm listening."

Isabella looked surprised. She never expected such a response.

Mr. White trembled with relief. His grip on the bars loosened.

"We did not kill Saskia or Heru," he insisted calmly. "There is no reason for us to kill them."

"Liar," Isabella claimed. "They want to control Ardana again, but we possessors stood in their way. Kallikratés seeks to kill us, starting with Saskia."

The older man shook his head. "Not only was Saskia her sworn enemy, but so was Heru," Mr. White revealed. "Lady Isabella planned to make Hema werewolf-free."

"Why?" Mara questioned.

"A werewolf's bite is fatal to a vampire," he explained. "The true purpose of the cure is to save vampires from their bite. And earlier versions were fatal to werewolves, which was why Heru despised the cure."

Mara turned her gaze onto the ruler of Hema. The latter froze upon hearing the older man mention this. The look on Isabella's face was evident that Mr. White was telling the truth. Mara spotted the key and took it. She approached Mr. White's cell and opened it. Strangely enough, Isabella did nothing to stop her.

"You failed to mention this," Mara addressed her while freeing Mr. White.

Isabella shrugged. "I do not deny it."

Hema's ruler approached the machine. Taking a wine glass from a shelf, Isabella placed it below the tank where a faucet sat below. After turning the tap, blood flowed into the glass. "Creating the cure required sacrifice, but I did it for my people. Over the years, the survival rate improved and many lived normal lives."

She turned the faucet off and lifted her wine glass, filled with Commander White's blood. Mara and Mr. White watched her drink. After taking a long sip, Isabella glanced over at Evan. "Why not ask him?" She gestured to him. "Evan was one of the unfortunate souls afflicted with lycanthropy, and now he lives a normal life."

Evan nodded. "It is true, Your Highness." The steward gazed at the two. "I had the infection until Lady Isabella cured me."

Isabella gazed at Mara. "Despite what others think, I have always extended my hand to those less fortunate. And I can also help you."

"What are you talking about?" Mara questioned.

"You are cursed. Such a sad state. Not human, yet not supernatural like the rest of us." The ruler of Hema smiled. "How would you like to become a vampire?" Isabella lifted her wrist and bit into it. She walked up to Mara, holding her bloody wrist out. "You shall never suffer again."

All of a sudden, Mr. White dashed in between them and frowned at Isabella.

"No, you must not take her offer," he addressed Mara.

Mara watched him in confusion. "Mr. White, what are you doing?"

He gazed back at her. "If she turns you, you will be sired to her. Obey her every whim without question! Is that what you want?"

Isabella smirked. "You think I would do that? I am offering to help her."

"You imprisoned us!" Mr. White cried. "Look at what you're doing to Karl."

Mara gazed back at the commander's unconscious form. His face was almost as pale as the moon, as the machine continued to drain his blood. Even without her humanity, something deep inside was bothering her to save him. While gazing at Commander White, Mara listened to their argument.

"If I agree to this treaty, Hema shall be subjected to oppression once again," Isabella claimed. "I saw what they did to my people—murdered them and enslaved the survivors. Hema fell into poverty. My people starved and froze while you and your gods did nothing! I brought them back to prosperity by removing this cancer, known as Kallikratés."

"How dare you speak of Queen Kal—"

"Say their names, and I will kill you where you stand!" Isabella screeched.

Mara snapped her gaze back onto them. She saw the face of Hema's queen, her red eyes glowing with rage. The vampire bared her fangs and released a low hiss.

Mr. White became frozen upon seeing the angry face of the vampire ruler.

Isabella calmed down and looked at her. "You do not have much time left. I know your curse. It is a horrendous fate to die over and over again. Your sanity will erode, turning you into a monster that preys upon humans."

Mara gazed at Isabella. Then she looked at Mr. White, seeing his pleading eyes. Mara did not care for the older man. But when her eyes fell onto the commander, she could not look away from the prince. She stared at his closed eyes, seeing how relaxed his face was due to losing more than a pint of blood. Commander White did not have long to live.

Isabella smiled and approached her. "Well, what is your decision?"

Mara looked back at Isabella. "Let him go."

Three simple words stunned Isabella. Shaking off her shock, Hema's queen smiled. "Your infatuation remains," she teased. "Even after losing your humanity."

Mr. White glanced at Mara. He seemed surprised to know about Mara's attraction to his son.

"You lied to me," Mara pointed out. "We were supposed to find the truth, but you decided to abduct the two. For what? Make an ultimatum to the High Priestess? Or make an example of the two when things don't go your way?" She shook her head. "As far as I'm concerned, the treaty will allow the worship of Kallikratés in Hema, not remove you from power." Mara reached for her sword and unsheathed it. "You also shut off my humanity. Sorry if I come off as rude, but I'll not ask again."

Isabella gaped at her. She did not expect to be insulted. Taking her wine glass, Isabella threw its contents into Mara's face. The blood permeated the cloth cover, reaching her lips. She felt a tingling sensation on her face. She pulled the mask down and wiped the blood from her eyes. Mara glowered at Lady Isabella. She was not going to let the vampire get away with this. Isabella glared at her, still holding the empty wine glass in her hand.

"What a fool you are! How could you take their side?" Isabella threw the wine glass to the floor, shattering it into several pieces. "Thanks to the gods, we are cursed! Ardana is in this mess because of the Faith!"

Mr. White frowned at Isabella. "How dare you? The gods are not at fault."

"What did I say before? Do not ever mention them again!" Isabella raged, lunging at Mr. White.

The older man cried out in fear.

Mara had no clue what she was thinking, jumping in front of Mr. White. Isabella's hand tore through her chest. Mara stood frozen. Her left hand grasped the arm that impaled her while her right hand gripped her sword. Blood seeped from the wound. Even the older man and the vampire were stunned at her selfless act. Nobody knew how she remained standing.

Soon, a smile crept upon Lady Isabella's pale face. "You have taken a massive injury, my dear. Better take my offer while you still can."

"No…"

Mara's breathing began to intensify while she glared at Isabella. Her canines elongated, resembling the fangs of a wolf. She gripped her sword. Isabella pulled away before the undying could slash her arm off. Clutching her hand close to her chest, the vampire gazed down to see black blood staining it. Isabella gazed back at the wound she created. Black ooze poured out of the hole in Mara's chest before closing up. Isabella saw the dark markings on Mara's face. A bright yellow glow from her eyes pierced the shadow cast by her hood. A dark aura emanated from her body in the form of black smoke.

"What is this?" Isabella questioned, sensing the aura.

Mr. White stared in astonishment until he saw his son.

Commander White had lost nearly two litres of blood. His breathing was laboured, his face drained of all colour.

The old gentleman grew horrified. "Karl is dying!"

Mara frowned at Isabella, taking a step towards her. "Release him."

Isabella remained frozen. After getting over her shock, she looked daggers at Mara. "How dare you talk to me like that?"

She stared at Isabella with glowing eyes. "Guess I didn't make myself clear."

Mara took another step, pointing her sword at Isabella.

The vampire suddenly released a screeching sound as she transformed into a hideous bat-like creature. Her dress tore away while her body grew twisted. Bat-like traits graced her face, making her look more like a beast. Her fingers elongated, ending in razor-sharp claws. Large leather wings burst from her back. She was nine feet tall as she towered over them.

Mr. White was horrified. Mara would have shared a similar reaction if not for her lack of humanity. The hideous creature was the opposite of the beautiful and elegant ruler of Hema.

Isabella grabbed the tank. With relative ease, she tore it from the blood-draining machine. Raising the tank over her head, she punctured it with her long sharp fangs. Blood flowed down her throat. The two looked on, mystified and disgusted. After she finished, the vampire tossed it aside and turned her attention to the two.

"I shall kill you both and have the commander for dinner," Isabella hissed in a deep and raspy voice.

Mara glanced at Mr. White. "Leave now! I will deal with her."

"What about Karl?" Mr. White cried.

Mara snapped her head around and snarled, "Get him out of here!"

Mr. White became paralyzed. Seeing her face, Mara appeared more beast than human. Eventually, he snapped out of his shock and scrambled to free his son. Mara turned around and faced Isabella. She pointed her sword at the vampire, forcing her away from the machine and allowing the older man to free his son. Mr. White managed to get him out of the room while the castle servants fled. Mara stood alone against the vampire.

Isabella snarled. "You dare draw your blade?" She flew into the air. "Such a hypocrite! You would rather hunt and kill our kind?"

The vampire grabbed Mara by the neck and slammed her into the wall. The impact produced a gaping hole. Mara ended up in the main halls. Fleeing servants watched Isabella slap Mara around like a rag-doll. She hit the ground, stunned for a short while. She managed to get up and started running.

The bat-like beast laughed. "Where do you think you're going?"

Mara ran down the hall and found a flight of stairs. Getting into the stairwell, she turned around and saw that Isabella could not follow in her current form. Even with folded wings, she could not squeeze through. The vampire swiped at her in a futile attempt to hit her. Mara stared at her briefly before ascending the stairs. Reaching the top, she found herself in a very extravagant room covered in dust. Looking out the window, Mara found herself very high up in the castle. A snowstorm brewed with howling winds.

Mara noticed her reflection. She saw a pair of glowing eyes staring back at her. For some reason, seeing her face made her think of the White Lady. The rotting visage of that creature faded away to show a more human face—a face that looked similar to Mara's own.

A hand burst through the window. Isabella found her. Grabbing Mara by the neck, the vampire threw her out of the tower. The undying hit a snow-covered roof. She tried to recover, but Isabella landed beside her and grabbed her neck again. She lifted Mara into the air and began to strangle her. Mara was losing air; her vision began to blur.

Isabella laughed at her. "Go ahead and die! I can wait."

Unable to breathe, Mara closed her eyes. *'Not like this...'*

Somehow, Mara regained her strength and opened her eyes. Lifting her sword, she swung it into Isabella's arm. The vampire screeched. Mara fell to the ground with the severed hand wrapped around her neck. She tossed it aside. Vampire blood stained the snow red. Looking up at Isabella, Mara saw her face twisting in agony and fury.

Isabella growled at her, holding her wound. "You will pay!"

The vampire swung at Mara, sending her flying. She grunted while hitting another roof. Snow kicked up around her. Tiny drops of her blood created small black circles in the snow. Her sword landed beside her. While recovering, she saw Isabella flying around. She landed beside Mara, ready to finish her off.

"Time for you to join Saskia and Heru!" Isabella roared.

THE LOST & CURSED

"So it was you?" Mara questioned.

The vampire smirked, baring her razor-sharp teeth. "They were my greatest enemies! Saskia, that foolish woman—she swore to protect humans from creatures like me. Humans are nothing but cattle. They only live to feed and serve us!"

Isabella showed her true colours. This whole "protecting her people" was an act, so her food supply was not endangered.

"What of Heru?" Mara then asked.

"He was nothing but a mongrel! His existence was a threat to me. Everyone knows a werewolf's bite is fatal to a vampire. I am glad he's dead! That's what he gets for slaughtering my kin!" The ruler of Hema smiled. "I wanted to thank you for killing that mongrel and hoped you would take my offer. But since you refused, the only thing I can offer is death!"

Isabella lunged at her. Mara snatched her blade and pointed it upwards. The vampire noticed, but it was too late. Once the blade penetrated her heart, Isabella released an ear-piercing scream and fell onto Mara. She became still. Mara pushed her body to the side and got up.

She watched Isabella revert to her human form, then her flesh dissolved. Red fumes rose from the remains. Mara stared at Isabella's bloody skeleton, then fell to her knees. With her injuries taking a toll, Mara collapsed as the darkness claimed her.

Chapter Ten

Blood of the Great Lord

The tingling sensation in her nerves caused her hands to twitch. Soon, it became a burning sensation, setting fire to every inch of her body. The familiar feeling awakened her. Opening her eyes, Mara saw Dr. Simon towering over her. He held a lantern while examining her.

"Ah, you're awake," said the doctor. "We meet again."

She looked at him before gazing at her surroundings. She somehow returned to Hemal Clinic. It was still nighttime. The last thing she remembered was being on the rooftop of Bartharoy Castle. She glanced back at the doctor and noticed they were not alone. Mr. White watched her in silence. Commander White was awake and receiving a blood transfusion. He sat in a chair while hooked up to a large vial of blood. The commander frowned with folded arms.

Dr. Simon gestured to Mr. White. "He requested your retrieval. You succumbed to your injuries, but somehow revived."

Mara tried to move, only to discover the thick leather straps holding her down. Then she gazed at the three men with glowing eyes.

"What is this?" Mara hissed.

"It is a precaution," the doctor told her. "I also hear you fell victim to the glamour. And since Lady Isabella is dead, it will be impossible to undo it."

She raised an eyebrow. "You know I killed her?"

"The general public knows," Dr. Simon replied nonchalantly.

"Aren't you going to arrest me?"

"Lady Isabella was as cruel as they came. I'm sure most are pleased with this outcome. Evan will serve as interim chancellor until a new leader is elected."

"I didn't just kill Isabella, but Heru as well—two seals to the Dark One," Mara murmured.

Mr. White nodded. "I sent a letter to Greyward Hold, telling everything that transpired. We shall escort you back to Grey Mountain."

She stared at the father, then to his son. Commander White looked less than thrilled about travelling in the same carriage with her.

Mara glanced back at the older man. "Thanks, but I'll return myself."

"Nonsense," Mr. White said. "It'll be much better if we go with you. I think Master Harold will understand if we are there to explain."

The doctor prepared a syringe containing a clear liquid. She reckoned it was a sedative, as she watched him insert the needle into her arm.

"If I wanted to sleep, I don't need drugs to help me," Mara said flatly.

"It's a safety precaution," Dr. Simon said, injecting the contents into her arm.

"What? Am I dangerous?"

Nobody answered her question. Everything went dark. Yet a part of her brain remained awake.

"This room will be isolated," Dr. Simon said. "No one is to enter under any circumstances."

Mr. White and Dr. Simon helped the commander to his feet. Commander White looked back at her as they vacated the room. Now alone, Mara fell asleep.

* * *

Mara found herself within a forested area, on a cold winter night.

"Show yourself!" shouted a man.

She looked up a hill and saw a group of men holding lanterns. Mara ran from them. She later saw them setting up a camp. One wandered away while the others slept. She crept up to him, only to be attacked by him.

"You can't even speak, can you?"

She heard the familiar male voice again. There were flashes of silver and steel.

"I have nothing to say to the likes of you," Mara hissed. She could see herself punching him in the face, slashing him in the chest, and even kicking him in the backside. She shoved her opponent against a tree. "She will never take you away from me, ever again."

Mara heard the man scream and saw a red haze. Then she was thrown to the ground. Another man had attacked her. The last thing she saw was a sledgehammer stained with her blood.

* * *

Mara jolted awake. She was still lying on the examination table. The sedative remained in effect. Mara wondered how much the doctor pumped into her. Her body remained asleep, yet her mind was wide-awake. She tried to comprehend the unusual dream. That man she bit—she recalled seeing a dark grey overcoat sporting a red cape and golden plates of armour. She could not see his face, but the voice remained familiar. Speaking of which, she heard voices in the distance. Mara recognized them as the commander and his father.

"Oh, there you are," Mr. White called. "How are you feeling?"

"Better," the commander said in a bitter tone.

"Where are you going?"

"I'm just going for a walk."

The footsteps grew louder, coming closer to her room. From the corner of her left eye, she saw an image of a man appearing in the door window. Commander White looked inside. The doorknob turned before he entered her room. He gave a sour look as he approached her. She saw a flask in his hand. He had been drinking again. She snapped her eyes shut and pretended to be asleep. Whatever he planned, she could do little about it.

She sensed Commander White towering over her, the smell of alcohol drifting in her direction. He placed his fingers on her eyelids, then pushed them up. Mara could see his bright green eyes staring at her face. He moved his hands from her eyes. She snapped her eyes shut, making it look like she remained unconscious. He reached for her mask and pulled it down. Her body tingled, the sedative began to wear off. Her right arm broke free of the leather bind and grabbed the nape of his neck. It caught him off guard. He tried to pull away, but she held on tight.

She opened her eyes to see his startled face. Pulling him closer, she exhaled. She could tell he was unhappy but didn't care. She parted her lips and brushed them against his own. Commander White tried to pull away again, but she refused to release him. Her lips pulled into a smile as her canines elongated. Playfully, she bit his lower lip and pulled away. One of her fangs pricked the flesh, making him flinch. Mara drew his lifeblood. She extended her tongue to lap it up. Her body began to shudder as the tingling sensation returned. When Lady Isabella splashed his blood onto her face, Mara tasted his blood by accident. It made her feel alive. Now she wanted another taste. Opening her jaws, Mara chomped on his neck.

The commander screamed as his blood flowed into her stomach. Her entire body shuddered again. Every cell came alive and sang with joy. She felt an itch underneath the surface of her skin, growing stronger by the second. Her prince tasted like roast beef with a hint of alcohol. Her feeding frenzy blocked out the screams of her victim.

All of a sudden, she was tackled by three men. Two guards restrained her free arm while the doctor pried her jaws away from Commander White's neck. The commander staggered backwards, holding his wound. Mr. White rushed to his side.

"Karl! What happened?" He gazed at his son's neck.

Dr. Simon inspected his injury. "She missed the carotid artery, but the wounds are deep."

The doctor had Mr. White hold a cloth to the wound and put pressure on it. He left to retrieve some medical supplies. The commander sulked at Mara.

Mr. White gazed at his son while pressing the cloth to his neck. "What happened?"

"What do you think happened?" Commander White hissed, reaching for the cloth.

Mr. White looked at her while the guards restrained her to the examining table.

Mara stared back at them, noticing the surprise and horror. They all gazed at her in shock. She wondered why they were gawking at her like this. By the time Dr. Simon returned, the electric feeling had faded. Even the doctor saw her face and grew mystified.

Mr. White glanced at Dr. Simon and asked, "What is going on?"

The middle-aged doctor approached her. After observing her, he turned around and looked at the two men. "I shall dress your wound in another room."

Mr. White nodded and helped his son to his feet. The commander kept glaring at Mara. She stared back at him with wide glowing eyes.

One of the guards looked at her. "What about her?"

Dr. Simon glanced back at them. "Don't worry. I will determine what she is."

Mara glared at the doctor in response.

The doctor noticed her reaction. "I wish to run a few tests. They shall not hurt for the most part." He gazed at the guards. "Watch this room until I return."

The guards nodded.

The doctor guided everyone out of the room. Commander White scowled at her as he left. The guards placed her free arm back into the strap, securing her. She watched them leave her alone.

Mara remained on the table after an hour. It was all she could do since being strapped down. Staring at the leather binds holding her arms, she began to writhe. While pulling at the straps, Mara heard voices. Focusing her ears, Mara recognized Commander White and his father. Despite them occupying a different room, she heard them crystal clear.

"She bit you," Mr. White said. "And she transformed!"

"Great," Commander White murmured. "The last thing I need is that rumour going around."

"I think it's too late. Word of you possessing the blood of the Great Lord is circulating."

Unbeknownst to them, Mara was listening. It was her first time hearing about this rumour but did not know what it meant. While she continued to pull on the strap, the door opened. She looked up and saw Dr. Simon entering the room.

"Now, where were we?"

She stared at him and became still. The doctor approached her with some gloves and a small brown book. The notebook was for recording any details worth noting. She eyed the book.

Dr. Simon took notice. "I assure you the tests won't be terrible. A little pain may be involved, but it will help us determine what you are." He first observed her face. "Consuming human blood restores your humanity? That's a neat trick."

She just stared at him, oblivious to what he meant.

He noticed her reaction. "Don't believe me? Here, take a look at yourself."

Retrieving a mirror from a cabinet, he reflected her image onto her. Mara almost looked human, save for the glowing eyes, fangs, and the dark markings on her face. As far as she was concerned, only an undying's soul or a healing stone could restore her. How did this happen? The doctor put the mirror away and continued his observation.

"Only a few creatures feed on human blood," Dr. Simon spoke. Using a rag, the doctor wiped the gore from her lips and chin. He reached for her mouth and got her to open her jaws. He observed her fangs. "Vampire or werewolf comes to mind, but they do not feed on blood to maintain a human form."

Mara watched him in silence.

Dr. Simon removed his hand from her mouth and examined her left arm. He reached for her glove and began to remove it.

"Vampires must feed to remain functional," he revealed. "The ability to appear human is determined by age. The older they are, the more powerful they become. So the vampire is ruled out." He removed her glove to find a very human-looking forearm and hand. Though her fingernails were black, possessing small pointed tips. "Werewolves, on the other hand, are driven by insatiable bloodlust. So, maybe you're a hybrid of both?"

Dr. Simon took a silver surgical knife and lowered it to her arm. She flinched upon feeling the blade against her flesh.

The doctor gazed at her. "Relax, this is part of the test."

Mara inhaled as the sharp edge sliced into her flesh. Blood, black as night, poured out.

Dr. Simon had never seen this before. He was also stunned to see the cut close up and heal as if it never existed. He turned to his notebook and jotted down some notes.

"Not a vampire," he said, "or a werewolf for that matter."

She stared at him. "Could have told you that—I'm one of the undying."

Dr. Simon glanced at her in surprise. "You are?"

She nodded.

He gazed at his notes, continuing to add more words. "How strange. The undying originated in Thoron, but due to the imposed isolation, much of that knowledge remains there."

She shrugged. "To regain my human form, I need to absorb the soul of an undying or use a healing stone. Don't know how consuming his blood did this."

He examined her for a while, then went back to his notes and continued to write.

"You bit Commander White?" Dr. Simon asked. "Maybe the rumours are true?"

"Is it about him possessing the blood of the Great Lord?" Mara asked.

"So, you've heard?" Then, "It is unconfirmed. But considering your transformation, it may be true." He changed the subject. "These notes will be sent to Dr. Moen. He studies all the monsters in Ardana. Quite the eccentric, dabbling in many inventions and claiming to improve the lives of many Ardanians. He might know what kind of creature you are."

Mr. White entered the room. "We shall leave soon."

Dr. Simon nodded and released Mara from her restraints. Once freed, she took back her glove and put it on. While doing this, she witnessed the doctor handing the notes over to Mr. White.

"I would appreciate it if you delivered this to Dr. Moen," said the doctor.

The old gentleman took them and nodded.

Mara placed her mask back on and left the clinic. Mr. White followed her out.

Chapter Eleven

Lost and Found

The sun rose on November 17. The snow fell to the ground like light feathers. Leaving the clinic, Mara found Commander White waiting with a group of Holy Blades. She recognized the men in golden armour from the other day. The Holy Blades stared at her, expressing apprehension at her unusual appearance. The commander remained quiet as he held his hands behind his back, gazing at the main road to Terra. Looking at Commander White, Mara saw that he was in uniform. Then the commander turned around to give his classic glare. Walking up to Mara, he reached into his left pocket and pulled out a rope.

"What's that?" Mara asked, pointing at the rope.

"This is a rope," Commander White answered in a matter-of-fact tone. "You're to be bound and restrained."

She stared at him in disbelief.

"A necessary precaution," Mr. White said, appearing by her side. "It's for everyone's safety."

"Necessary precaution…" Mara rolled her eyes. "My ass! I think I'll just walk."

She began to walk away. The commander stared forward nonchalantly.

"Very well," Commander White spoke. Then he glanced at his subordinates and shouted, "Blades!"

The Holy Blades swarmed Mara, tackling her to the ground. One of them hit her in the back of the head.

Commander White gazed down at her with his hands behind his back.

"You do not have any choice in this matter. We are on a tight schedule."

The commander crouched down and took her hands. He wrapped her wrists with a tight rope. Mara showed no resistance due to being disorientated from the knock on the head. After he finished, Commander White pulled her up to her feet and directed her to a carriage.

"Now move." He began to push her.

She reluctantly moved.

Before boarding, Commander White gazed at Mr. White. "Please go to the other carriage, father."

Mr. White looked confused but obeyed his request. Mara watched the older man enter the other carriage.

"Get in," the commander ordered.

She glanced back at him and then turned to enter the transport. Once everyone was in place, the carriages began to move.

* * *

Mara looked out the window as their carriage travelled to Grey Mountain. She could see his reflection on the glass. The commander was scowling at her with his arms folded.

"Did you enjoy my blood?" Commander White questioned in a cold tone.

Mara refused to answer. A hand grabbed her face, forcing her to look at its owner. The commander glared at her while holding her face in his grip.

"Look at me when I talk to you." Commander White released his grip and pulled her mask down. Staring at her face, he was stunned by Mara's transformation. The commander then raised an eyebrow. "I see you've become easier on the eyes again." He frowned at her. "But you remain a beast. I should have known better than to let my guard down last night."

"Now we're even," Mara replied coldly, "after you hit me."

Commander White scowled at her. "You remind me of this she-wolf." He reached for the left side of his neck. "This is the same place she got me." The commander lowered his hand. "Ever heard of the Black Smoke?"

Mara shook her head. The commander rolled his eyes but continued to speak.

"The Black Smoke was a beast," he said. "Parading as a vigilante, she killed many people. The Faith sought to stop this creature. I was in charge of the investigation. The Holy Blades and I searched for her in the woods surrounding Ghost Mountain. She attacked me. Luckily, my men were nearby." He gave a smug look. "One of them smashed her skull with a sledgehammer."

Mara's eyes remained on him. His tale perfectly matched the dream she had last night. She wondered if it was a memory, but could not remember such an event.

"And that's why you do not trifle with Kallikratés." He pointed to his neck. "I'll let this pass, seeing how my blood made you less repulsive."

Reaching over, he pulled her mask up. The two remained silent during their journey.

* * *

After a long and uneventful ride, Mara saw Greyward Hold drawing closer. She also spotted the other transports. It appeared Master Harold had invited others to this meeting. Once they reached the iron doors, the carriage stopped. The commander was the first to leave.

"We're here. Get out!" Commander White shouted at her.

Mara sighed and left the carriage. The commander stayed behind her, grasping her arm tightly. Holy Blades surrounded them while they walked to the large iron doors.

"Open up," called the commander. "We've come for the meeting."

The doors opened, allowing them entry.

Walking through the grand hall, Mara saw the remaining Silver Thorns gawking at her. They were stunned by her appearance. Entering the meeting room, she grabbed the attention of Master Harold, Chancellor Davis and Dr. Moen, and Morgan. Even High Priestess Alena and some of her disciples were present. Commander White placed her in the centre of the room before joining his father and the priestess. He never bothered to untie her ropes. After a moment, Mara freed herself.

All eyes were on her. Dr. Moen, however, was studying the notes obtained by Mr. White a few minutes ago.

Harold stood up. "We have gathered here again to discuss more troubling matters," he began in a solemn tone.

The chancellor stared at Mara. "What happened to her?"

"We shall get to that." Then, "With regret, I announce the deaths of Lady Isabella of Hema and Heru of the Old Hunting Ground."

Everyone was stunned. Taken aback, Davis looked at Harold.

"How could this be?" The chancellor glanced back at Mara. He opened his mouth to say something, but Dr. Moen approached her with the notes in his hands.

"Whoa," Dr. Moen said, staring at her with wonder.

She gazed back at him while he began to examine her. Others gave the middle-aged doctor a strange look.

"Dr. Moen, what are you doing?" Chancellor Davis cried. "You are embarrassing me!"

The doctor ignored him. He reached for her mask, but Mara backed off and made a low hissing sound. Dr. Moen pulled his hand back as he stared at her. She made it clear that she was not to be observed or prodded. She had enough already.

Commander White stood up. "What is she?"

The doctor glanced at the notes. "From what I could gather, these undying are normally formed based on the environment they're in." Then he addressed the Silver Thorn master. "Where was she when she transformed?"

"She was in the Dark Labyrinth before meeting Saskia in Ozin," Master Harold replied.

Dr. Moen gazed at him with wide eyes. "The Dark Labyrinth? That's not much to go on." The doctor rubbed his chin. "That's a place of highly concentrated magic. Some of the most dangerous monsters are born there." He looked at the notes. "She has wolf-like traits but is not a werewolf or a vampire. She also has some regenerative abilities. I suspect a shadow beast albeit partially transformed." Dr. Moen nodded. "Shadow beasts can teleport, leaving behind black smoke, and have regenerative abilities. But it is uncommon, like the darkling."

Murmurs filled the room.

The commander folded his arms. "Shadow beast? Darkling? Are you making this up?" Commander White questioned.

The doctor sulked at him. "We do have a darkling living among us," Dr. Moen said condescendingly. "Sealed away in the Black Tower, near the abandoned City of Cerebell."

"You know your history," Morgan commented on Dr. Moen's knowledge. "Anna of Cerebell was sealed away for posing a threat."

"And for many years, the Silver Thorns have dealt with creatures no human has ever laid eyes upon," Master Harold added.

The commander gazed at Harold. "Is that so?" Commander White asked indifferently.

Harold nodded. "Yes, there are creatures even you may have never seen during your time as Commander."

The chancellor turned his gaze onto Master Harold. "What else is down there?"

"The Dark Labyrinth is home to a past long forgotten, not just a prison for the Dark One." The Silver Thorn leader turned his gaze onto High Priestess Alena and her disciples as if he were directing his words at them.

The priestess stood up. Commander White and his father watched as she rose to her feet. Ignoring Master Harold's words, she gazed at Mara.

"So, another demon is among us?" Alena questioned, staring at Mara through her veil.

Mara scowled at the older woman with glowing eyes. A dark aura exuded from her body.

Unfazed by Mara's response, Alena gazed at Master Harold. "This creature is dangerous to mankind."

"Never mind that," Master Harold said. "We have some pressing issues to talk about." He gazed at Mara. "She is believed to be responsible for their deaths."

Gasps and murmurs filled the room again.

"See, I knew she was trouble! Not only did she kill two possessors of the seals, but she must have killed Saskia as well."

Hearing a familiar male voice, Mara gazed at the one who said those words. She recognized the young man with black hair. Boyd stood with the Faith. She reckoned they took him in after being kicked out of the Guardsmen.

The chancellor and the doctor glanced at him.

"I thought we determined that she didn't kill Saskia?" Davis questioned.

"Yes, the Watcher made sure of that!" Dr. Moen glowered at Boyd.

"You believe in that thing?" Boyd demanded.

Dr. Moen kept frowning at him.

Davis sighed and looked at Mara. Everyone turned his or her attention on her.

"Is it true?" Harold asked her. "Did you kill Lady Isabella and Heru?"

Mara gazed at him and nodded. "I did."

Boyd slammed his fists on the table. "See? She even admitted herself!"

Mr. White stood up. "She killed them, but not with ill intention."

Alena turned her head to look at him. The commander glared at his father. They looked as if they never expected the older man to speak. Everyone gazed at Mr. White.

"Go on," Master Harold said. "We are all listening."

Mr. White took a deep breath. "Heru turned my son into a beast." He gestured to Mara. "And she administered the cure. The next evening, Lady Isabella took us hostage, demanding that the Faith withdrew the treaty, or else she would kill us. If not for the young lady, both Karl and I wouldn't be standing here."

Harold nodded. "Yes, you mentioned this in the letter. But it does not explain why Heru and Isabella died."

"Both threatened me," Mara said. "For curing the commander, Lady Isabella gave me the cure as one of my rewards. But Heru abducted me, thinking I wanted to remain a werewolf. He saw me take the cure and tried to kill me, so I stabbed him in self-defence."

"He saw you take the cure?" Harold questioned. "It is no secret he despised it. Both Morgan and I know the lengths Lady Isabella went to create it. The cure's existence caused Heru to not see eye to eye with Hema's ruler."

"Before Heru died, he gave me a letter, claiming I wanted to remain a werewolf," Mara continued, "but I did not write this letter."

"Then who did?" Morgan inquired.

"The same guy who ripped it up after hitting me," Mara answered, turning her glare onto the commander.

Everyone stared at her, then to him. Commander White rose to his feet, staring back at her in anger. He held his hands behind his back.

"I did not write this letter, nor did I give it to him," he insisted coldly.

Mara scowled at him. "Your father identified the handwriting to be yours, and the steward saw you give the letter to Heru."

The father gazed at him. "What about the glamour?"

The commander looked back at him in confusion. His mouth opened. "I... I do not remember," he murmured.

Mr. White watched him in concern. "I believe Lady Isabella orchestrated Heru's death," he told everyone. "All evidence may point at Karl, but I believe he was hypnotized into writing and giving the letter to Heru. She offered to use her glamour to remove any lingering signs of lycanthropy. I allowed it as long as Karl was fine with it. But I was not present when she performed it since she requested to be left alone with him."

Everyone gazed at Commander White. Becoming aware of their stares, the commander nodded. "I gave consent, but do not recall anything from that night."

"Lady Isabella harboured a deep hatred for both Saskia and Heru," Morgan said. "They caused the Aristocracy's demise. The Aristocracy comprised of high-born vampires created by Isabella. They assisted her in reclaiming Hema."

Harold nodded. "This happened four centuries ago," he revealed. "One of the vampire nobles attacked a young man, unaware he was a werewolf. The man transformed and bit him. The others could only watch as he died a slow and painful death. Upon learning that a werewolf's bite is fatal to a vampire, Lady Isabella hired scientists and doctors to create the cure. Not only did it cure lycanthropy, but it also saved vampires from the fatal bite. Nobles took to nightly hunts. Many werewolves died. It escalated to a vicious war with humans caught in the crossfire. Heru once sought the aid of the Silver Thorns. Saskia led a small group to help him. She helped many humans escape their oppressive ruler while Heru and his pack slaughtered the Aristocracy."

Mara tilted her head in confusion. "What about the incident in Marrow? Lady Isabella claimed she had the cure created after a rogue slaughtered the whole village."

"That incident happened eight centuries ago," Harold revealed.

"So, she lied to me?" Mara asked.

"She may have twisted the truth, especially when it came to her not seeing eye to eye with Saskia and Heru," he admitted.

"She was not pleased with what those two did and might have decided to act recently," Morgan said. "To avoid suspicion, she probably mesmerized some poor fool into killing Saskia, and then hypnotized the commander into orchestrating Heru's death."

Some expressed surprise, although this was an undeniable fact. Most were aware of Isabella's hatred of Saskia and Heru.

"The Silver Thorns could not find the one responsible for Saskia's murder," Harold added. Then he gazed at Mara. "And what of Lady Isabella?"

"I stood in her way," Mara replied. "She shut off my humanity and offered to turn me. I refused and sided with the commander and his father, so she tried to kill me too."

"Very well, but speaking of glamour," Harold said, "I offer my humble apologies. With Isabella dead, there is no way to turn your humanity back on."

Silence filled the room.

"It may be possible," Dr. Moen broke the silence.

Everyone stared at the doctor.

"Is that so?" Harold asked.

"No, don't tell me you brought that thing here again!" Davis cried, his face twisted in a frown.

Dr. Moen laughed. "Of course not, but…"

He took out a gold pendant with a glowing blue gem. He held it out in front of Mara and gazed at her.

"The Watcher's psychic powers may be able to neutralize Isabella's glamour," Dr. Moen addressed Mara. "Can't guarantee it will work, but it is better than nothing. I can use this communication stone to call her here, but only if you want it. Do you want our help?"

She stared at the doctor and shrugged. "Sure, why not?"

Dr. Moen smiled and gripped the pendant. All of a sudden, everything went black.

* * *

Mara woke up to find herself lying on the floor. Rising to her feet, she looked around. Greyward Hold was silent and empty. Everyone left her alone.

"Mara…"

Hearing her name, Mara looked behind to see two people. A man and a woman appeared to be in their fifties, looking similar to her. She recognized the man from an earlier vision when she was training with Saskia. She stared at them in confusion. Who were they? Mara opened her mouth to say something, but a thought emerged in her mind. She knew these people.

"Mom? Dad?"

A flood of emotions and memories washed over her, tearing down the wall that locked away her humanity. It was the first time seeing her parents after becoming lost and cursed.

Her name was Mara Ashwood. Her mother, Daniella, had white skin and black hair. Mom often coloured her greying hair to hold on to her youth. Her eyes were pale blue. Her father, Mathias, was nicknamed Bear because his strength rivalled such a creature. A member of the Stone Mage Tribe of the Outer Frontier, he possessed dark skin and greying hair that was once black. Mom groomed her to be a wife and mother, while Dad trained her to be a hunter. He wanted Mara to take over his workshop someday. Her parents' different views often clashed. Their fights sometimes bothered her. Even though her memory was incomplete, she got to remember her family.

Mara wanted to run to them, but her vision became obscured by thick black smoke rising from her body. When the smoke faded, her parents had vanished. She felt fingers on her head. Mara turned around and found the Watcher standing behind her, pulling her hands away. She gazed at the armoured woman in confusion. What did the Watcher do to her?

Dr. Moen gazed in awe as the smoke began to dissipate. "Whoa," he uttered.

Gazing at the doctor, the middle-aged man reminded Mara of a friend she once knew from college, but could not recall the name yet. The others looked on in surprise.

"The dark aura is dissipating," Harold said.

Mara looked at her hands. She thought she saw blood, but another look showed her hands were clean. Her heart began to twist in guilt. What was she thinking? What would her family think? She gazed at the Watcher. Mara began to realize the importance of her human side. She was grateful that the Watcher brought her back from the brink. Mara would not have a second chance.

"What happened? What did you do to her?"

Recognizing his voice, Mara turned her head to see Commander White approaching. Once their eyes met, she could not look away. Mara believed he cared until she saw his typical glare.

She glanced down at her hands. "I... I remember," Mara murmured.

Dr. Moen gazed at her in curiosity. "What are you talking about?"

Mara looked back at him. "It's just... I could not remember anything before the curse."

The doctor looked intrigued. "So, remembering your human life triggered your humanity to return?" He gazed at his creation. "And the Watcher did that?"

The Watcher looked back at him and nodded.

Dr. Moen stared in surprise. He turned away and rubbed his chin. "I know of a patient in Mirahyll Hospital. Maybe the Watcher can help?"

Mara gazed at the doctor in confusion, then noticed Davis' apprehensive look. People were wary of the strange creature. And allowing the Watcher near patients in a hospital was out of the question.

Commander White gazed at Dr. Moen and the Watcher with indifference. "Oh, is that it? I see." He held his hands behind his back and looked at Mara. "She must answer for her crimes."

Dr. Moen looked surprised and confused. "What?"

Ignoring the doctor, Commander White scowled at her. "She broke two seals. She must be the Cursed Herald!" He turned to Davis. "She shall be handed over to the Faith for judgment."

The doctor stared at the commander in anger. "Are you serious?"

The chancellor gazed at Dr. Moen. "With all due respect, she did kill them."

Dr. Moen frowned. "She didn't hypnotize the commander into setting up Heru's death. Nor did she create the situation leading to the death of Lady Isabella."

"That is true," Morgan agreed.

"I also agree," Master Harold said. "There is more evidence that Lady Isabella was the mastermind. Concerning Hema's ruler, it was an unfortunate accident."

"No," Alena said, pointing at Mara. "Three possessors died in her presence. She killed two of them. She must be the Cursed Herald."

Mara sulked at the priestess. "Why should I face judgment while your commander gets a free pass?" She turned her scowl onto Commander

White. "I didn't turn into a beast and slaughter many innocents, including small children!"

The commander's face turned red. Mara thought she saw smoke billowing out of his ears.

"You committed a far worse crime," he growled. "You have placed all of Ardana in danger!"

"She does have a point," Master Harold said calmly. "If not for your status and position, you would have been executed without question." He looked at Boyd. "And you have a suspect among your ranks. The Silver Thorns were searching for him, but he mysteriously disappeared. Now here he is, as a member of the Holy Blades."

Boyd frowned at Harold. Commander White turned his glare onto the old master.

"He did not kill Saskia," the commander insisted, "and he's under Kallikratés' protection. We will not hand him over to you."

"Is that so?" Harold asked. "It is my understanding that he was an accomplice to the murder."

Commander White gazed at Boyd. "Like the others, the real murderer promised Masterson a full bag of gold for framing her."

Mara looked at Commander White, and then to Boyd. She felt unsure if this was true, but knew that most of Boyd's actions were for selfish gains. Financial motivation seemed believable, considering Boyd's past.

The commander then scowled at Mara. "She, on the other hand, killed two possessors."

He took a step towards her, but Harold approached her as well.

The Silver Thorn master gazed at him through his mask. "She is not going anywhere. I declare her to be under my protection."

Everyone glanced at each other, appearing baffled.

Commander White frowned at Harold. "How could you defend her after what she did?"

"We have our evidence. Lady Isabella orchestrated the deaths of Saskia and Heru." Harold gestured to Mara. "She was merely caught up in all of this."

"And I believe him," Morgan added, rising from her seat. "The young lady had no reason to want them dead. It was just a series of unfortunate events."

The commander turned his spiteful gaze onto Morgan. "You as well? I think you're both making a grave mistake."

Morgan folded her arms. "Why do you seek this woman's arrest? Heru was critical of Kallikratés. Lady Isabella opposed the treaty. And with her gone, the Faith will finally have a presence in Hema. To you, their deaths should be a blessing."

No one expected Morgan to stand up to the disciples of Kallikratés. Commander White gazed at her in annoyance.

"Well, at least we have not forgotten their roles," the commander hissed. "They were seals to the Dark One. Two seals that she broke!"

The two glanced at him, appearing unfazed by his words.

"She will not go unpunished. I will deal with her myself." Master Harold looked at Mara and declared, "For killing Lady Isabella and Heru, your punishment shall be… to slay all the undying in this land."

"Excuse me?" Commander White protested. "What kind of punishment is that?"

Mara gazed back at Harold. She wondered the same thing as well, but the commander took the words right out of her mouth.

Harold looked at him. "I believe she'll be of greater use here, rather than rotting in a prison cell." He gestured to Mara. "She is the only one who can kill them permanently and demonstrated her worth by slaying the White Lady."

The commander snapped his gaze onto Mara. She noted the hint of surprise as if it were his first time learning of the White Lady's permanent death. He stared at her in silence before his face fell back to the classic glare.

The Silver Thorn master addressed Davis. "What do you think? Is this acceptable?"

The chancellor cleared his throat and gazed at Mara. "Yes, I agree, as long as it means less dangerous monsters to deal with."

Commander White glanced at the two men. "As Commander of the Holy Blades, I express my disappointment in your decision to let this creature roam. It will be a matter of time before another seal fails."

Mara sulked at him for calling her a creature. She had a name.

Harold chuckled. "Are you concerned that the Dark One will awaken?"

"The prophecy forewarned this," Commander White claimed.

"Does the prophecy also tell of the return of Kratés and Kallisto?" Harold asked. "That they shall save the world? If so, then why worry?"

"We don't know what sort of chaos the Dark One will bring once it awakens," the commander admitted. "Or if it is possible to stop it."

"Perhaps we should seek a way to stop it for good?" Master Harold suggested. "We can reopen an alliance with Thoron. Their sages possess more knowledge on the Dark One than anyone in the world."

"Out of the question!" High Priestess Alena scorned.

Everyone looked at the older woman. Some were stunned by her sudden outburst.

"Thoron is a land ruled by demons," claimed the priestess. "As long as I draw breath, I will not allow the slaves of those pretenders to step foot on Ardana!"

Mara gazed at the priestess in confusion.

The commander nodded. "We will not make amendments to the laws our gods placed to protect us."

The chancellor sighed. "What else can we do?" Davis asked, glancing back at Master Harold.

"There is another way," Harold said.

Everyone gazed at him, expressing interest.

"The Dark One is an entity of pure magical energy," said the Silver Thorn master. "It is kept alive by a core, its heart. This core contains its life force. Severing or destroying the heart will kill the leviathan. We can send someone inside to do this."

Some expressed surprise while others gave incredulous looks. Mara looked at the old master, noticing his gaze on her. It sounded like he was addressing her.

"Kill the Dark One?" Davis asked.

"In theory, it could work," Dr. Moen said, "but it's never been done before."

"Impossible!" Commander White exclaimed. "Lord Kratés fought the Dark One and died."

"And last I recalled, Lord Kratés was unable to kill the Dark One for good," Harold responded. "What do you think will happen when it awakens? With Godstruck, there may still be hope."

The chancellor looked at Dr. Moen. "If it is possible, then maybe we should consider this as a course of action?"

The doctor nodded. "Yes, but getting inside and destroying its heart won't be easy, let alone finding someone who can pull it off."

Mara stepped forward. "I can do it," she said, "I can destroy its heart."

Everyone looked at her as if she was daft.

She ignored their stares and looked at Harold. "You said you needed someone who can do this. I can."

"Please, what a delusional girl," Commander White hissed. He gave a mocking smirk. "She thinks she can kill the Dark One?"

Mara looked at the commander.

"The Great Lord Kratés fought the Dark One and died," he scolded her. "What makes you think you can do it?"

She glared at him. "I fell from a cliff and survived. Hanged, slashed open, mauled, and even impaled! And I came back because of this curse." Mara glanced at everyone. "Can any of you say the same?"

Master Harold shook his head. "No, I'll not hear any more of this," he said. "Do not think ill of me for saying these words. You may be one of the undying, but there is no guarantee you will succeed." He changed the topic. "We shall conclude this meeting. Before we part ways, there is one more thing I must address."

Everyone gazed at him, anticipating what he had to say.

"It is with regret that I announce the disbandment of the Silver Thorns."

Some expressed surprise. Davis gave a questioning glance.

"For over a millennium, we have been protecting mankind from monsters," Harold revealed. "But over the years, other organizations and independent hunters emerged." He gestured to the priestess and the commander. "The Faith also specializes in monster hunting with the Holy Blades."

Alena nodded. "That is true. It is our creed to rid the world of all monsters. Fulfilling this task will bring this land closer to returning to the

Golden Age. Our lords shall return to their thrones, and peace and prosperity shall reign."

Mara noticed Commander White looking at Alena with absolute devotion. She felt jealous that the older woman received so much admiration from him. Mara then thought about the memories she retrieved. In addition to remembering her family, Mara recalled Dad's training and some parts of her time in college. Knowing where her parents lived, she hoped to see them soon in Mirahyll.

As the meeting came to an end, Commander White had one more announcement to make.

"We are always looking for more recruits. To any men who are no longer Silver Thorns, you are welcome to join the Holy Blades."

After making his announcement, the commander approached two female Silver Thorns. He gazed at them dismissively. "I'm afraid you two are unsuitable to join," he said to them.

Mara witnessed this and raised an eyebrow. *'What makes him think they want to join?'*

"Women have no place in the Holy Blades. The Silver Thorns and the Guardsmen allow them to join, though not many survive," the commander stated. "Women should not be on the battlefield or fighting monsters. I hope you ladies consider my advice."

The two women looked unhappy when he said those words. Commander White stood there, not caring if he offended them. His face was devoid of an apology.

His words hit pretty close to home, reminding Mara of her mother. Mom never approved of her becoming a hunter. The scars received from hunting always set her off, creating a schism between them.

Mara glanced up and saw the commander glaring back at her. He walked towards her.

She folded her arms. "Let me guess—you're going to give me the same lecture. Even though I am the reason why you are still alive."

Commander White's face remained frozen in a scowl. He stopped before her, holding his hands behind his back. "I still believe you are the Cursed Herald. You being around when three possessors died is no mere coincidence."

"So what?" Mara asked. "You have no proof."

The commander gave a dark gaze. He took another step, invading her personal space. "Make one wrong move. I will end you."

She looked down and saw his left hand tightening around the grip of his sword. She gazed up at him. Mara never expected to be threatened. He kept his eyes on her.

"I'll be watching you." He turned around and left.

Mara watched him join his father and the priestess. She sighed as the tension lifted. She felt she could finally breathe. As Mara watched them leave, Harold approached her.

"You can stay here, but we won't have as much as before," the former master said.

She looked back at him. "Heard the Silver Thorns were struggling."

Harold nodded. "Over time, our numbers dwindled. Some left to join other guilds while others died during hunts. Losing Saskia was a fatal blow. I intended for her to be the next leader. However, things changed that night."

She gave a grim look. "I'm sorry."

"Oh, that is fine. There was not much you could do to change that. Before long, only I shall remain in these empty halls."

Mara's expression lightened up. "I suppose I should get a start on finding these undying?"

"Yes, I will help you. With whatever knowledge I can gather, I believe killing them and absorbing their souls is the key." Harold handed her a piece of paper—a work order to slay a monster. It had the name of the creature and the location.

"The Siren?" Mara read the work order.

"That is correct," he told her. "This creature existed for over one hundred fifty years. She has caused many deaths in the waters around Har' Yhan. The Silver Thorns had slain the creature before, but she returned each time. It is my belief she is another undying." He then advised, "You should leave as soon as possible. Not only will it take some time to get to the town, but the Siren only appears at night. Meet with Har' Yhan's alderman, Jonathan. He issued the contract."

Mara gazed at him. "So, that whole punishment speech was an act?"

"Perhaps," Harold replied. "After you slay the creature, please return to me. I shall search for the next one."

She nodded. Mara headed to her room to gather her things. Before returning to her quarters, she went to the crates in the far corner to take some provisions. It was far less than before. Mara was not surprised to know that the food deliveries would cease.

* * *

On the way back to her room, she noticed Talon packing up his stuff. Mara approached him with curiosity.

"What's going on? Where are you going?"

The old blacksmith gazed at her. "Didn't you hear the master? The Silver Thorns are no more! There is no reason for me to stay in Greyward Hold."

She now realized what Harold meant by not having as much as before. They were also losing the blacksmith. "Where will you go?"

Talon shrugged. "I plan to open up shop in Mirahyll, though it'll be tough since the city already has a blacksmith." He watched her. "I'll see you there?"

She nodded in response.

"Good, great to know I'll be getting a return customer." With that, he chuckled.

Mara decided to use his services one more time. After he repaired and upgraded her gear, Talon packed up his bags and left.

Greyward Hold had become empty, save for the former guild master and the undying. Mara headed to her room to make her preparations. She spotted a mirror. Walking up to her reflection, Mara removed her mask. She still looked human. After a moment, her tanned skin began to pale. Her cheeks grew sunken as dark circles formed underneath her eyes. Her lips turned dark grey and scars formed on her face. She was horrified to see her human form decaying before her eyes.

Fighting back her tears, Mara placed her mask back on with a shaky hand. There was no way she could face her parents like this. The commander's blood offered temporary relief. Her only hope was the soul of the undying. She turned around to make her preparations.

When ready, Mara left Greyward Hold and headed for Har' Yhan.

Chapter Twelve

The Siren

While Mara descended the mountain, she had the luck of not encountering any snow beasts. She also realized that she had not seen Talon, who left not too long ago. Mara thought she could catch up, but it seemed the old blacksmith had quite the head start. Reaching the foot of the mountain, Mara spotted someone in the distance. It looked like Talon as he headed south.

With her hand to her mouth, Mara shouted out to him. "Hey!"

However, the person in the distance didn't respond. Mara grew disappointed they could not hear her. Then again, she was far away.

She spent much of the day heading south. It would be easier to travel through Mirahyll to get to Har' Yhan. But she refused to pass through a populated area in her current state. The Guardsmen or the Holy Blades might attack her on sight.

As usual, Mara stopped and ate some food. She sat below the same tree, which she used during her first journey to Greyward Hold. The shade of the tree made her inconspicuous. Bread and dried fruit were on the menu again. The meal was tasteless as usual, but it no longer surprised her. Mara had to learn to get used to her predicament. Even though the provisions were unappetizing, it was better than nothing. While eating under the shade, Mara thought about all that happened. The vast landscape before her looked more familiar. She used to travel these roads with Dad. Mara wondered how her father was. Still forging weapons in the Ashwood Workshop, she hoped. Thinking about her parents, Mara still had to figure out how to explain her situation to them. She could not exactly tell them that she became cursed. But if she could find a way to lift it, then everything could go back to normal.

Mara then thought about Doctor Moen's words. She was unfamiliar with the shadow beast. Even when she worked for Dad, she had never seen one before. Mara glanced down at the bestiary, recalling Saskia mentioning them. Taking the book, she opened it and flipped through the pages. She happened upon an image of a dark shadowy beast. It resembled a werewolf, but stood on hind legs and possessed horns on its head. The illustration looked a little creepy, thanks to the glowing eyes the black creature possessed. Wisps of black smoke surrounded it. Just as Dr. Moen mentioned, the bestiary spoke of the creature's healing capacity and the power of teleportation. As far as Mara was concerned, she had faster healing but lacked the ability of teleportation.

For a supernatural being, she did not own many capabilities. Vampires could fly, while werewolves had strength. Even the White Lady devastated a whole village. What kind of powers did Mara have? Supposed immortality, or becoming a beastly creature upon getting angry or endangered? Then again, Mara planned to free herself from this curse. After finishing her small meal, she rose to her feet and continued to Har' Yhan.

Travelling further south, she saw the crossroads and Ozin Village over yonder. Stopping before Ozin, Mara watched the villagers go about their business while the children played outside. With the White Lady gone, everyone was free and happy. Security was beefed up by the Holy Blades, who replaced the village guards. The people could rest easy knowing they were safe. Unfortunately, they executed one of their saviours. Mara had her doubts they knew the truth, nor did they care. She felt like storming into that village to confront Nigel. But with so many Holy Blades around, all she could do was glare at the place. Mara sighed and moved on.

Travelling the eastern road, Mara passed by Golden Mountain. Looking up at the mountain, she saw the cave entrance to the Dark Labyrinth. Then her eyes drifted onto the ivory and golden temple, which sat on a higher elevation. Pillars holding flames lit up the trail to the temple. She never noticed it before because she never looked up. Several Holy Blades guarded the path, while people dressed in fancy attire ascended the mountain. Mara assumed this to be the Temple of Kallisto, home of the Faith of Kallikratés. It was once the grand palace the gods ruled from before the Dark One razed much of it to the ground. According to legend, the disciples of Kallikratés gathered at the remains of the palace to witness Kallisto's departure from this world. The place felt familiar to Mara, but her memory remained incomplete. Nevertheless, she moved on.

* * *

By November 19, she spotted the harbour town of Har' Yhan. Getting there was not as treacherous as she thought it would be. Mara figured she was getting more comfortable getting around—it took two days of travelling. By the time she arrived, the sun was setting. Walking in, she ignored the stares of the townsfolk. The dark hood and tattered cape made everyone suspicious of her. In the heart of the town, Mara found Har' Yhan's alderman standing with two guards.

Jonathan was a middle-aged man with dark hair and a full beard. Small pieces of grey were setting in. Not many wrinkles were present on his pale face. He stared at her with dark grey eyes. She stopped before them and glanced at Jonathan.

"I'm here for the Siren," Mara began.

Everyone gazed at each other. Some appeared impressed while others shrugged. Jonathan opened his mouth to talk, but his eyes glanced past her shoulder.

"What are you doing here?"

Hearing a familiar voice, Mara turned to see Commander White, who greeted her with contempt. Boyd stood by his side. Ten Holy Blades accompanied them, equipped with armour and weapons.

Boyd gave a malicious smirk. "What do we have here?"

Mara frowned. "Could ask you the same question."

"We came for the Siren!" The commander stormed past her. "And you are wasting our time."

The Holy Blades followed suit and walked past her as well.

She sulked at them. "Why are you here? You can't kill the Siren!"

Boyd shrugged. "This town already paid us half in advance. We'll get the other half once we kill the creature. Nothing personal, but we Holy Blades can't leave a job half-finished." He then joined the others.

Before boarding a tall ship, already prepared for them, the alderman spoke up.

"Excuse me, gentlemen," Jonathan called.

The Holy Blades stopped and gazed back at him, except Commander White.

"It might be in your best interest to take her with you," the alderman recommended.

The commander snapped his head around, setting his fiery gaze upon Jonathan. Turning around, he stormed up to the older man.

"Excuse me?" Commander White hissed. "Unless I am mistaken, you're suggesting we take her with us?"

Mara glanced at the alderman. He looked intimidated by the commander's bold and aggressive demeanour, though he held his ground.

"Considering what you're dealing with," Jonathan said.

"I know what we are dealing with, but why should we take her?"

"The creature's song enchants the hearts of men. She lures her victims and feeds on their life force." Jonathan gestured to Mara. "However, women are unaffected. The last person who came close to killing the Siren was female."

The commander kept scowling at him. "Was she successful?"

The alderman shook his head. "The Siren used her song to control the monsters from the Dark Labyrinth. They killed the woman. Since then, the creature knows better than to be near women."

The Holy Blades murmured among each other.

The commander raised an eyebrow. "So, the Siren appears before men and never women?" He looked at Mara. "If we bring her, we will never find the creature."

The Holy Blades murmured in agreement.

Commander White glared at her before leading his men onto the ship. Boarding the tall ship, the Holy Blades departed to search for the Siren.

Mara's right hand tightened into a fist. She never expected to see the Holy Blades here, let alone interfere with her task. Thanks to them, she might be unable to kill the creature tonight. She watched as they began to drift into the dark ocean.

Jonathan sighed, also watching them depart. "The Siren will be well fed tonight." He gazed at her. "I apologize. You wasted your time coming here." Then he walked away.

Mara looked back at him. "I came to kill the Siren," she insisted.

Jonathan stopped yet didn't look at her. "Did you not hear the conversation? The Siren will not appear before women!"

"I know," Mara replied, "but if they kill the creature, she'll come back."

Jonathan gazed back at her. "Everybody knows that! The Siren is no mere mermaid. It's an evil spirit wanting revenge."

"Revenge?" Mara asked.

He revealed the tale of the creature. "A long time ago, there lived a songstress in this town. She was known for her beautiful voice until some thugs silenced her. She was under the care of a man, whom she loved unconditionally. However, her lover went away to study in Corlin, claiming he would return. She waited three years, but he married another and wanted nothing to do with her. Distraught and heartbroken, she took her own life by throwing herself into the ocean."

As tragic as the tale was, Mara received some crucial information. "That's when the Siren appeared?"

The alderman nodded. "She will never stop until she has the man who betrayed her."

Mara took a step towards him. "What if I can kill the Siren for good?"

Jonathan looked at her with a questioning glance. "Then I'd reckon you are no mere hunter. Who are you? What organization do you identify yourself with?"

Mara shook her head. "Harold, formerly of the Silver Thorns, sent me to kill the Siren."

Jonathan looked surprised. "He did? You must be a good hunter."

"I slew the White Lady in Misty Valley," Mara said.

His eyes widened. "We've heard. And now you have come to Har' Yhan to slay the Siren?"

Mara nodded. "That is correct. Chances are, the Holy Blades will lure her out. If I can find the Siren, I can kill her."

"Very well. Follow me." He led Mara to a small fishing vessel. It could only sit one or two people. "The Siren has her home in a nearby cove in

Ghost Mountain. You can use this boat to follow the Holy Blades. You might be unable to save them. But if you can kill the Siren, the town will be forever grateful."

Gazing at the small boat, Mara figured this was not going to be an easy task.

* * *

After Mara took the helm, the wind filled the sails, causing her boat to drift away from the port. The moon became her guide in the night. At last, she found the Holy Blades' vessel. The ship remained still in the moonlit night. The Holy Blades were searching for the Siren. As she drew closer, Mara heard a voice carried in the wind. It was unlike anything she ever heard—the haunting song of the Siren.

The Holy Blades' vessel drifted towards the voice. Mara began to follow, only to hear a loud crash. The ship smashed against the rocks, tearing the bow off. Everyone ended up in the ocean. One by one, the Holy Blades were dragged down into the churning sea. Their cries for help grew silent as the sea became still.

As her boat drifted to the wreckage, a body rose from the sea. Mara found a skeleton with skin stretched across the bones. The culprit had sucked out all the muscles and fat. Another mummified corpse rose to the surface, then another and another. Looking around, Mara saw a cove where the ocean spray swept along its entrance. As she pushed the rudder, the current tugged at her boat, drawing her into the creature's lair.

Reaching the cove's entrance, Mara found bones and corpses riddling the ground—all victims of the Siren. Some wore the golden armour of the Holy Blades. She reckoned these were the men Commander White led on this hunt. But the commander was not among them. Also missing was Boyd, who likely cowered out. In the distance, Mara heard the faint voice of the Siren. Getting out of the boat, she followed the sound.

For every step taken, the voice grew louder. Mara arrived at a large cavern where she found the creature. The Siren, now silent, could be mistaken for a mermaid. The lower half was a long, dull gold fishtail while the upper part was human. Her hands possessed long slender fingers, with webbing in between, and sharp claws. Sharp spines ran down the middle of her back. The fins and frills had little tears. The torn remains of a white dress covered her upper body. Mara could not see a face, thanks to the long dark hair that plastered it. She stepped forward, only to realize she was not alone. A survivor of the sunken ship was present as well.

Commander White approached the Siren with a drawn sword. The creature sat silently, appearing unaware of him. He lifted his sword, ready to strike her down. She looked back at him and sang. So haunting and sad, her song froze the commander in his tracks. Lowering his sword, his hand began to relax. His sword fell to the ground. A loud clang echoed throughout the cavern. The Siren reached out, longing to hold him. Falling deeper into a trance, Commander White fell to his knees. She snared him in her arms. He lay beneath her, her face hovering over his own. The creature held him in her arms as she sang her enchanting song. Her tender caress made him sigh as he closed his eyes. She leaned in and kissed him on the lips.

His entire body began to convulse while the Siren drained his life. Witnessing this, Mara knew she had to save the commander. She dashed at them, shoving the creature off Commander White. The commander lay stunned but remained alive. Gasping for air, he stared at the ceiling with wide eyes. Mara turned her gaze from him and looked at the Siren. The creature hissed at her, realizing Mara was not a man and thus immune to her song. The Siren began to scream. Her eyes turned black while her distorted mouth opened wide. The skin tore apart at the corners of her mouth. She opened her maw to reveal a row of razor-sharp teeth.

The Siren dived into the water. Mara tried to catch her, but she was too slow. Then she heard the Siren's song and the sounds of monsters growling. Mara turned around and saw a black beast charging at her. At eight feet tall, it possessed the snarling face of a wolf. Horns protruded out of its head as its eyes glowed yellow. Mara recognized the creature from the bestiary. The shadow beast stalked her while flexing its claws.

Mara swung her blade at the beast. The monster evaded her attack and took a swipe. She backed away, only to tumble into the water. Unable to swim, she drowned in the darkness. While sinking deeper, she sensed a presence nearby. A leviathan slept in the ocean. Spots of blue gleamed in the dark as black scales glistened. Then she was bewildered by a large blue sphere of light. As a gigantic eye watched Mara, her body felt like it was burning.

Mara rose from the water, her clothes darkened and soaked. She grabbed onto the shore, her nails digging into the ground. The shadow beast returned to whence it came, leaving her with the main target. She saw the Siren with Commander White, planning on draining his life again. Glowing, wolf-like eyes stared at her prey. Mara released a low guttural growl. She clenched her teeth and snarled at them. Rising to her feet, Mara wrapped her right hand around the hilt of her sword and unsheathed it. The Siren had yet to notice her, for she was busy with the commander. Her lips came closer to his.

"Get away from him!" Mara roared, dashing at them.

In a blind rage, Mara swung her sword at the Siren. The creature took notice and pushed Commander White away. She tried to flee again. Mara plunged her sword into the Siren's tail, pinning her to the ground and preventing her escape. The creature released a loud screech. Mara came closer, pulling her mask down to reveal growing fangs. The Siren glared back and hissed. She slashed at Mara with her claws, inflicting three new scratches on her face. The attack caused Mara to flinch. The Siren swiped again, but Mara lunged at her with an open maw. Her teeth sliced through the creature's fingers, severing them from her hand. The Siren screamed in agony.

Mara glared down at her, the severed fingers still in her mouth. She spat them out while her injuries healed. The Siren struggled from the sword and crawled away. Refusing to let the creature live another moment, Mara grabbed her tail. The Siren responded by thrashing about, but Mara did not let go. She held on tight while lifting her. With the creature high enough, she slammed the Siren onto the rock hard floor, head first. A loud cracking sound echoed in the cavern. Soon the Siren stopped struggling. Looking over her prey, Mara opened her mouth. She lunged at her neck and bit into it. She completely blacked out.

Regaining her senses, Mara found herself crouching over the creature. A massive bite wound on the Siren's neck squirted blood. Mara could taste blood in her mouth. She had no idea what came over her. Her heart was pounding, her head spinning. A glowing orb rose from the Siren's body. Mara lifted her hand to touch it. Once the soul shot into her, her body began to tremble. Mara felt like she was on fire again. She fell beside the Siren's body and lost consciousness.

Chapter Thirteen

A Fair Reward

For half an hour, Mara laid beside the Siren's corpse. With a pounding head and a lack of strength, she had no desire to get up.

"Aria," she uttered in a half-lucid state.

The pain eventually faded. Regaining clarity, Mara gazed at the Siren. Just like the White Lady, she transformed. Her scales fell off to reveal tanned skin. The tail disappeared, allowing her legs to form. Even the white dress reformed, adorning the waterlogged corpse. If not for the large gash on her neck, the Siren would appear to be sleeping peacefully. Despite the wet black hair plastering her face, she looked more human than before.

Mara rose to her feet and looked around. The commander was absent. She wondered where he went. He just left her here with no regard for her well-being. Not even a simple thanks for saving his life. Well, she had to kill the Siren anyway. That monster threatened humanity for many years. And according to Harold, killing the undying was supposed to help her. She completed her task. It was unfortunate many lives were lost tonight, but at least Mara obtained the Siren's soul.

She wiped the blood off her face with her glove. Mara returned to the entrance, only to discover her boat was missing. She knew she left it here. Commander White likely took it to escape the cove, to add insult to injury. Sighing, she returned to the cave to find another way out.

Mara saw her reflection in a pool of water. In spite of being restored, her face remained bloody. The coppery taste lingered in her mouth. She scooped up some water to wash the blood out. After washing her face, Mara placed her mask back on. Searching the cavern, she found a tunnel. A draft came from it.

Mara looked back at the Siren's body. A little voice whispered in her head, telling her it was wrong to abandon the corpse. She approached the body and noticed a crumpled note in her left hand. Mara took it and folded it out. The old letter was difficult to read due to the discolouration and almost faded words.

Her eyes grew wide when she saw the words. "I am breaking up with you," Mara read. "I was married for a while... what's this?"

A part of it was illegible. Mara lowered the letter, then gazed at the body. The little voice begged her to keep the relic and not forget Aria. She kept the comb from the White Lady. She did not have the heart to throw it away. So, she stashed the letter away with the tarnished comb. Mara gathered some rocks to entomb the Siren. After making the grave, she entered another tunnel to see where it went.

Mara kept her guard up. Since encountering the shadow beast, who knew what else lurked in the Dark Labyrinth. She lifted her gaze to see holes and cracks in the ceiling. Light poured in. While wandering the labyrinth, Mara spotted some boxes and barrels. She peered into one of the crates, finding various goods and imports.

"What are these?" Mara looked at some of the products, but they were no use to her. She put them back and moved on.

She saw an opening. Peeking out, she found a large grove within the mountain. Light poured in from an opening in the ceiling. She was underneath Ghost Mountain, north to the towns of Désir and Har' Yhan. Strange flora grew under the mountain, giving off light in the darkness. A lake was in the middle of the grove with a lone island and a large tree. She stared in awe of the strange but beautiful paradise. Unfortunately, Mara had to return. She looked once more upon the grove before leaving.

* * *

Mara emerged at the foot of the mountain. Har' Yhan was a fair distance away. Gazing at the town, Mara walked towards it. As she drew closer, some townsfolk noticed and approached her warily.

An elderly man asked, "What are you doing here?"

Mara gazed back at him. "I killed the Siren."

The townsfolk looked mystified.

A young man stepped forward. "Then you must see the alderman."

The woman behind him nodded in agreement. "Yes, Jonathan must know."

They beckoned her to follow them. Mara joined them to meet Jonathan.

"Hope we're not too late," said the elderly man.

Mara gave a questioning glance. "Why do you say that?"

"Commander White and a Holy Blade returned to the town earlier, claiming to have killed the Siren," the young man answered.

Mara gaped at him. It was bad enough they took her boat and stranded her, but now this? "No, they didn't!" Mara exclaimed. "They couldn't get close without being entranced."

The townsfolk were stunned to hear that, though not too surprised.

The older man looked at her. "So, it is true? Women are immune to the Siren's song?"

"Yeah, they should have taken you with them," the woman admitted. "At least more could have survived."

"Oh, they also claimed you died," the young man added.

Mara opened her mouth, but her words got stuck in her throat. This scenario became familiar. She quickened the pace and followed the townsfolk to Jonathan's home. Mara was not going to let this happen again. While running through the town, she grabbed the attention of others. They followed her as she reached the alderman's home.

Allowing the small group to enter the house, Mara saw them. Commander White and Boyd were with Jonathan, about to get credit for the work she did. Before the alderman gave them their money, the townsfolk barged in. Jonathan and Boyd took notice. The commander did not turn around, refusing to acknowledge their presence.

"What's going on?" Jonathan asked. "Why are you here?"

The older man stepped forward. "Sir, there's something you must know."

The alderman shook his head. "Well, can it wait? I must finalize the payment."

The townsfolk parted, allowing Mara to walk through. Jonathan's eyes widened. His mouth dropped open, but he was rendered speechless. Boyd looked at her with wide eyes and sealed lips.

The alderman found his voice at last. "You... You're alive?"

Mara gazed at Jonathan's shocked face before looking at the back of Commander White's head. The commander snapped his head around to look at her. Rage radiated from his face while his eyes burned with intense hatred.

Boyd leaned over to his ear. "So much for stranding her," he whispered.

The commander kept his glare on her.

Mara heard Boyd's words and glowered at them. Her suspicions were confirmed. Somehow, Boyd was nearby and helped Commander White while she slaughtered the Siren. They stole her boat, stranding her on purpose.

Jonathan looked at Commander White and Boyd. "What is going on? You told me she didn't survive."

"They lied," Mara said, looking at Jonathan. She turned her attention to the two and folded her arms. "And they didn't kill the Siren. I did."

The alderman looked back at her in shock.

"No, you did not!" Commander White stormed up to her. "We killed the creature."

"Yeah, what a great job you did," Mara retorted. "If not for me, you would have joined your men!"

Jonathan looked at the commander, then to Mara. He sighed and gazed down at the bag of gold in his hand. He began to approach her, lifting the bag to offer.

The two men scowled at him.

"What do you think you're doing?" Commander White demanded.

"That's our money!" Boyd exclaimed.

Jonathan stopped and looked back at the two. "I'm paying the one who killed the Siren."

The commander's face darkened. "We have an agreement."

"And I upheld the agreement. You got fifty percent in advance, but did not kill the Siren." Jonathan looked at their clothes. "Your clothes are damp, but nary a spot of blood." He looked at Mara's outfit. "Her attire is soaked in more blood than water."

"Well, she's not who she says she is," Boyd claimed.

Commander White glared at her and began to circle her. "Yes, it is true."

Mara gazed at the two, realizing they were going to expose her. Before she could do anything, Boyd grabbed her arms from behind and restrained her.

"Let me go!" Mara shouted.

The commander reached for her cover. "Behold, this woman is just like the Siren!"

He tore her mask off.

Mara squeezed her eyes shut upon hearing the gasps. Then it grew silent.

After a moment, Jonathan spoke up. "She doesn't look like the Siren at all."

Mara opened her eyes. She noticed the lack of reaction from the alderman and the townsfolk.

Commander White and Boyd appeared to be the only ones surprised.

The shocked expression on the commander's face melted away. He sulked at Jonathan.

"Did you not hear me? She is a monster!" Commander White glared back at her.

"Seems plenty human to me," Jonathan said as he shrugged.

An elderly lady smiled at Mara. "She's a pretty doll."

The commander whipped his head around and looked down at the townsfolk. He folded his arms and rolled his eyes.

"Only peasants will think that," Commander White grumbled.

Boyd stole a glimpse of Mara's face. "Hmm, they have a point," he admitted. "She isn't hard on the eyes."

The commander snapped his gaze back onto Boyd, who released his grip on Mara.

"You have low standards." Commander White scowled at Mara and began to walk around her. "Why would anyone consider this beautiful? Her skin is mixed and imperfect. The hair is a messy mop." He looked at her body. "Her bottom is big and round, and her thighs belong on a horse!" His eyes drifted to her lips. "And her lips are huge! She belongs in a whorehouse!"

Mara's jaw dropped. She felt like punching the commander in the face. A few compliments and this man went on a rant. His comments reminded her of a so-called nice boy, who Mom wanted to introduce her to. Mara could not remember his face but recalled his cruel comments. They were similar to the words the commander used to describe her.

Boyd raised an eyebrow. "Odd, I thought she's your type? Wasn't your wife—"

He froze upon seeing the commander's death glare. Even Mara noticed—if looks could kill.

"Sounds perfect to me," spoke a feminine voice.

Mara saw a woman, with a smooth and pale curvy build, approaching them. Long black hair framed her slightly rounded face, with some strands tucked behind her ears to show off her golden earrings. Her evenly parted hair showed her steel-blue eyes. Her nose was quite thin, and she possessed full lips. Her red and black dress showed a deep cleavage. White pearls and a ruby pendant adorned her neck.

The alderman and the townsfolk watched as she approached them.

"Lady Lorelei," Jonathan addressed her. "What are you doing here?"

Lorelei gave a wry smile while placing her hands on her hips. "I came to thank whoever slew the Siren." She gazed at Mara. "Well, I'll be," she continued. "Aren't you a very charming young lady."

"Thank you," Mara replied. It felt great to get a compliment. Too bad Commander White had to ruin it with a mocking grunt. Mara turned around and looked at him. He stood there with his arms folded. The commander closed his eyes and frowned. It was clear that he did not share the older woman's view.

"Do not take him seriously," Lady Lorelei advised. "He only said those things because he's not good enough."

Mara looked back at her. "I don't."

Lorelei nodded. "Good, you should also know that he said similar things to other women. I've heard he saw Kallisto."

"And it is a great privilege," Commander White proclaimed, opening his eyes. "Her beauty so great, none can compare."

Both women looked at him.

Lady Lorelei shook her head. "Did anyone tell you that gazing upon her will turn your heart into a lump of ice? Or skew your vision to see even the most beautiful as plain and ugly?"

Mara looked intrigued. If true, no wonder why he acted like a jerk.

The commander rolled his eyes. "Please! Only the jealous would make such excuses."

"Or is it a coping mechanism?" Lorelei argued. "It must be so hard to keep that vow of celibacy."

Some of the townsfolk caught onto the woman's crude humour and laughed. Boyd also snickered, prompting a sharp frown from his superior. Only Commander White and Jonathan were unamused. The commander's right fist tightened. He looked as if he wanted to hit this woman for humiliating him.

Mara looked confused. "What is that?"

Lorelei gazed at her. "A vow taken by the Holy Blades, to make sure they're devoted only to Kallisto. That means no sex. Rumour has it—Commander White takes his vow most seriously."

Commander White glared at Lorelei. "How dare you mock me?"

"My apologies, Commander," Lorelei addressed him, "but I am not mocking you. I'm just stating facts. This woman risked her life to save you, only to be insulted. I've seen your kind, how they speak poorly of people like her." She gestured to Mara. "Yet, hypocritically, those same nobles walk into my brothels and drown my girls in gold. Jasmine is a popular one."

Mara glanced over at the commander and saw his humiliation.

Commander White's face began to turn red as he folded his arms. "What do you know?"

"I am a woman of pleasure," Lorelei proudly claimed. "I own a substantial part of the town, including all the brothels and most of the inns." Changing the topic, Lady Lorelei looked at Jonathan and asked, "Did you pay this lady yet?"

Jonathan shook his head.

Lorelei cast a sharp gaze onto him. "Well, pay her already!"

The alderman complied, rewarding Mara. She received a bag worth three thousand gold.

"It was my money you gave to those boys. A pity considering that all but two perished." Lady Lorelei gazed at Commander White and Boyd. "It's only fair she gets the other half. You got half your payment in advance, so it's not like you're walking away empty-handed."

Commander White and Boyd stared at the older woman. The commander's angry expression lightened up, though not by much. He regained his composure once again, holding his hands behind his back. The commander looked at Lady Lorelei with a nonchalant expression.

"Very well," Commander White said.

Mara also gazed at Lorelei. "Thank you."

"No need to thank me. I'm sure this town is grateful for what you did." Lorelei glanced at the other townsfolk, who nodded in agreement. She gazed back at Mara. "Would you like to stay the night? I'm willing to pay for your meals and lodging."

In spite of being surprised by the offer, Mara acknowledged that Lady Lorelei had a point. It would take two days for a return trip to Greyward Hold.

"Sure," she replied.

Lady Lorelei grinned. "Good," she said, then looked at Commander White and Boyd. "What about you two?"

Before the commander could say anything, Boyd piped up.

"Sure! We'll accept your offer. Who can turn down a free meal and bed?"

Commander White gazed at him with an annoyed stare. "I rather not."

Mara, as well as a few other people, were taken aback by his response. Even Boyd took notice and turned to Commander White.

"Karl," Boyd spoke.

"No!" Glaring at Boyd, Commander White lifted his right hand and pointed at him. "You shall refer to me as Commander or Sir." He lowered his hand. "And I have misgivings about staying here. I hear this is the prowling grounds of the Succubus."

Mara grew confused. "The what now...?"

"You don't know?" Commander White grew annoyed. "The Succubus is a vile demon that drains the life force of the men she seduces! It will be a mistake to stay the night."

Lady Lorelei shook her head. "That is untrue."

The commander scowled at her. "How would you know?"

"It's a creature from the old world," Lorelei explained. "The story of the Succubus is meant to scare would-be cheaters. Besides, no man has ever died at my brothels. All your fears are for nothing."

"Sir, the lady is willing to pay for our meals and lodging for tonight," Boyd added. "Besides, don't you think this would serve as compensation for half of the money we didn't get?"

Commander White pondered his words. After giving it some thought, he turned his gaze onto Lady Lorelei. "Fine, we'll take your offer."

Lady Lorelei smiled and beckoned them.

* * *

The three followed their hostess to an inn for their meals and lodging. At the end of the dining hall was a large fireplace with a roaring fire. The warmth of the flames took the chill away. Several people sat at the tables, having a good time and drinking. Some had a little too much to drink. One man was passed out at a table, snoring loudly as a cat crept by his head.

Mara was unsure what to think of this establishment. She never stepped into such a place or at least remembered being in one before. Looking at Boyd, she could tell that he was thrilled. He saw good food and beverage. He also spotted some courtesans—hired women of pleasure, brought in by Lady Lorelei to entertain guests. Boyd liked this place.

However, the commander did not share their views.

"What a dump," Commander White spoke with disdain.

Everyone within earshot heard his words, but he could care less.

Ignoring him, Lorelei turned around and greeted her guests.

"Welcome to the Black Smoke Inn," she announced cheerfully.

A female innkeeper walked up to them.

Lorelei looked at her and instructed, "Get the special table ready. They shall also stay the night."

The innkeeper nodded and left to make the arrangements.

Commander White stood beside Mara. He gave a scrutinizing look while folding his arms.

"The Black Smoke Inn?" Commander White asked.

Lady Lorelei glanced back at him. "Yes, I named this inn to celebrate a hero."

"Hero?" The commander narrowed his eyes. "You mean murderer?"

"Maybe to you, but not everyone thinks this way," she argued. "Bandits and killers were the only victims. The vigilante never went after innocent people."

"True, they were the lowest of the low, but they were still human," he defended.

"And if a man is willing to kill an innocent, he's no better than a beast," Lady Lorelei said sharply.

Before the commander could retaliate, a woman wearing a dark purple bustle dress approached the three. The black hood and veil obscured much of her face.

"My dear Lorelei, you speak with great wisdom," the woman said. "It was a great time to be anything except a thief or a killer." She looked at Commander White with a visible smile. "A pity the Black Smoke was sentenced to death."

He stared back at her, looking disturbed to see her here. Mara recognized her. So did Lady Lorelei, who curtsied to her.

"Ah, Lady Morgan of Désir," Lorelei addressed.

Morgan laughed in a light tone. "My dear, there is no need for formalities; we are friends after all." She turned her gaze onto Mara and Commander White. "I see you have brought guests."

Mara noticed the older woman's look on the commander and his increasing discomfort.

Lady Lorelei nodded. "Yes, for helping the town, their meals and lodging are on the house tonight," she explained. "Perhaps you'd like to join us?"

Morgan smiled. "I'm here for a different matter," she hesitated. "Once I finish this errand, I will join you." With that, she left.

Lady Lorelei looked to her guests. "I suppose we'll have you seated. Please, follow me."

However, the commander didn't budge. He stood there with his hands behind his back.

"Excuse me, but I'd prefer to eat at another table," Commander White said.

Mara looked back to find a look of disdain on his face.

"Very well," Lorelei sighed. "You're more than welcome to." She gestured to another table. "I see your friend already made some accommodations for himself."

He turned to notice that Boyd was not with him. Looking around, the commander spotted him at a table. Courtesans surrounded his subordinate while he flirted with them. Commander White seemed annoyed. Without saying a word or looking back at the two women, he joined Boyd. Upon taking a seat, the courtesans swarmed him.

Mara saw how unhappy the commander was. He sat there with a frown. Folding his arms, the commander ignored the courtesans as they fawned over him. It looked amusing to see such an unpleasant person in an awkward situation. Mara felt a hand on her shoulder. Turning around, she looked at Lady Lorelei.

"Come, let's be seated," said the hostess.

Chapter Fourteen

A Night in Har' Yhan

The two women sat at a private table, decorated for an elegant feast. Colourful tapestries hung from the ceiling, as shadows danced upon them in the light of the flickering flames. The menu had a medley of meats and vegetables, while various liquors sat on one end.

Lady Lorelei sat beside Mara, giving her a strange look.

"Aren't you going to remove your hood?"

Mara looked back at her. "What? I…"

Lorelei reached for her hood and pushed it backwards. "You are not hard on the eyes." After pulling Mara's mask down, Lorelei studied her face. "Are you from Thoron?"

Mara shook her head. She never ventured outside of Ardana in her life.

"Oh, my apologies," the inn owner said. "Judging by your appearance, I reckoned you're from Thoron. At least Southern Thoron…"

"I was born here," Mara explained.

A male server arrived. Mara watched him cut into some red meat, seeing how rare it was. The aroma filled her nostrils, making her mouth water. Her scleras turned dark grey as her irises glowed bright yellow. The markings around her eyes grew darker, spreading down her face. Mara opened her mouth to reveal her lengthening canines. She released a slight growl. Realizing what she was doing, Mara stopped and changed back. Her fangs shrank. The server turned to look at her but seemed unaware of her transformation. After serving them, he left. Mara watched him walk away.

"So, it is true?" Lorelei asked. "You're a creature like the Siren?"

Mara locked her gaze onto Lady Lorelei, who witnessed her transformation. She then looked away.

"Then you know why I hide my face," Mara murmured.

The inn owner seemed unfazed. "You look nothing like a monster." Lorelei changed the topic. "In my homeland, there are witches with beast-like traits. They can even transform into beasts. You resemble one, but I've never seen a Thoron Witch in Ardana."

"I'm one of the undying," Mara responded.

Lorelei looked surprised. "One of the undying?"

Mara nodded, then turned to her plate. "Harold is helping me. He believes killing the undying is the key. Every time I claim one of their souls, I regain my humanity. So far, I've killed the White Lady and the Siren."

Lady Lorelei watched her. "I know about the undying."

Mara looked back at her. "You do?"

"It's an old Thoron tale—a tragic love story about a young woman."

"What happened?" Mara asked.

A shadow loomed over her.

"She loved a man who would never return her feelings," said another woman. "So, she went on a journey to find the rose that could grant any wish—the Blue Rose of Immortality."

Mara looked behind to see Morgan gazing at her, her expression unreadable.

"However, she encountered Lonely Cenobia, the rose's guardian," Morgan revealed. "The angry goddess bit her, the venom slowly killing her. Her heart and lungs were shutting down, yet she did not want to die." The older woman broke her gaze and walked around the table. Morgan sat across from Lady Lorelei and stared at Mara again. "As she drew her last breath, the rose granted her wish. It transformed her into the first undying. She became cursed while the man she loved married another and started a family. Unloved and cursed, she left her home village and never returned. All who crossed paths with her met with misfortune."

Many thoughts ran through Mara's mind. In spite of being more aware of herself, she still had trouble wrapping her head around the tale of the undying and the curse. Her mind drifted back to her visit to Hema, recalling the words of the late vampire queen.

"Lady Isabella told me about her," Mara said.

Morgan froze. It was hard to see her face, but judging from her stillness, she seemed surprised to hear that. The older woman's lips parted. "She did?"

Mara nodded. "She said the original undying split her soul in two after a failed attempt of lifting her curse. I'm one of her reincarnations. I inherited her curse."

"Is that so?" Morgan paused for a brief while and then nodded. "Yes, I did share the tale with the late ruler of Hema," she continued. "The soul of the original undying was scattered across time, giving new life. But none could tell when a reincarnation would appear."

"Who was the original?" Mara asked.

Morgan stared at her for a minute before answering. "Thalia of Thoron…"

"Haven't heard that name in a long time," Lady Lorelei murmured, shaking her head.

Mara looked at the inn owner. "Why?"

"Thalia disappeared two thousand years ago," Morgan explained. "In this part of the world, her name had been forgotten. But Thoron still remembers her." She then gestured to the inn owner. "Like Lorelei, I am also from Thoron. I came to Ardana many years ago."

"How old would she be?" Mara asked.

"Around five thousand years," Morgan answered candidly. "The immortality took a toll on her, and she lost the will to live. The Thoron Sages refused to help because the rose was considered sacred. Desperate to lift her curse, she used a very dangerous spell. Hoping to free her spirit from her cursed vessel and enter the land of the dead, Thalia ended up breaking her soul in half. One half remained with her, while the other half created the first reincarnation. Thus it created a vicious cycle." Morgan looked at Mara. "But it appears you found a loophole."

"You mean killing the undying and claiming their souls?"

Morgan nodded. "Maybe one day, you will find a way to break this cycle, once and for all."

Mara watched Morgan. She was impressed by the immense knowledge that the older woman possessed. After obtaining more information, Mara wondered out loud, "If the rose did that to her, could it also reverse the curse?"

"Perhaps," Morgan frowned, "but Kallikratés' laws will make travelling to Thoron impossible."

"Why?" Mara asked.

"Thoron is the only nation the gods could not conquer," Lady Lorelei explained. "The gods called upon Thoron to renounce their worship of the Seven Divines and the Mother of Gods. Not only did the Thoron Sages refuse, but they also called Kallisto and Kratés fake. Provoking the gods' ire, the Faith sent a mighty army to conquer Thoron. But Sea God Mantos destroyed their fleet, and not a single soldier survived. It's a black stain in Kallikratés' history." Lorelei smiled. "It's even taboo to mention it."

Changing the subject, the inn owner passed a plate over to Mara. It appeared to be fried fish. "This is the house special for tonight—Mermaid Meat, great for the ailing undying."

Mara stared at the dish. "What?"

Lorelei laughed. "It is not the flesh of a mermaid. It's just called that."

"The first undying was immortal, thanks to the rose and mermaid meat," Morgan revealed. "The rose gave immortality yet took away her humanity. According to legend, consuming mermaid meat granted immense longevity, but turned the consumer into a mermaid. Thalia ate mermaid flesh to regain her human youth and beauty. She could still die. But unlike you, she remained human. Since discovering the abilities of their flesh, humans hunted mermaids to extinction."

"Oh…" Mara stared at the dish. "That's okay. I'm not a fan of fish."

"A pity… it could help you stay human," Morgan said.

Mara glanced up at her. "Well, at least I've got undying souls and healing stones, until the next death." She recalled another thing. "Oh, and there's drinking the commander's blood."

"Is that so?" Morgan asked with intrigue. "The rumours are true?"

"You mean him possessing the blood of the Great Lord?" Mara asked. "What does that mean?"

"Rumour has it that Commander White is a direct descendant and the reincarnation of Lord Kratés," Morgan explained.

Mara gawked at her in shock. "What?"

"A little known fact about the Great Lord Kratés—he fathered many children, but only a few descendants remain today," Morgan said. "It is believed that the commander is from one of the old bloodlines."

"Is Commander White a demigod?" Mara asked.

"It is unconfirmed," Morgan replied, "but if his blood could restore you, even temporarily, then the rumours must be true."

"Another interesting thing about him," Lady Lorelei added. "He was once married."

Mara nodded. "I heard about that. She died. Since then, he drinks heavily."

"Upon discovering his true origins, he had to choose between his destiny and his wife," Lorelei explained. "He left her with a broken heart. She took her own life, or that's what I heard."

The women heard a loud thud. Through a small crack between the curtains, they saw the commander bolting up from his table, knocking over his chair.

"How dare you touch me?" Commander White shouted.

Mara saw a courtesan sitting across from him. Even Lady Lorelei and Morgan noticed his eruption of anger.

Lorelei shook her head. "That girl is forward in her advances."

They watched him scowl at the courtesan before storming away. While he walked by their table, Lady Lorelei opened the curtain.

"I hope you're enjoying yourself, dear," called the inn owner.

Commander White stopped and sulked at them. "Having a prostitute's foot on my crotch is not something I'd describe as enjoying oneself! And the service is deplorable. I have not eaten."

"My apologies, but you did request to sit elsewhere," Lorelei told him.

"Perhaps he can join us?" Morgan suggested. "There is plenty to eat and drink."

The commander looked at Lady Lorelei, then Morgan. His eyes finally fell on Mara, who looked back at him and wondered what his answer would be. He did request to sit elsewhere and far away from her. The hard look remained in his eyes. Not wanting to see his face anymore, Mara turned around and ate her dinner. She hoped he would refuse.

"Perhaps, I will."

Mara stopped eating while hearing him approach the side of their table. She never expected him to say those words.

"If that is all right with you," Commander White spoke.

Knowing he was not talking to her, Mara did not look at him.

"I do not have a problem with him here," Morgan said.

"Neither do I," Lorelei agreed. "As long as he is good company." She gazed at Mara. "What do you think, dear?"

Mara looked at Lady Lorelei and Morgan, who sought her approval. She gazed down at her dinner plate.

"Sure, as long as he doesn't act like an ass," Mara grumbled. She never bothered to look at him but noticed the positive responses from the other women.

"Ah, that's great to hear," Lady Lorelei said.

Morgan beamed at her in silence.

Mara sighed, looking down at her plate. At least the other two women were happy to have "Prince Charming" sitting with them.

Commander White took the seat across from her. Morgan seemed pleased to have him beside her. Mara hoped the rest of her dinner would go by smoothly. She glanced up to see the commander helping himself to the food. Then she looked back at her plate and continued to eat.

"This is pretty decent considering the establishment," said the commander.

Mara was stunned, for this was the first time he ever gave a compliment about anything. She turned to her plate and ate her meal. The commander was right; this was delicious. Every bite was worth savouring. While eating, Mara sensed his gaze on her. Commander White was watching. A knife could slice through the tension, being so thick. Mara lifted her gaze to confront his own. He observed every detail of her face with scrutiny. She grew weary of his judgmental gaze. He made her uncomfortable but never cared. Mara spotted a glass of wine before him. Grasping it, the commander lifted his glass to his lips. He kept his eyes on her as he took a sip. Mara took a deep breath. With the addition of alcohol, things could get worse.

"Remarkable," he spoke. "Never realized you are associated with those savages from the Outer Frontier."

Mara stayed quiet. Not only was he sexist, but he was also racist. She was surprised that he could identify her as a member of the Stone Mage Tribe.

Commander White gazed at her, his face devoid of emotion. "Your skin is lighter. I assume you are born of two races, and thus impure."

He was right—Mom and Dad's union was unusual. And it was also rare to produce such offspring. Mara put her knife and fork down.

"And I remind you of your wife," Mara replied in a low tone.

He frowned at her. "What did you say?"

She hit a nerve. Mara saw his eyebrows furrow in anger.

"Your father told me about her." Mara gestured to his glass. "It's why you drink."

Commander White glanced at his wineglass. "He did?" He looked up at her and nodded. "Yes," he admitted solemnly. "I pray to the Goddess, hoping to forget that day."

"I'm sorry," Mara said softly.

He glanced at her while reaching into his pocket. In his hand was a glowing white stone.

Mara's eyes widened. "That's a healing stone!"

Commander White gazed at the stone.

"I hear these help you," said the commander. He stretched over his hand to offer the healing stone. "I found it on the Siren's corpse, but I have no use for it. It will benefit you more."

She reached out and received the healing stone. Mara took great care to put it away. She glanced up at Commander White. "Thank you."

Lorelei began to serve drinks. Taking the green and blue bottles, she opened them. Mara looked at the bottles with curiosity. Lady Lorelei smiled while pouring the drinks.

"How about we celebrate?" asked the hostess. "Ever tried absinthe?"

She prepared the drink by placing a unique spoon with holes on the rim of the glass.

Mara shook her head.

"It is strong alcohol," Morgan said.

"Not if you distill it." Lady Lorelei placed a sugar cube on the spoon. Taking a pitcher of water, she poured it into her glass, distilling the absinthe. She served out the drinks to Morgan and Commander White.

The commander snatched his glass and began to chug eagerly. The three women watched in shock. Realizing what he did, the commander stopped, then placed his glass on the table.

"Sorry," he said softly. "It's one of my favourites."

Lady Lorelei watched him before pouring a second glass for him. "Careful how you drink it. It is strong stuff." After distilling the drink, she passed it to Commander White.

When it came to Mara's glass, Morgan stopped Lady Lorelei. "I think the young lady should have the other one."

Lorelei looked at her, and then to Mara. "If that's all right with you, dear?"

"What's the difference?" Mara questioned, offering her glass.

"Just the colour," Lorelei answered, pouring the blue absinthe. "Kept this for a while, considering the heavy taxes I had to pay to import this from Thoron. It's called Blue Rose."

"Like the story?" Mara questioned. Lorelei nodded.

The commander sat there, folding his arms. "What story?"

"An old Thoron tale of a young woman seeking the Blue Rose of Immortality," Morgan told him, "to prove her love to a man who never loved her."

Commander White looked back at Morgan.

Mara gazed at him until he noticed her gawking. She looked away and turned her attention onto her drink. She could not recall trying alcohol before. Reaching for her glass, Mara lifted it to her lips. As soon as she took a sip, she tasted the combination of herbs and botanical ingredients.

"How is it, dear?" Lady Lorelei asked her. "Is it too bitter?"

Mara looked back at her and shook her head. "Never drank absinthe before."

Lady Lorelei nodded and offered some advice. "Don't drink it too fast. The last thing I need is you passed out on the ground."

* * *

Some time had passed, and Mara had yet to finish her first drink. She took Lorelei's warning to heart. However, the man sitting across from her ignored the valuable advice.

Commander White was on his fifth drink, already showing signs of drunkenness since his third. His face was flushed. His green eyes were glazed over.

The three women looked mystified.

"Why hasn't he succumbed to alcohol poisoning?" Lady Lorelei questioned.

Mara watched him. Aware of his alcoholism, she wondered if she should have stopped him.

Commander White looked at Lady Lorelei and passed his glass to her.

"Give me more," he slurred.

Lorelei's jaw dropped. "I think you had enough."

He shook his head. "No, I'm not drunk."

The three gaze at him with concern.

"We shouldn't have given him more," Mara told the others.

The commander scowled at her. "How dare you? I'm the Commander of the Holy Blades!"

Mara shook her head. She could not take him seriously in that state.

Lady Lorelei picked up the empty green absinthe bottle. "Well, too bad. You finished it off!"

Commander White looked at the empty bottle and then gazed at the blue absinthe, which remained plentiful.

"What about the other one? You still got lots." He tried to reach for the other bottle, but Lady Lorelei snatched it away from him.

"No, I'm cutting you off."

"No, I want one more!" Commander White cried, acting like a small and whiny child. "One more!"

Mara shook her head in embarrassment before reaching for her glass. But it was snatched away before she could grab it. Commander White had stolen her drink and chugged it before anyone could react. He finished and stared at Mara with glazed eyes.

"What is this?" He looked at Lady Lorelei. "Why did you give her a better drink?"

Lorelei grew confused. "The only difference is the colour."

"No, this one is sweeter and more fragrant," Commander White slurred. "Why did you give this savage half-breed the better drink? What makes her so special?"

Mara stared ahead, tapping her fingertips on the table. With her dinner ruined, there was no hope of salvaging the rest of it.

She got up and looked at Lady Lorelei. "Don't mean to be rude, but I would like to go to my room now."

"Very well," Lady Lorelei sighed. She beckoned some servers to take Mara to her room.

* * *

The innkeeper led Mara to a luxurious suite. It contained two bedrooms and a washing room in between. How generous of Lady Lorelei—this had to be very costly, but a good night's sleep would help her forget the lousy dinner. After a few moments, she heard shouting and knew who it was.

"I refuse to sleep in this filth!" Commander White yelled.

"Come on!" Boyd shouted back. "It's not that bad!"

"Not only did you invite those whores to our table, but you also brought them here?"

The commander was livid.

"What's going on?" Lady Lorelei confronted Commander White.

All this yelling had to be disturbing the other guests. They were a few doors away, yet Mara could hear everything.

"I demand better accommodation! I refuse to sleep in this dump!"

"I apologize, but we just gave our last room away," Lorelei said with a lowered voice.

"To who?" Commander White demanded.

Within a few seconds, Mara heard three loud knocks on the door. She hesitantly answered, only to be greeted by the commander's glare. His eyes remained glazed, his face flushed. He stormed past her and inspected the suite. To her surprise, he could walk around without staggering.

"What are you doing?" Mara questioned.

Commander White looked around. "This will do," he murmured. Then he turned his head and scowled at her. "You! Get out!"

Mara's jaw dropped. As if her night could not get any worse! But she stood her ground. Mara no longer took him seriously.

The commander stormed up to her. "How dare you? How does a savage half-breed get—"

Mara lost it. She swung her hand across his face. Her palm slammed against his left cheek. He tumbled to the ground in an instant. Mara stared at him. It was reminiscent of the incident in Hema, but the roles reversed. A profound red mark formed where she slapped him. At first, Commander White barely reacted. He sat there stunned before sneering at her.

"You dare hit me?" Commander White barked, the rest of his face turning red.

"Yes, I think you deserved it," Mara admitted. She pointed to the door. "Now, get out!"

"She hit me!" Commander White raged while trying to get up. "She hit me!" He snapped his head around and scowled at her. "How dare you? You heathen! Vile creature! She-devil!"

Mara did not know if she should be offended or amused, for he remained drunk out of his mind.

Lady Lorelei stepped into the doorway, placing her hands on her hips. "I swear you two fight like a married couple."

The two frowned at her.

The commander rose to his feet and stormed up to her. "Why did you give her this room? She does not deserve this at all!"

"You deserve better?" Mara argued. "You tried to claim my kill as your own, threw insults at me, and ruined my dinner!"

"It matters not!" He gazed at her in anger. "You are a low creature!"

"At least I'm not like you," Mara hissed in a low tone. "A petty and shallow noble, and a drunk who hides behind his men." Her right hand tightened into a fist. "I bet I've slain more monsters in the past few days than you ever had in your career."

"Stop fighting," Lady Lorelei interrupted.

The two stopped and stared at her.

Lorelei addressed the commander. "I apologize for any inconvenience this caused you. If you wish, you can stay here."

Mara could not believe her ears. The inn owner was going to give her room to him.

Lorelei paused and looked at Mara. "But I gave this place to the young lady, and I won't force her out." She then addressed Mara. "Do you wish to stay? The choice is yours."

Mara stared at Lady Lorelei, then to Commander White. He wanted her gone, but she was not going to give him the satisfaction. She stood her ground and folded her arms.

"I am staying." Mara sulked at him. "And I'm not changing my mind!"

The commander scowled back at her.

Lady Lorelei shrugged. "Well, I guess that's final. You both can share the place."

He whipped his head around and frowned at the inn owner. "What?"

Lorelei began to walk away. She had enough of him. "You have two bedrooms. You don't need to look at each other. I'm sure you can make it work." With that, she left them alone and closed the door.

Mara stared at the door in silence.

Commander White took a step forward. "Very well."

She gazed back at him.

The commander gave a cold look, holding his hands behind his back. "I shall see which bedroom is more satisfactory." He turned his back.

Mara sighed. He wanted the superior room, leaving her with the inferior one.

Chapter Fifteen

Human Nature

Frankly, there was nothing wrong with the inferior room. A queen-sized bed sat in the middle of a sizable room. The sheets were soft and comfy. Mara needed a bath, so she headed to the washing room.

However, someone else occupied it. Commander White began to remove his garb. His sword sat at the side of the tub while the coat came off. He wore a white shirt under a dark grey vest. The commander rolled up his sleeves. The lower half of his garb stayed on. He became sober enough to hog the washing area. The commander did not acknowledge her at first, but her relentless watching finally drew his attention. He turned his head to frown at her.

"What do you want?" Commander White demanded.

"Why are you washing your coat?" Mara asked. "It doesn't look dirty."

The commander gave a sour expression. "I see you're still bragging about the Siren." He turned to his coat and began to wash it.

"I am not bragging. It's just a question."

He stopped and scowled at her. "You fail to see the grime defiling this garb of mine. Then again, I do not expect a low creature to understand."

She shrugged. "It was just a bunch of courtesans."

Her reply earned her the commander's scorn. "Is that all you have to say?" He folded his arms. "Maybe you should join them?"

Mara ignored his cruel remarks. "Are you at least done? I'd also like to clean my clothes."

"No, I am not," he replied coldly. "I must also perform a cleansing ritual upon myself."

Mara gaped at him. She never heard of this before, and it sounded ridiculous. But judging from the commander's face, he was serious.

"Okay, what is this ritual?"

Commander White turned to face her, holding his hands behind his back. "It is sacred to the followers of Kallikratés, so I doubt you understand its significance."

She rolled her eyes. "Fine. I hope this isn't going to take all night? I do not want the stains to be permanent."

"I will need at least an hour for adequate cleansing. Besides, you lasted this long. I'm sure you can wait for another hour or two."

The commander lifted his right hand, gesturing her to avert her gaze. He was about to strip down. Turning around, Mara shook her head. She was less than thrilled about having to wait.

"Might as well go to a nearby river," she muttered.

"Maybe you should. It'll be more appropriate for you."

She rolled her eyes. Before leaving, she took the key to the suite. The commander would probably lock her out. Mara left the room.

* * *

While Mara searched for a place to clean her clothes, she ran into Lady Lorelei.

"Ah, fancy meeting you again," Lorelei began. "What are you doing out here?"

"Looking for a place to clean my clothes," Mara explained. "Where's the nearest river?"

"What are you talking about?" Lady Lorelei paused for a few seconds. "Oh, let me guess. Your roommate hogged the washing area?"

"He's also doing a cleansing ritual."

"Oh, dear," Lady Lorelei sighed. "I never realized he would be difficult." She beckoned Mara. "Come with me."

Mara followed her to another room, where some servers took her clothes for cleaning. In the meantime, Mara obtained new attire. The low collar on the white shirt showed off much of her chest. A black corset covered much of her torso. She got black pants as well as brown boots and gloves.

After getting dressed, Mara walked out. She spotted Lady Lorelei speaking to Morgan. Mara was surprised to see the older woman still here. Morgan took notice of Mara and stared back at her. Her face was unreadable.

Lady Lorelei turned around and saw Mara. "Oh, my dear! Don't you look charming," she cooed. She glanced back at Morgan. "Don't you think she looks charming?"

Morgan stared at her. After a few seconds, a smile began to spread on her big and full lips.

"Yes, she indeed does," Morgan replied.

Mara stared at her. Morgan's smile seemed forced as if something was bothering her. Mara wanted to say something, but Morgan interrupted.

"I heard about your eviction."

"He's doing a cleansing ritual," Mara corrected her.

Morgan looked intrigued.

Lady Lorelei glanced back at her. "You know what that means."

Morgan gazed back with a smile, and then the two watched her. Mara looked puzzled.

Lady Lorelei smiled. "Are you coming with us?"

"Where are we going?" Mara asked.

"To see Commander White."

Remembering the key, Mara retrieved it from her pocket. "I'm not sure if it's a good idea."

"He won't even know that we are watching him," Morgan told her.

"I have some secret corridors," Lady Lorelei revealed. "They are accessible from the outside, allowing one to peer into a room without the occupant being aware." She looked back at Morgan. "We're going to use them to watch him bathe and…" Lorelei gazed at Mara. "We want you to join us."

Mara shook her head. "I don't think I—"

"Don't you want to see how beautiful he is?" Morgan interrupted her.

Mara was speechless. Lorelei looked amused by her silence.

"Why do you want to see him like this?" Mara finally asked.

Morgan grinned. "I shall explain if you come with us."

Mara was reluctant but decided to go. She put the key away as she followed them.

Lady Lorelei guided them to a door hidden in the bushes. She opened it and led them through the dusty old corridors. They kept going until they found her room.

A hole in the wall allowed one to peer into the washing area. Lorelei and Morgan were the first to take a look. They kept their voices low, making sure he remained unaware of their presence.

"Oh my, he's something else," Lady Lorelei murmured.

Morgan was silent while her eyes took in his image. They gazed at Mara, gesturing her to join them.

Mara shook her head in silence.

"If you look, I will explain," Morgan whispered.

Mara stared at them. She thought if she came with them, Morgan would explain why they were doing this. There was no mention of having to look at his naked body. She was not one to cave into peer pressure but was a little curious. She approached the hole in silence, hoping not to blow their cover. Just a tiny peek.

Lying in the bathtub, the commander leaned his head back while resting his eyes. The water rose to his muscled chest as his arms rested on the edge of the tub. He had a nice build to go with his attractive face, yet there was nary a scar or blemish on his skin. Mara suspected he didn't get his body from hunting monsters. Maybe he hid behind his Holy Blades.

"What do you think?" Lady Lorelei asked.

"He is handsome, but I still think he's an ass." Mara looked at Morgan. "Why are we here?"

Morgan stole another look at him. "He is special."

Mara looked at her with curiosity.

Lorelei leaned in to whisper into Mara's ear. "He's the sort of man she's seeking."

Mara glanced at the inn owner and then stared back at Morgan.

"Oh, so you're interested in him?" Mara asked.

"Yes, but not for the same reasons as you," Morgan replied, looking back at her.

Looking confused, Mara folded her arms. "What do you mean?"

"I've seen how you look at him," Morgan said. "To you, he is a prince. He cares for his appearance more than most men. He has a nice body, but you try to see his worth on the inside."

Great, another one saw her ogling the commander at the first meeting.

"And I've yet to find," Mara grumbled.

"True…" Morgan smiled.

"What about you?"

"It is not so much the inside I care about, but the outside," Morgan said. "I want him whole rather than the sum of his parts."

They were like opposites. Mara's attraction to him was no secret, but she never knew Morgan wanted him too. Mara gazed back at him. The commander opened his eyes and tilted his head forward. He rose from the tub. Mara looked away. The other women kept looking, for they did not want to miss the show.

* * *

Once the three women had enough to see, they left the corridors. Mara came out to be approached by a server holding her black Silver Thorn armour. It looked nearly clean and almost free of bloodstains. Then again, the stains were barely noticeable on black.

"I suppose you want the other outfit back?" Mara asked Lady Lorelei.

"No, keep it, dear," Lorelei replied. "It was an old attire I used to wear when I first came to Ardana. It no longer fits me. I think it will suit you better."

"Okay…" A thought crossed Mara's mind. "Can I ask you a question?"

Lady Lorelei looked intrigued. "Sure… what is it?"

"I used a tunnel within the Dark Labyrinth to return and came across all these crates and barrels. What are those?"

Lorelei froze, for she knew what Mara meant. After a while, the older woman relaxed. A wry smile formed on her face. "I shall tell if you promise to keep it a secret."

Mara nodded, "I won't tell."

"It is a smuggling operation," said the inn owner. "As mentioned before, Thoron is blacklisted by Kallikratés. Travelling there is forbidden, while imported goods or people are taxed. So I helped create this to bypass those unfair laws. But the Siren interfered with our operation."

"What?" Mara felt confused. She had her reasons for killing the Siren, but now it seemed others had their ulterior motives.

Lorelei looked indifferent. "I made myself clear. Besides, she was a monster, and all monsters must die. You, of all people, should know that."

Mara clenched her teeth as her hand curled into a fist. Intense hatred began to boil. Then she stopped. Why was she angry? Mara could feel her canines elongating, ready to tear into flesh. After calming down, her fangs shrank down. Mara saw the worried expression on Lorelei's face and with good reason. She felt like killing the inn owner on the spot. Regaining control, Mara stormed up to Lady Lorelei, having one thing to say to her.

"I… I apologize if I scared you, but the Siren was no mere monster—her name was Aria."

Mara looked at Lorelei's shocked face. The hostess seemed surprised that the undying gave a name to the monster. With that, Mara walked away.

"Wait," Lorelei called out to her.

Mara stopped and gazed at her.

The inn owner began to approach. "Maybe I was a little insensitive," Lorelei apologized. "Nobody asks to be cursed."

"Wise words," Morgan said, appearing beside Mara. The older woman had witnessed their conversation. "A monster may be a monster, but no one should ignore the capacity of evil in every human being."

Mara looked at Morgan with curiosity. "What do you mean?"

"Humans are more willing and capable of committing more atrocities to their own," Lorelei explained. "Aria is an example."

Mara looked back at Lorelei. "You knew Aria?"

"Come with me," Lady Lorelei beckoned the two. "I want to show you something."

The inn owner led the two women to her private room. Lorelei crouched down and pulled a floorboard out. Mara looked on in confusion, wondering what she was doing. Morgan remained still and quiet. Lady Lorelei took out a box and opened it, revealing several articles inside. Most were letters.

"Aria often sent letters to her lover while he was away in Corlin," Lorelei spoke solemnly. "It was the only way she could communicate since losing her voice. At first, she would get a response, but they became sparse over time. By the third year, he never responded to any of her letters. She wrote to him each week, though it seemed he disappeared from her life."

The letters reminded Mara of the one found from the Siren. She reached into her satchel.

"The Siren had this one."

Taking out the faded letter, Mara showed it to Lady Lorelei. The inn owner's mouth dropped open, but no words came out. She eventually found her voice.

"May I see it?" Lorelei asked.

Mara passed it to her.

Lorelei studied the letter. "I don't believe it. She had this the whole time?" The inn owner looked back at Mara. "This is the final letter from him." She glanced down at it. "I know the full story. Aria's lover was behind the destruction of her voice. In truth, he hated her and found her voice annoying. He paid those thugs to harm her. His cruelty and callousness drove Aria to suicide."

Mara stared at her in shock. She felt upset to hear this part of the tale. Lady Lorelei gazed at her with sympathy and passed the letter back.

"Keep it," she said. "You were meant to preserve her memory."

Mara shook her head. "If he never loved her, why didn't he just leave her alone?"

"As I've said before, humans have a capacity for both good and evil," Morgan said.

Mara looked back at Morgan.

"What about all the wars humanity waged upon one another?" asked the veiled woman. "What about the Golden Age at the cost of millions of lives? What about bullies in school?"

Mara never expected to talk about school bullying, which was a familiar topic. She remembered the bullying she endured in elementary school. Some children threw rocks at her. When a boy hit her and drew blood, she picked up the rock and threw it back at him in retaliation. She hit him on the head and knocked him out cold.

Then she remembered her time in junior high. A group of students played a prank by stealing her book and not giving it back. They ridiculed her, claiming she was illiterate. It was a big mistake on their part. Mara threw a chair at the ringleader and knocked her down. The lackeys stood slack-jawed while she approached the ringleader with another chair and beat her with it. The girl was bruised, but not bleeding. It was the first time Mara made anyone cry. It was satisfying.

In high school, a drunkard attempted to rape her. She beat him with a large schoolbook, then stabbed him with his knife when he tried to defend himself. She did not get into much trouble for that one since the pervert was known to be a serial rapist and alcoholic. Despite the heroic act of defending herself, Mara had gained criticism from her parents. Her mother was disturbed by Mara's sudden violent behaviour. According to Mom, Mara was never the same after getting that mysterious illness as a toddler. Her father seemed more understanding, though he did not approve of her ways of handling those situations.

Finishing her thoughts of the past, Mara looked at Morgan and nodded. "I suppose you are right."

"Yes, but there is nothing wrong with holding onto your humanity," Morgan said to her. "If anything, it will help you from becoming like the others."

"In the end, you did help Aria and put an end to her suffering," Lady Lorelei added. "You know what? I might rename one of my brothels."

Mara gazed at her with a raised eyebrow. She thought it was strange to change the topic in such a weird way, but decided to go along with it.

"Okay, like what?"

"I think I'll call it The Siren," Lady Lorelei announced.

Mara kept giving her a strange look. "I... I don't know what to think of that."

"I think it's a fine idea," Morgan said. "The Siren had power over men with her song and was often mistaken for a mermaid. Mermaids were said to be beautiful creatures, irresistible to men."

Mara raised an eyebrow. "Okay..." She changed the topic. "It's getting late. I should head back. I have a two-day journey to Grey Mountain. Maybe Harold has found the next undying?"

"Goodnight, my dear," Lady Lorelei said. "I wish you well in your endeavours."

Mara nodded. Looking at Morgan, she noticed the same unreadable expression from before. The two gazed at each other for a while. Mara broke her gaze and left. She still felt the other woman's eyes on her while walking away.

* * *

Entering the suite, Mara noticed the silence. She suspected Commander White had gone to bed. It was late in the night. She walked to the washing area and saw that it was now vacant.

A glimpse of a bare arm drew her attention to the other room. Mara looked inside to see Commander White dressed only in his pants. He was on his knees with his hands resting on his legs. The commander kept his eyes closed as his breathing was deep and slow. It looked like he was meditating. She gazed at him with curiosity. A few seconds later, his head began to shudder and twitch. Mara noticed and wondered what was happening. The strange convulsions grew more frequent. Growing concerned, Mara approached him to see if he was okay. After taking a few steps, his head stopped shuddering. His eyes flew open to see Mara standing before him. He rose to his feet with a frown on his face.

She was stunned. "I thought...?"

Commander White grabbed her arm and forced her out. He glared at her and slammed the door in her face.

Mara stood perplexed. The commander acted as if nothing had happened. It was none of her concern. She sighed, then entered the washing room.

The water seemed decent. The servers probably changed the water after Commander White finished. She began to remove her clothes. Mara took off her gloves, seeing the black and pointed fingernails. It looked like paint. She tried to remove it, but it refused to come off. The doctors mentioned this as abnormal, but it never bothered her. She continued to strip down.

Her abdomen had some muscle tone from working for her father. There were fewer scars, possibly due to her curse. Mara was part shadow beast, known to have regenerative healing abilities. It might explain how she survived getting impaled by Isabella. Either way, it was a blessing, or she would never hear the end of it from Mom. The most notable scar was on the lower abdomen. She could not recall where she got the ugly vertical deformity. It was healing, but very slowly. At least it was not painful to touch. Mara decided not to dwell on it. She saw more of the faded spots decorating her skin. Mara went into the tub to wash her body.

After she finished, Mara returned to her room. She kept only her white shirt and underwear on. Looking around the room, she saw a mirror and approached it. Mara saw her messy hair, which became tangled during the bath. Recalling the comb, Mara searched her belongings. After pulling it out, she felt unsure about running it through her hair, knowing where she got it. Mara returned to the washing area and cleaned it. It remained tarnished, but at least she could use it. Mara returned to her room. Sitting on the bed, she began to brush her hair. The tangles were very stubborn. It felt like a long time since she last combed her hair. Mara never had this much difficulty, but she managed to get the tangles out. While straightening her hair, she thought about her parents. Were they looking for her? If she had some time, she could go to Mirahyll. After she finished, Mara put the comb away and went to bed.

* * *

An hour later, Mara awoke to the wind's howling. She also heard a faint but audible voice. It sounded like the Siren, even though the creature was dead. The song grew louder until she realized it came from the commander's room. She also heard a man moaning. Someone was having a good time. As she listened carefully, Mara realized it was Commander White.

Wide awake, Mara got out of bed to investigate. She snuck out of her room and headed for the other. The moans grew louder with each step. The door to his room was open by a crack. In silence, she leaned over and took a peek. Mara first saw a dark purple bustle dress abandoned on the floor. Then she looked up to see Morgan and the commander—together and naked. Mara could only see Morgan's backside. Long black hair flowed down to the middle of her back. Shimmering scales of green and blue decorated her tanned skin. Morgan mounted Commander White as if he were a stallion. With their genders locked, she rode him up and down towards an orgasm. He responded by pushing his hips up, diving deeper into her.

Mara froze, while many emotions rushed through her mind. She felt upset and betrayed. Deep down, she should not care. Commander White was never interested in her—he made that clear on many occasions. She also knew Morgan wanted him.

The commander wrapped his hands around her waist, holding Morgan tightly. He groaned with every push. Morgan looked down at him in silence as she clung onto him. In one final thrust, he erupted like a volcano. Commander White arched his back while moaning from the release.

Mara looked at Commander White and saw his joy. He appeared to be moving on from his dead wife. Mara could have been happy for him but felt her heart was breaking. Seeing them together was not only shocking but very agitating. Mara also felt disgusted, knowing that she stood there and watched their sexual union. She wondered if she should have stopped it, but it might have made things worse.

Mara could not stay another moment. Backing away from the door, she hurried to her room. She closed the door behind her and made her preparations in silence. Mara wanted to avoid the commander. While donning her attire, she heard the door open and close. She peeked out the door to find Morgan missing. Mara emerged from her room. The other room remained open. Peeking inside, she saw Commander White sleeping peacefully. He laid in bed naked but did not seem to care. Mara closed the door gently. She double-checked her room, making sure she left nothing behind. Leaving the suite, she took extra care not to wake him.

On the way out, Mara encountered Lady Lorelei.

"What are you doing out here?" Lorelei questioned.

Mara frowned under her mask. "I'm sorry," she said quietly. "I have to go."

Lorelei looked confused. "What? At this hour?"

Mara nodded and turned away.

"Wait," Lorelei called.

Mara ignored her. Taking a few steps, she ran into Morgan and froze. The older woman looked back at her. They watched each other in silence. Mara then stormed past her, still feeling Morgan's gaze as she left Har' Yhan.

Chapter Sixteen

A Tale of Misfortunes

Mara travelled north for two days. She still felt numb. The images of that night were burned deep into her mind. Weariness began to set in—she only received an hour of sleep since that night. She didn't want to stop until she reached Greyward Hold.

She shook her head, trying to get the images out of her mind. However, they refused to go away. Mara knew Commander White was not interested in her, but she felt hurt and betrayed. Tears began to well up in her eyes. She could not fight them. Mara wiped them away, but they still kept coming. Strong emotions sapped her strength and the lack of sleep caught up to her.

As she reached the mountain, the snow began to fall. A winter storm brewed. The air became colder as the wind whipped around her. She had to focus on returning to Greyward Hold.

Traversing the mountain path, Mara heard a growl in the wind. She looked up to see a snow beast baring its razor-sharp teeth. It leapt from the wall and landed in front of her. She wondered if this was the same creature from earlier, seeking retribution. Mara unsheathed her sword. She was unsure about taking on this creature alone, but there was no going back.

The snarling beast lunged at her, but Mara dodged its swing. It attacked again, this time hitting her left arm. Dropping her sword, Mara held her arm while falling to her knees. Three ugly gashes bled profusely.

While Mara watched the snow beast's approach, a black mist drifted towards them. It enveloped the snow beast, causing it to roar in pain. The creature swiped at the air, trying to get rid of the mist. Its white fur darkened and fell off, as the dark blue skin began to decay. Its amber eyes rotted into a sludge that trickled out of its sockets. The snow beast kept roaring and swiping at the air in a futile effort. Finally, its strength gave away. The snow beast fell to the ground where it continued to rot. All that remained was a bloody skeleton with flesh hanging from its bones.

Mara was stunned at the grotesque sight until she realized that she also stood in the mist. It entered her lungs, burning them from the inside. She could not breathe. She tried to escape, but the haze sapped her remaining strength. It burned her skin like acid, forcing her to the frozen ground. In the cold darkness, she spotted a man in grey robes and holding a staff. Her vision faded as the wind's howling grew distant.

* * *

She awoke to the burning sensation coursing her veins. Opening her eyes, Mara recognized her bedchambers in Greyward Hold. She looked around and blinked. As her vision cleared, the first thing she saw was his mask. Harold gazed at her while moving closer. He held a wooden cup in his hands.

"Take this," he instructed softly. "Drink it slowly."

After pulling down her mask, she reached for the cup. Mara was so weak she needed to hold it with both hands. Upon lifting the cup to her lips, a strong minty taste made her cough and sputter. Some of the concoction went down the wrong way. Even the smell invaded her nostrils. Then a gentle tingle descended her throat. Soon, she began to feel better as some strength returned.

"This should help remove the poison from your body," Harold explained.

Mara gazed at him with a questioning glance.

He noticed and sighed. "My apologies, you were never the target."

"That was you?" Mara asked.

The former guild master nodded. "I am a lich, an undead like you. I have lived for over two thousand years. A bringer of death and disease, my miasma will rot the flesh of any creature," he said solemnly. "I intended to save you." Harold reached for the mirror. "I assume you were returning after your victory against the Siren, only to have all your efforts undone." He showed her reflection. "I am sorry."

Mara saw her face and became horrified. No longer was she human. The decayed skin and black scars returned. But deep down, she knew it was not his fault.

"It's okay. I've got a healing stone." Recalling the healing stone Commander White gave her, Mara could use it to restore herself.

"Very well," Harold spoke, "but you should use them wisely. Those stones are rare."

Mara frowned at him, but he had a point.

"Fine," Mara murmured. She changed the topic. "You lived for two thousand years?"

"Yes, I have."

"If you don't mind me asking, what were you before you became this?"

He looked away. "Once, I served an ancient order, which was to protect humans from monsters and the magic blight. Its principles and foundation helped build the Silver Thorns. Even Kallikratés and the Holy Blades trace back to the same guild." He looked back at Mara. "It is a very long story from long ago. Perhaps I will speak more about it another time. For now, you should rest and regain your strength."

He exited her bedchambers and closed the door behind him. His footsteps grew silent.

Mara glanced down at her pouch and opened it. The healing stone shone in the darkness. She wanted to restore herself, but Harold's advice stopped her. It would be a stone wasted if she died. She was better off searching for the next undying. Looking at her face in its current condition, Mara felt ashamed. She wanted to see her parents, but they would never recognize this undead creature. With so many thoughts running through her head, Mara returned to her rest.

* * *

After having enough rest, Mara got up and left her bedchambers. She strolled through the grand halls and entered Harold's chambers. The former master was meditating while she walked in.

Harold lifted his gaze to her. "Ah, you have awakened. Are you feeling better?"

She nodded. "Yes, I am. Have you found the next undying?"

He rose to his feet. "Don't you need more rest? You just got here."

"I want to find the next undying," she said firmly. "Please, tell me where she is."

"I do not think you are ready," he hesitated. "If you die, it'll be over."

"I know the risk," Mara insisted, "and so do you. You gave me this task."

"I did," Harold said, "but if you are lost, it will all be for naught."

She sulked at him. "Fine, but I'm not going to sit here, twiddling my thumbs!"

Harold sighed. Reaching into his robes, he pulled out a letter and handed it to her.

"What's this?" Mara took the letter from him.

"Something else you can do in the meantime," said the former master. "Chancellor Davis requests your presence. Since Heru's death, werewolves have now wandered south, close to nearby villages and the Delta Farms. You are to meet him at the Council Hall in Mirahyll."

Mara looked up at Harold and sighed.

"Fine, I'll go see him," Mara said, walking back to her bedchambers.

Even though she was bitter with Harold's refusal, he was right about one thing. The rules of the undying also applied to Mara. At least this task involved werewolves. She gathered her things and left for Mirahyll.

Travelling down the mountain path, Mara saw the dead snow beast. It continued to decompose as the rotten stench assaulted her nostrils. Mara cringed. She never deemed the former Silver Thorn master would be capable of this. Although grateful for Harold's help, Mara remained a little upset about getting caught in the deadly haze. After staring at the corpse for a while, Mara walked away. She travelled to the road and headed for Mirahyll.

* * *

On the morning of November 23, Mara stood before the gates of the second-largest city in Ardana. She remembered living here before, but since losing her memory, it felt like her first visit to Mirahyll. The street lights decorating the roads were more impressive at night. Now that she recalled, an electric variant of moonstone powered them. The city shared some gothic architecture with Hemal but was more lively and elegant in comparison. The most notable locations were the Grand Cathedral, the College of Ardana, Mirahyll Hospital, and the Council Hall. Her parents lived here, and she wanted to visit them. However, with her current appearance, she felt unsure about seeing them. She still didn't know how to explain her predicament. Besides, her presence at the Council Hall was urgent.

Walking to the Council Hall, she spotted an information board. Of the various postings, one stood out from the rest—Ardana was cutting ties with the southern nation of Corlin.

"A rash of stolen goods?" Mara asked herself, reading the notice. "Main items targeted are general goods and weapons. Corlin's chancellors have halted trades until further notice." She felt perplexed. "What are the Guardsmen doing?"

It was one of the many troubles this land faced. Now Ardana had to rely on the Delta Farms, the Lilystone general stores, and the dwindling number of blacksmiths. She stared at the notice, then walked away.

Mara happened upon a blacksmith's shop at the edge of the noble quarters. An older man hammered away at his newest creation. He had a balding top while sporting a short beard. A long thin nose sat on a loose and wrinkled face. The round glasses adorning his face hid the colour of his irises.

Mara reckoned this was Master Blacksmith Edwin. Approaching him, she noticed his sour expression.

He ignored her at first. "Hmm, I haven't seen you around these parts," he began. "If you're interested in my services, show me some gold! If not, then don't waste my time."

Mara was taken aback by his rudeness. Her eyes drifted onto the beautiful and elegant weapons on display. Talon was not lying—this man's work was a piece of art, but very expensive. The cost of these weapons rivalled her tuition fees. Even Dad would never demand such abhorrent prices. She turned around and left the blacksmith's shop.

She looked for Talon, who came here to set up shop. With no other blacksmiths in the area, she wandered into the lower quarters of the city and found an old dusty building. The sign hanging above the door depicted an anvil and a hammer—a blacksmith's workshop. Talon had to be here. It would be a great idea to repair her weapons and gear before meeting the chancellor. Mara went inside.

"Hello?" Mara called.

Following the sound of striking metal, she found Talon at his forge.

He looked up at her. "Ah, great to see you again," Talon greeted. "Hope it wasn't much trouble finding the place?"

She shook her head. Then she asked, "Is business much better?"

Talon gazed down at his weapon with a sombre look. "To be honest, no."

"Why?"

"You must've seen him?" Talon questioned. "Edwin's workshop is here as well. Not only does he forge superior weapons, his customers include the Holy Blades, the Guardsmen, and various nobles who can afford his wares."

Mara passed her sword over to him for repair. "I think you're a great blacksmith," she said. "You forged weapons for the Silver Thorns. You even made my weapon, which helped me defeat some of the most dangerous monsters."

Talon smiled and took her sword for repairs. "Aye, that is true." After a while, he finished repairing her weapon. "Good to know you're my most valued customer." He returned her sword. His face fell back to a frown. "Still, it's not enough."

"What do you need to help your business?"

Talon rubbed his chin. "Hmm, it'll be great if others knew about my workshop." He looked at her. "I'd appreciate it if you spread the word around. Start with the chancellor. He controls what weapons go into the guardsmen's hands. Tell him I'll offer reliable weapons for a more reasonable price."

"Okay," Mara replied. "I was heading there anyway."

She sheathed her weapon and went on her way.

* * *

To get to the Council Hall, Mara had to travel through the noble quarters of the city. The houses were huge manors. Her parents were middle-class citizens and unable to afford such a place. While walking towards the Council Hall, Mara began to notice all these eyes on her. Nobles dressed in their elegant attire paused to gawk at her. Even the children playing in the streets were staring. One of the mothers took her child home, watching Mara with caution as they hurried to the door. How long were these people watching her? She stuck out like a sore thumb in a place of prestige.

Two male guardsmen approached her.

"State your business," one of them said with a bold voice.

She raised an eyebrow. "Is it normal of you to accost random people in the streets?"

"Only if they're suspicious, which you appear to be."

"A concerned citizen notified us," the other explained, "that you are up to no good."

Mara stared at them. Now she was being profiled. Then again, they had a right to be concerned. She was not exactly human. She reached into one of her pouches and retrieved the letter from the chancellor.

"Chancellor Davis requested my presence." She handed the paper to the guardsmen.

One of the guardsmen took the letter. While reading it, he spotted the signature and seal of the chancellor.

The other guardsman looked at her. "Wait, aren't you the Huntress?"

Mara gazed at him in confusion. "The Huntress?"

She never gave herself a name before. It had a nice ring to it.

The guardsman nodded. "Yeah, the Huntress! You slew the Siren and the White Lady?"

"You know about that?" Mara asked.

The other guardsman looked up from the paper. "We knew a while back. After discovering who killed the White Lady, we made sure to expel that weasel. We've also received word about the Siren." He looked at her attire. "Based on the descriptions of the slayer, we figure that you are the one."

Mara glanced down at her outfit before looking up at them.

"True," she replied.

The crowd began to murmur. Mara looked around, seeing the city folk surrounding her. Some nobles grimaced at her appearance.

"That's the Huntress?"

"She looks so raggedy."

"I was expecting something else…"

Mara ignored their comments. Not everyone could be pleased. At least the children showed appreciation.

"Mommy! Mommy! That lady killed those monsters," a small boy said, pointing at her.

A little girl jumped in glee. "She's a hero!"

The mother shushed her children as she ushered them into their house. She gazed at Mara suspiciously before closing the door.

Mara looked away and focused her gaze on the guardsmen.

One of the guardsmen nodded. "Very well, we shall take you to the Chancellor."

"Thank you." Mara followed them. She thought about those children, especially the one who called her a hero.

"Hmm, a hero," Mara muttered under her breath.

Many people called her different things before, but a hero was not one of them. Then again, how many lives did she save since killing the White Lady and the Siren? In truth, this was the first time thinking this way because of how she saw those creatures. They were not just monsters, but victims of a cruel and terrible curse. They were the undying and Mara was one of them. If these people knew of her true nature, they would treat her no different from the monsters they feared.

On the way to the Council Hall, Mara saw the Grand Cathedral—a large gold and ivory building deep in the heart of Mirahyll. The large wooden doors were open to welcome worshippers. Mara visited the place a few times before. One of her friends called it an eyesore, but with reason. That cathedral was built with taxpayers' money, an idea by the previous chancellor who favoured the Faith. Not everyone agreed and spoke with their votes. Mara admitted it was large and extravagant. It had several gardens, showcasing an impressive array of flowers during the spring and summer. Her mother once brought her here to meet that jerk. Dad refused to step foot near that place, calling it an abomination and an insult to the people of Ardana.

By the time Mara reached the Council Hall, the chancellor was in a meeting.

"Please wait," said the first guardsman. "We shall let him know you're here."

In less than a minute, Mara heard Davis. "Let her in."

Entering the council chamber, Mara froze at the sight of Commander White, who stood beside the chancellor's desk. A few Holy Blades accompanied him. The commander glared at her while folding his arms. Mara felt awkward—seeing him brought back the memories of that night. She frowned at him as tensions began to flare. Davis cleared his throat. Removing the scowl from her face, Mara gazed at the chancellor. A few guardsmen stood behind him. Davis lifted his right hand and beckoned her. She walked forward until she stood beside the commander. She ignored him while looking at the chancellor.

"So, you're the Huntress?" Davis questioned.

"Yes," Mara said.

He stared at her, then to Commander White. "You may go."

Commander White shifted his gaze onto him. "I recommend our expertise."

"With all due respect, I would like to explore other alternatives," Davis argued.

The commander sulked at him. "I see." He turned to Mara and sneered at her. He stormed past her and addressed his men. "We shall return to Golden Mountain."

The Holy Blades followed their commander out of the office.

She looked at Davis. "They were also here to deal with the werewolves?"

The chancellor sighed and rose from his desk. "They were. But if I chose them, I'd be forced to raise taxes throughout Terra to pay their fees, and that is the last thing I want."

Mara reckoned Davis was a frugal man. Recalling her conversation with Talon, she spoke up. "Speaking of alternatives, have you heard of Blacksmith Talon?"

Davis gazed at her. "Who?"

"Blacksmith Talon," she repeated. "He used to serve the Silver Thorns. He just arrived in Mirahyll after the guild disbanded."

"Is that so?" Davis questioned. "We have used Edwin's services for the past decade. As great a blacksmith as he is, Edwin asks way too much and can be difficult to deal with at times. This Talon—is he willing to forge weapons for the Guardsmen?"

Mara nodded. "They may not be as elegant, but are very reliable." She gestured to her sword. "He forged my weapon."

Davis eyed her blade. "Hmm, I shall consider it," said the chancellor, rubbing his chin. He changed the subject. "Now, the reason why I called you here…" He gazed at her. "I will offer a thousand gold for each werewolf slain. You shall be required to collect each head as proof. We'll even provide a horse. Do we have an agreement?"

"I'll do it, but couldn't they be cured?"

Davis shook his head. "Only Lady Isabella had that knowledge. After the cure's creation, she had the scientists and doctors killed to keep the formula a secret. When she died, she took the cure to the grave."

Mara felt guilty. "I'm sorry," she said quietly.

Davis looked surprised for a moment. He never saw a supernatural act so human.

"I'm sure you had to do what was needed," Davis said. "However, those at the Delta Farms had an unfortunate encounter. Considering what happened in Hemal, I'd hate to see it happen here."

"Oh, okay…" Mara murmured.

One of the guardsmen approached her and handed over a brown sack to bag the werewolf heads. She headed for the exit.

* * *

A guardsman guided her to the stables to obtain her horse. Mara saw a black mare with a white diamond shape on her forehead. Her dark mane fell past her eyes. Black pools watched Mara as she entered the stables.

The guardsman stopped and held up his right hand. "Wait here, miss. I'll get the little lady."

"Little lady?" Mara raised an eyebrow.

"Why, yes…" The guardsman took a saddle and some reins, then equipped them onto the mare. "That's what she is—a lady." He took the reins and began to lead her out, but the horse was unwilling to move.

She took notice of her new ride's behaviour. "What's going on?"

Mara began to approach them. A big mistake. The mare pulled away, causing the guardsman's grasp to falter. The horse reared up and neighed. Breaking free, the little lady almost ran over Mara while galloping out of the stables. Mara fell onto the hay.

She stared at the guardsman in shock. "What the hell was that?"

The guardsman shrugged and scratched the back of his head. "I'm sorry, but that's the only horse we can offer. If you go after her now, you may be able to catch her."

"Are you kidding me?" Mara grew annoyed, knowing she had to chase after the horse. She sighed while getting back up.

* * *

144

The horse fled through the southern gate. Mara chased after her. She saw the horse run west, which she needed to take anyway. The so-called lady galloped away until she stopped at the crossroads. The mare turned her head and gazed back at her. The huntress slowly approached her. If she could calm the horse, Mara could mount her. Unfortunately, the little lady had other plans and dashed away. Every time Mara approached the horse, the mare bolted. She ran circles around the huntress. Mara sighed, wondering if it was worth the trouble to get the mare under control.

The horse stopped and stared at the huntress. Mara watched her. Were all her efforts starting to pay off? She approached the mare with caution. Somehow the horse did not run away. As Mara placed a gentle hand on the coarse hide, the mare winced and whined. Mara took a firm grip on the reins. She wanted the horse to know she meant no harm, but she needed the animal's cooperation.

After appearing to gain the horse's trust, Mara mounted her. The process was smoother than expected. Now on the horse, she pulled on the reins to guide her west. The mare showed some resistance but went along. Now, getting the little lady to move forward was the next challenge. But Mara had no experience with horses.

'How do you get this thing to move?' Mara wondered.

She then gripped the reins and shouted, "Yah!"

The horse remained still. Okay, that didn't work.

"Uh, giddy up?" Mara asked.

Instead, the horse turned her head to give Mara the stink eye. Then she whined and balked. The little lady had no desire to move. Mara was losing her patience.

"Move, you damn horse!" Mara shouted, kicking the sides.

The horse reared up on her hind legs and neighed, throwing the huntress off. Mara heard a sickening crack coming from her skull as she fell to the frozen ground headfirst.

Chapter Seventeen

The Huntress

At least Mara took Harold's advice and did not waste a healing stone. Waking up, she groaned to the burning pain in her body. She closed her eyes and felt the back of her head for any damage. Her skull healed, though the pain remained.

"Well, aren't you the professional hunter?"

Upon hearing the familiar voice of the commander, Mara opened her eyes. A group of Holy Blades, who sat atop their steeds, stood before her. Commander White came forward while mounted on a white horse. Stopping before Mara, he gazed down at her with disdain.

"Wouldn't the chancellor be thrilled to know that you are sleeping on the job?"

The Holy Blades began to chuckle.

Mara stood up and scowled at him. "I wasn't asleep! I fell off my horse…" She looked around. "Wait, where's my horse?"

The lady was nowhere in sight.

Commander White gazed at her with indifference. "That is none of my concern. The horse was your responsibility. It's your fault you lost it."

She glared back at him. "Why the hell are you here?"

"If you think we came to do your job, you are sadly mistaken. Although we are better equipped and more capable of dealing with werewolves than you."

Mara shook her head. "So, why are you here again?"

"We have a different business to attend to, which is none of your concern," Commander White said, his face remained frozen.

Rolling her eyes, Mara turned around and walked away. She was not going to waste any more time talking to him.

"Where do you think you're going?" Commander White demanded.

"I have some business to attend to as well," she replied in a cold tone. "The people at the Delta Farms depend on me."

She heard the gallop of a horse coming from behind. Mara looked back and saw the commander approaching her. His glare remained on her.

"I've noticed that you entered Mirahyll in your true form," Commander White said.

She looked away. "That's none of your concern."

"Perhaps," he said. "I trust you didn't use that healing stone."

She checked her pocket. The gemstone remained intact and ready to be used.

"No, I still have it," Mara said, looking up at him.

"You did not use it?"

Mara frowned. "I only have one. Death can be a few steps away, and it'll be a stone wasted."

"I see," the commander responded. "You are smarter than I thought."

Mara raised an eyebrow. "Thanks, I think."

He changed the subject. "I heard you left Har' Yhan in the middle of the night."

"So?"

"Why did you leave?"

Mara was surprised at his question. "Why do you care?"

"Did you see us?"

Looking at his face, she could tell that the commander demanded a response. Mara nodded.

Keeping his eyes on her, Commander White dismounted from his steed. The frown remained on his face as he approached her. Stopping two feet before Mara, his eyes studied her with scrutiny.

"So, you did?" Commander White asked. "It must hurt so much..."

Mara froze. He knew she had seen him with Morgan. She looked up at him. The commander's face was devoid of emotion.

"Hopefully, you'll get the point," he said unsympathetically. "I could never love a monster."

His words drove Mara over the edge as her right hand tightened into a fist.

"You didn't seem to mind fucking Morgan," she said lowly.

Those words spilled out of her mouth, but she stopped as soon as she saw his death glare. His face turned red. His subordinates, who murmured among each other, likely heard her comment. The commander cleared his throat, silencing his men. He focused his glare on Mara.

"And if I were you, I'd keep what happened that night a secret," Commander White hissed, then returned to his horse. After mounting his steed, the commander kept scowling at her. "Now, if you excuse me, you are wasting our time as well as your own." With that, he snapped his head forward and rode past her.

He led his men down the road. Mara shook her head—what nerve he had threatening her. She looked around once more, seeing no sign of her horse. Sighing, she walked down the road to the Delta Farms, trailing behind the Holy Blades.

* * *

Reaching the Delta Farms was straight forward, but much of the day was lost. The sun was setting. She met a group of farmers who were waiting for her.

"I'm here to deal with the werewolves," Mara began.

Truthfully, she was exhausted. It was a long day, dealing with a disobedient mare and the commander. And she had a job to do on top of it all.

An older man with a grey beard stared at her. He wore a worn and stained shirt, and his pants were dirty from working in the field. He wore a cap on his head. Mud caked his boots. Standing before the other farmers and their farmhands, he folded his arms in disappointment.

"The Chancellor sent you?" he asked. "What took you so long?"

"Had some difficulty getting here due to an uncooperative horse," she explained.

The farmers murmured and exchanged glances.

Mara took notice. "Is there a problem?"

The older man frowned at her. "This task is beyond you. We encountered five beasts!"

"We should have got the Holy Blades heading to Medulla," a woman suggested.

Mara looked at them in silence. They did not think she was capable of this task.

"I've dealt with beasts and monsters before," she reassured them. "Where did you see them?"

The older man looked at her with caution. "Well, if you say so," he hesitated. "The beasts are in the woods, where the creek flows. That's where we found Nate and Jon."

Mara shook her head. "I'm sorry for your loss."

"Aye, that's why we called upon Mirahyll to deal with this," he said. "The Delta Farms supplies much of Ardana's food. Without us, this land will face famine as well as her monster scourge."

"Very well, I'll deal with the beasts right now."

"Do it quick," the older man warned her. "Lupine Woods becomes very dark at sundown. You can lose your way with ease."

Mara nodded, appreciating the advice. She followed the creek into the forest.

* * *

Lupine Woods was a vast forest spanning over much of western Ardana, dividing the Outer Frontier from the rest of the nation. The Hema portion, north of Grey Mountain, was named the Old Hunting Ground. The Old

Hunting Ground was home to Heru and his werewolves. The forest also housed the most diverse population of plant life and herbs. Now it was home to dangerous predators and monsters.

Within a few minutes of entering the woods, Mara encountered the first werewolf. The beast spotted her and charged. She stepped to the side, evading the monster's gnashing jaws. The werewolf stood on all fours while pacing back and forth, watching and growling at her. She stared back at the creature with glowing eyes. Removing her mask, the markings on her face darkened. As she bared her teeth, her canines elongated. The beast did not seem to register the changes in its opponent—she still looked human.

The werewolf lunged at Mara again. She unsheathed her sword and slashed at the creature, hitting a vital spot. Despite its injury, the beast was not willing to give up. Standing on its hind legs, it made one more attempt to lunge at her. She slashed at the creature once more, taking off the head and left forearm. The body crumpled to the ground, its blood seeping into the soil. Mara stared at the beast, unfazed by the gore until the scent of blood reached her nostrils.

Mara began to cringe while approaching the head and picking it up. She placed it inside the sack. She remembered being used to this when working with Dad and helping him deal with nuisance pests and dangerous predators. Dad believed hunting was a valuable skill. People needed to learn how to survive in Ardana.

Soon, she heard the howls of the others. The pungent smell of the beast's blood permeated the air, attracting them. Two werewolves had arrived, making the hunt more difficult. Both were aggressive as they lunged at her. She evaded their attacks, biding her time until the moment was right to strike. That was easier said than done. When she thought she could attack one, the other lunged at her to protect its companion. One of the werewolves slashed her arm. Mara jumped back and held her arm, fearing the attack had connected. Moving her hand away, she saw that the beast's claws only grazed her sleeve. Being infected was the last thing she needed.

A strange sensation washed over her while dashing at one of the werewolves. Mara did not know what it was, but it no longer mattered when her sword slashed across the neck of the beast. The headless body slumped to the ground. She turned to the other monster and stared it in the eye. The creature was still willing to fight. Good, it would be easier to kill it. Mara never felt so alive. She dashed at it, slashing the head off with her sword. Another headless body crumpled to the ground. Taking deep breaths, she could feel euphoria rushing through her brain. The thrill of the hunt—Mara remembered enjoying it. That feeling seemed to be amplified by the curse.

However, a single thought of her parents drove the joyful feelings away. It wasn't so much the scars Mara received, but the look in her eyes while coming home stained in blood. Mom saw her transform into the huntress, becoming like the creatures she killed. It made the mother fear for her daughter, believing that the world would see Mara as a savage.

Mara frowned at the two werewolf corpses. Then she picked up each head and bagged them. Three down, two to go.

A loud screech pierced her eardrums. Mara lifted her head and scanned the area. Following the sounds, she found a werewolf and a wolf pack chasing a single horse. She recognized the uncooperative mare from earlier. Amazing that the horse remained alive, but not for long if Mara did not save her.

The beast's lack of awareness was its undoing as Mara rushed in and decapitated it. After dealing with the werewolf, she went straight for her horse. She stood between the mare and the wolves. The beasts tucked their ears down while baring their teeth. Her face darkened as her eyes glowed brightly. Baring her fangs, Mara answered with a growl as a dark aura exuded from her. The wolves dropped their aggression, their faces scrunching up in fear. They ran off with their tails tucked in between their legs. Her attempt to scare them away worked. Mara did not wish to kill the noble creatures.

The huntress turned around to see the mare standing behind her. The lady remained alive yet frightened. Mara glared at her.

"Is this what you saw when you looked at me?" Mara asked her.

The huntress took a step forward. The mare backed away.

She could sense the horse's fear. "Get out."

The frozen horse kept staring at her.

The huntress lost her patience as her eyes glowed with rage. "Get out!"

Terrified, the mare neighed and dashed past her. Hopefully, the horse knew her way out of the woods. The huntress strolled over to the body of the werewolf, picking up the head and bagging it.

Upon hearing a low growl, Mara turned to see the final beast. This one looked different from the previous four encountered. It was an alpha, standing on its hind legs and glaring at her. Its posture made it appear taller than the other beasts she slew.

"I should have known it was you, the murderer of our lord," the beast growled in a low male voice.

Mara was stunned. "You can speak?"

The werewolf bared his fangs while laughing at her. "We were always capable. But to humans, a beast is nothing more than a beast." He gazed at her. "Hmm, you are a monster hiding in human flesh..." He approached her. "I should free you from your human skin and show the world what you are."

Mara gripped her sword tightly. The creature began the fight by lunging at her. She dodged and countered, slashing at the creature's arm.

A few minutes into their fight, the werewolf grew more aggressive and chanted, "Die. Die! Die! Die!" The creature went after Mara with a flurry of swipes. "Humans commit more atrocities to their own... and they call us the monsters?"

Even though his words fazed Mara, this was not the time for contemplation. In her distraction, the beast rammed his claws through her torso. Mara became frozen.

'Not again,' she thought.

It was just like that incident with Lady Isabella, except there was no one to save. Black blood began to rise in her throat, forcing her to cough it up. Her life was slipping away. She looked up at the creature as he snarled at her.

"Do not worry. I shall show you mercy and reunite you with Lord Heru." He opened his mouth, ready to crunch down on her head.

However, she was not willing to give up without a fight. Her hand tightened around the grip of her sword. In a flash of silver, the forearm in her chest became separated from his body.

The beast roared and staggered backwards, holding the stump where his forearm was. He stared at Mara in anger and growled, "What are you?"

She removed the beast's arm from her torso and tossed it aside. Gripping her bloodied sword again, she dashed at him. In one swift motion, she took his head off. She watched as the body crumpled to the ground, releasing its final shudders. After it became still, Mara gazed to the severed head. She leaned over and picked it up. She looked into the bloodshot and glassy eyes of the creature.

"Monsters, every last one of us," she murmured, bagging the final head. The injuries caught up to her. Exhausted from the loss of energy and blood, she leaned against a tree and slumped down. She felt so weak right now and would not be surprised if she died.

However, the knowledge that she was an undying brought comfort. Any mistakes made, she could always return to life and fix them. As a human, she would never have a second chance. For the first time, she saw the benefits of her curse. She was also grateful she didn't use her only healing stone. She doubted it would help now. Mara tilted her head up and looked up at the night sky. The stars twinkled in the black velvet sky. It was unusually quiet where she sat. Mara wanted to close her eyes; no longer could she resist the urge to sleep. She lowered her head and fell into the darkness.

* * *

Later that night, Mara woke up. She recovered enough. It was time to return to Mirahyll. On her way out, she found Commander White slumped against a tree. She walked towards him. What was he doing here? Coming closer, she noticed a long sword impaling him. Her eyes widened in horror. Mara dashed to him.

Falling to her knees, she saw his colour-drained face. He looked unconscious with closed eyes and relaxed muscles. Reaching out with her right hand, Mara gently brushed her fingertips against his left cheek. He was as cold as ice. Then she noticed a red spot forming on the left side of his neck, staining his collar. Her right hand grabbed the collar and pulled it down. Blood gushed from a massive bite wound on his neck, turning his attire red. She had to help him, or he would bleed to death.

However, a coppery taste in her mouth stopped her. Sensing an urge to heave, Mara covered her mouth with her right hand. A foul and thick substance surged up her throat, making her cough. Splatters of red blood fell onto the snow. She stared at her bloodstained hand with wide eyes. Looking back at him, Mara realized it was his blood in her mouth. She tried to vomit the rest out, but her stomach would not relent. She eventually looked back at him. Commander White awoke, glaring back at her in silence.

Mara lifted a shaky hand to him. "I'm sorry—"

A strong force crashed into the back of her head. Thrown to the ground, Mara became paralyzed. Another powerful blow smashed the back of her skull. Blood and pieces of brain matter flew out and splattered onto the forest floor. The Holy Blades stabbed their swords and spears into her body. Her blood drained onto the frozen ground.

* * *

Mara's eyes shot open as she awoke to the sensation of fire in her veins. She was dreaming. Commander White and his Holy Blades were not here. They never attacked her. But the dream was disturbing. Mara now had another reason to remove her curse. Sometimes the commander irritated her, but she would never harm him. She looked up and saw the morning sky. The bag containing her kills was by her side, reminding her of her task. Mara stayed at least one night in the forest. She began to relax. Nothing was around. Mara can rest a little while longer. There was no hurry.

A rustling sound snapped her from her relaxed state. Mara reached for her sword. Even though she had yet to recover, the huntress braced herself for whatever new threat came her way.

The dark eyes of a black mare stared at Mara, her head sticking out from the brush. Mara released a sigh of relief. It was just the horse. The little lady stood there for a few minutes, staring at her and snorting. Stepping out of the bushes, the lady approached Mara. The huntress was unsure what to think of this. While sniffing Mara's face, the mare noticed her injuries. The smell of blood, both Mara's and the werewolves, made her whine. The horse lowered herself, offering access to the saddle. Mara stared at this strange display. She suspected the little lady was showing appreciation for saving her life. After some effort, Mara mounted the horse. The mare stood up and began to move.

Before riding away, Mara noticed something shining within the corpse of the alpha. She dismounted from the horse and approached the body. Searching the corpse, she found a healing stone. Mara looked in her pocket to make sure it was not the same one. It might have fallen out during the fight. But the gleaming gemstone in her pocket revealed that this was a new gem, which Mara claimed. Despite having more, the stones were rare. When she returned to Greyward Hold, Harold might give her the location of the next undying.

She mounted her horse and left. The mare kept walking until they encountered an unfrozen pond. Mara took the time to wash the blood off. The water was cold, yet very refreshing. Looking at her reflection, Mara could tell her gear needed repairing. She put her hood and mask back on. She mounted the mare and rode back to Mirahyll.

* * *

Riding back into the capital city, Mara noticed a new posting on the information board. A guardsman pinned it on and then walked away while another spoke to the crowd.

"As of now, all travel to Medulla is no longer advised."

"Why is that, sir?" asked a male citizen.

"An unknown illness has taken the village," according to the guardsman. "The Holy Blades are investigating. So far, Mirahyll is in no danger. There is nothing to worry about."

Mara watched the crowd while riding towards the stables. She dismounted to deliver the bounty to the Council Hall. She met the guardsmen, who escorted her to the chancellor's office.

"Ah, you have returned," the chancellor said. "We were getting worried."

She was perplexed. "How long was I away?"

"About three days," he replied.

Taken aback, Mara never suspected being gone that long.

Chancellor Davis eyed the bag.

Mara noted his gaze and offered it to him. "Five werewolf heads."

Davis gazed at the bloody bag and gestured for a guardsman to take it. The guardsman took the bag from Mara and peered inside. After counting five heads, he nodded at the chancellor with a disgusted face. Davis nodded back, then looked at her.

"Very good." He gestured for another man to step forward. This man handed a large bag of gold over to Mara.

"That bag is worth five thousand gold," said the chancellor. "You are more than welcome to count if you wish."

"I'll take your word. Thank you." Mara accepted the payment.

"You may also keep the horse," Davis added.

"Thanks," she replied. Before leaving, there was something on her mind. "What's going on with Medulla?"

"Ah, so you've heard?" Davis questioned. "Medulla has been gripped by a mysterious illness. The Holy Blades are investigating."

Now that she remembered, Medulla was not too far from the Delta Farms. It explained why she encountered Commander White and the Holy Blades.

"Okay," Mara said. There was no reason to stay any longer, so she turned around and left.

"Oh, and one more thing…" called the chancellor.

Mara stopped and looked back at him.

"Thank you for suggesting Talon," he spoke.

"So, you're going to choose him?" Mara questioned.

Davis nodded. "Talon might be a little rough around the edges, but he is very decent. Some of our newest guardsmen are from the Silver Thorns and offered positive testimonies." Then he cleared his throat. "As you mentioned, his weapons are not quite as elegant, but they are reliable and the price more reasonable. By going with him, we will save more money. It is a good thing considering our current predicament."

"Is this about Corlin?" Mara asked.

The chancellor nodded. "Once, we had our weapons imported, for it was cheaper and easy to mass-produce." Then he frowned. "But the transports were often subjected to attacks and thefts, mostly from the Blackthorn Guild. They also preyed upon many blacksmiths in this land, causing them to go out of business." He took a deep breath. "However, Edwin never had this problem. I believe it is because his workshop is within city walls. The Blackthorns would never dare enter. I am sure Talon will also benefit from this."

"So, you had issues with the Blackthorns?" Mara questioned.

"We haven't been able to do much," the chancellor admitted. "It seems they are always one step ahead of us. We wanted to act, but the Holy Blades are investigating, demanding that we don't get involved. So far, their investigation yielded very little."

A thought crossed her mind. "What about the Black Smoke? Didn't they put a stop to this?"

Davis nodded. "Yes, the vigilante did a number on the Blackthorns. But not everyone saw the Black Smoke as a hero. The Faith arrested the vigilante for taking human lives, and held a private execution."

"Oh, I see," she replied.

Once the conversation ended, she left.

* * *

Mara headed to Talon's workshop for gear repairs. Since being approached by the chancellor for the Guardsmen's weapons and gear, the place looked more like a professional blacksmith's forge compared to the dusty and run-down building Talon bought at first.

"Well, you must be very busy." Mara smiled underneath her mask.

He smiled back while repairing her gear. "Whatever you did, it worked!" Talon exclaimed. "How about I temper your blade for free? It's the least I can do to thank you."

She accepted the offer and allowed him to upgrade her weapon. Talon grew silent while tempering her blade. It was brief, but he finished.

"Thanks," Mara said, grateful for his services.

"Thank you," he responded, passing the sword back to her.

Sheathing her blade, Mara bid him farewell.

Now that Mara had some time, she thought about seeing her parents. She knew where they lived. Within ten minutes, she found her home. The wooden house was not too big, being only two floors. The parents' room was on the main floor while her room sat on the second floor. The window to her room was on the back of the house. Mara was both excited and nervous because she reached the cusp of one of her goals. She peered into her pocket and retrieved a healing stone. But there remained a problem. Not only did she have two of these gems, but it was also the fact that she was inhuman.

How would her parents even react? Would they accept her with open arms? Or would they drive her away and disown her? Mara did not know the answer to her questions, and that frightened her. Most had a black and white view of humans and monsters. But for Mara, it was not so easy, especially since she stood on the other side.

If she found the next undying and obtained their soul, she could appear human. And while her parents remained unaware, she would find the cure. Everything could go back to normal. Harold probably found the next undying. At least she should let them know she was here. Mara didn't have the keys to the house. She might have lost them when she ended up in the Dark Labyrinth. Before leaving, Mara wrote a note to leave at the door.

"Hi Mom and Dad," she read out loud while writing. "Wanted to let you know I'm okay, in case you heard anything happening to me. I'll come back later." She signed her name. Mara stuck the note on the door and left. She promised she would return.

Mara walked back to the stables and mounted her horse.

On the way out, she rode by the other blacksmith's shop. She heard a man shouting before storming out. His fancy attire hinted to his noble status. The thin middle-aged man had a handlebar moustache and oily hair slicked to the right as if it was a hairpiece.

"You expect me to pay for this?" The noble sounded high-pitched for a man.

Edwin emerged with a scowl on his face. "That's the price," he said in a cold tone. "Take it or leave it."

"Commander White was right about you. You are a crook! I refuse to buy anything from you ever again!"

"That's too bad… Either you have the coin, or you don't waste my time."

"Harrumph!" The nobleman stuck his nose up into the air and stormed away from the blacksmith. He noticed Mara and called out to her. "You there!"

She gazed at him with a raised eyebrow. "Uh… Yes?"

"You are an adventurer, are you not?"

Mara shook her head. "I'm a hunter for hire."

"Well, I must warn you about Edwin. He is a swindler! All his wares and services are far too overpriced."

She noticed the nobleman's stance with his hands held behind his back. It was the same stance the commander and his father used as well. Mara reckoned it was a nobleman thing.

She gazed at him. "I use Talon's services."

The nobleman looked perplexed. "Talon? I've never heard of him."

"He just set up shop after forging Silver Thorn weapons for twenty years," Mara explained. "His weapons may look plain, but they are reliable and affordable." She gestured to her blade. "The sword he made for me has never let me down."

The nobleman glanced at the sword. "I see," he murmured. "A reliable and decent weapon for a lower price. And you save money, which is a smart thing to do. Perhaps I shall look into this Talon." He gazed up at her with a stoic face. "Thank you for your kind suggestion. I shall consider spreading the word among my peers." Then he left.

Mara looked on in surprise, for it seemed not all nobles were cruel.

Edwin, on the other hand, looked sour. "Great! I'll lose even more customers. None of this would have happened if that damned Talon had not come to my city!"

Gazing at Edwin, Mara was not deaf to his cruel words. "Excuse me?"

Edwin glared back at her. "It was bad enough with the Guardsmen cancelling my contract. I had to raise prices on my weapons and services. Thanks to you, I'll have to raise them once again."

"That's not fair!" Mara exclaimed. "How can anyone afford your weapons?"

"Not fair? Not fair, you say? I have to make a living," Edwin growled. With that, he stormed back into his shop. He scowled at her once more. "Since you caused me to lose more customers, you are not welcome here! I shall never sell my wares to you, not that you could afford them anyway." He slammed the door.

In spite of being stunned at his behaviour, Mara decided not to dwell on it. She rode out of Mirahyll and returned to Grey Mountain.

Chapter Eighteen

Brain Drain

Mara travelled up the path to Greyward Hold on November 27. So far, the mare was cooperative but seemed wary of these surroundings. Mara reckoned she had never been in these parts before. Still, the horse managed, and they were fortunate not to encounter anything. They reached Greyward Hold by noon, where Mara spotted a coach. Someone was visiting. She looked at the carriage in curiosity while approaching the hold. After leaving the horse at the stables, she walked in. Mara entered the grand hall and saw the former master speaking with someone.

Harold noticed her. "Ah, welcome back. It seems we have a visitor."

Mara looked at the short and round nobleman, recognizing his snow-white hair.

"Mr. White, what are you doing here?" Mara questioned.

The older man gazed back, looking very tense. "Oh, you're here! That's very good. We have a great dilemma on our hands."

She could not help but feel surprised that he was looking for her. "What is it?"

"Karl is in danger."

"What?" Mara asked, feeling perplexed. "Wasn't he investigating an unknown illness in Medulla?"

Mr. White shook his head. "It was all a ruse."

Mara became stunned. "What happened?"

"The villagers swarmed them and took them to the Black Tower outside of Cerebell. One of the Holy Blades managed to escape and told the Faith."

Harold sighed. "This is troubling news," he said solemnly. "Anna must be behind this."

She looked at the former master in confusion. "Anna?"

"I came here, hoping you could save him," Mr. White said.

She looked back at the nobleman, astounded that he wanted her to save the commander. "Why not send another group to rescue them?"

The older man frowned. "We have, but none returned."

Before she could say anything, the former master spoke up.

"If you wish to save him, then you must know what you are going up against."

Mara and Mr. White gazed at him.

"Anna is a darkling who feeds on the brains of her victims," Harold explained. "Her immense psychic powers allow her to enslave others, causing the abandonment of Cerebell long ago. We sealed her away to prevent her from harming more innocents, but her powers continued to grow. Somehow, the seal within the Black Tower is failing. If left alone, her reach could go beyond Medulla. I would not condone challenging her, not just because she is a possessor, but I fear you will be no match." He looked at Mr. White. "And I also fear the commander may be lost."

Mara sighed as the former guild master walked away.

Mr. White looked at her with pleading eyes. "Please, save Karl. It could have been anyone."

She gazed at the older man. "It may be too late. He's been there for a few days."

"I would still save him. I won't leave him in that wretched place."

She pondered his words. "Okay, but there's something I need from you."

Mr. White's face scrunched up in confusion as if he never expected her to request a favour. "Okay, what is it?"

"I am looking for a way to remove my curse. I believe there's a cure in Thoron, but I need a passage."

Mr. White gave a sympathetic look. "And only the High Priestess can grant that," he murmured. Then he gave a serious look. "I'll see what I can do, but I want you to save Karl first."

"Okay, but if you fail to get me that pass, then I'll demand full compensation," Mara told him. "I won't do this for free."

"Very well, please save him," Mr. White said with a stern voice. Then he left.

While preparing to leave, Mara found it strange that she had to save Commander White again. It was also unusual Mr. White came to her. What was he planning? Well, it might bring her one step closer to removing her curse. Ready to go, Mara headed out.

* * *

She approached Medulla by horse. Travelling there was pretty straight forward, although it took a day from Greyward Hold. On the same road as the Delta Farms, the village was just over yonder.

As she approached the village, not a single soul was around. Mara dismounted from the horse and looked around. Within seconds, some villagers emerged from their homes. They slowly approached her, wielding farm tools or kitchen utensils like weapons. They shared a dark expression on their faces. These villagers did not look friendly. Realizing this, she unsheathed her sword and gripped it tightly.

"Stay back," Mara called. "Don't come near me!"

The villagers kept advancing, ignoring her warning. Mara did not want a fight, but there might be no choice. All of a sudden, they froze like statues. Confused, Mara walked up to a man with a stained shirt and leather pants. He didn't react to her. She gave a light poke on his shoulder. He released a groan while crumpling to the ground. Soon, the other villagers followed suit. She looked around in bewilderment until she found a man in golden armour. He was one of the Holy Blades, who were among the affected.

At the corner of her eye, Mara spotted a lone figure still standing. Looking up, she recognized the seven glowing eyes, dark armour, and red hood.

"You!" Mara stood up and stared at her in shock.

The Watcher remained silent while holding her arms out. She levitated in the air. Mara cautiously watched her and began to approach, but the creature disappeared in a flash of blue light. Left in her place was a strange device embedded in the ground. It looked like a metal staff with a glowing blue gem in it, resembling something old wizards use. Approaching the strange-looking object, Mara reached out and touched it, but nothing happened. Knowing there was no time to waste, she moved on.

Every villager remained unconscious. Mara suspected this to be the Watcher's handiwork. Doctor Moen mentioned her psychic powers, but this was amazing. Looking to the Black Tower, Mara ran through the abandoned city of Cerebell. The Watcher also knocked out everyone in the area. Arriving at the main gates, they opened upon her approach. She looked around with caution and walked into the tower. On the way in, Mara spotted another one of those strange staves but kept going, for she had an important task to do.

Several corpses inhabited the many cells lining the stone halls. Mara gazed to each cell, feeling uneasy about being in the hallway. She walked faster to get out sooner. She entered a large circular room with walls reaching high up. Mara stared up at the endless expanse of the room, unable to see the ceiling.

"You are too late."

Hearing her voice, Mara found the Watcher staring back at her.

"You cannot fight Anna," the Watcher warned. "You will die."

She stared at the creature. "I have to save him."

The Watcher gazed at her, sitting in the centre of the room. Countless candles surrounded them. Beyond the candles were the stairs leading further up into the tower.

"You care about him," the Watcher said.

Mara's face began to heat up. Great, another one noticed her ogling

Commander White, but it was not like that. "His father and I have a deal. He's going to help me get to Thoron, but only if I bring his son back."

"I know how you feel about him. I am psychic."

Mara's face grew hotter. She wanted to say something but heard whispers coming from everywhere. She looked around, but they were the only ones in the room. A shiver ran through her spine.

"Are we alone?" Mara asked.

"The darkling needs to be fed, for she is one of the seals."

Mara glanced back at the Watcher. "I still have to save Commander White."

"It is too late," the Watcher told her.

Mara closed her eyes. When she opened them again, the Watcher vanished with some parting words.

"She knows you are here."

Now alone, Mara looked to the stairs and began to ascend them.

* * *

Walking up the stairs, Mara heard a light hiss as if from a snake. Anna's victims wandered from their prison cells but lacked the clarity to acknowledge her presence. There was no need to fight them.

After searching the tower, she found a large pair of doors. Mara placed her hands on them. With enough force, she pushed the doors open to unveil a large, dark chamber. Inside sat a man, tied to a chair by his wrists and ankles. Getting a closer look, she recognized him.

"Commander White?" Mara called but got no response. She looked around, yet no one else was here. She began to approach him. Mara had to get him out of here, for saving him was the top priority. As soon as she reached him, Mara crouched down to undo his bindings. Eventually, he regained consciousness. She took notice while freeing him.

"Oh, you're awake. Mr. White sent me to rescue you."

Mara expected a snide remark from the commander but got nary a peep. Looking up at his face, she noticed the blank expression and glazed eyes. Commander White had joined the others in the tower. She looked at him in silence, unsure what to think. How would his father, or the Faith, react if they saw him like this?

"Can you stand?" Mara asked.

After rising to her feet, she tried to get the commander to stand up. His legs were very shaky as if he never used them before. Mara shook her head, for this would be a struggle to get him out of this place. She heard the hissing sound again. They were not alone. Before she could figure out where the sound came from, Mara was struck from behind and sent flying across the room. She cried out in pain as she hit the ground with a thud. At least no bones were broken. She got up and looked back at Commander White, but her gaze fell upon a shadowy figure behind him.

From the shadows came a strange female creature, who had the upper body of a woman and the lower half of a giant snake. Four red eyes graced

Anna's pale face. Red glowing spots decorated her dark body. Her hair was like writhing tentacles, as if from an octopus or a squid. Scales covered her long arms, while webbing connected each bony finger.

As Anna slithered beside Commander White, Mara noticed a bulbous appendage attached to her tail. A smile crept upon Anna's face while looking at the commander. The end of her tail hovered above his head. It opened up, resembling a fleshy flower. Then she plunged it onto his head, closing around the upper half of his skull.

Commander White appeared to have reacted but did not attempt to break free. Her tail pulsed and flexed. The darkling was pumping something into his head. His arms and legs twitched, but soon relaxed and hung from his body. He became paralyzed. The tail had stopped pumping the substance into his head. Anna smiled in a wicked fashion as Mara watched in horror.

Anna's head began to convulse violently. He released a terrifying howl of pain. Mara's eyes widened. He sounded like he was being flayed or burned alive. Anna continued to smile while lifting him. The darkling held him out in front of her, her head still convulsing. Commander White continued to scream with every fibre of his being. Tears flowed from his eyes.

Mara did not know what Anna was doing to him, but enough was enough. "Stop!"

Anna had stopped as if she could understand Mara. The commander was now wheezing from exhausting his vocal cords. Anna gazed at Mara and kept smiling. Her head convulsed again. The commander's eyes rolled back into his head while he released a groan of pleasure. His cheeks began to turn red. Mara looked on in confusion. She had no idea what Anna was doing or why, but she had a task to finish.

However, the darkling had other plans. Anna switched her gaze from Mara to Commander White. Her tail began to constrict the top half of his head. It looked like she was crushing his skull. The commander's eyes grew wide as he cried out in intense pain. Lifting his arm, he tried to reach for Mara. He cried for help but was unable to form words. The mouth in her tail began to pulsate. He froze, then screamed again. Anna gave a wicked smile as she sucked his brain.

A sticky fluid dripped down his face. His screams grew raspy as Anna fed. The suction grew stronger, pulling the commander's head into the circular mouth. His eyes rolled back into his head as his mouth remained agape.

Mara ran up to him. She grabbed the tail and tried to pull it off of his head. Anna's smile disappeared upon having her feeding disturbed. An unseen force knocked Mara away. She tried to get up, but it was too late. His body went limp while the mouth-like appendage remained attached to his head. Commander White became still as he gazed off into space. Mara stared into his hollow eyes. Tears welled up in her eyes, threatening to spill.

Anna smiled, satisfied with her meal. The darkling slithered up to him and placed both hands on his shoulders.

Something snapped within Mara when she saw the darkling touch him. Filled with an incredible rage, she bit her lip hard enough to draw blood. Mara rose to her feet and reached for her sword.

"Don't fucking touch him!"

The darkling tilted her head in confusion.

Mara trembled as she glared at her. Anna had to die!

Anna began to rise, towering over the commander. The end of her tail engulfed his entire head and began pulsating with wild abandon. His body began to convulse.

Unwilling to grasp what the darkling planned next, Mara unsheathed her sword and dashed at Anna. But the darkling dodged all of her attacks effortlessly. As they fought, Anna released Commander White. Seeing him fall, Mara ran to his side.

"Karl—"

Anna struck Mara with her tail and sent her flying several feet. Upon landing, the huntress heard a loud crack. An intense pain shot up her left leg. Mara looked back and saw Anna lifting the commander. His eyes fluttered open to see Anna's face. He stared at her with adoration. Anna lowered his body to the ground. He took a few steps before bending the knee. Taking her hand, he kissed it. Anna pointed to Mara, who had yet to recover. Commander White nodded and gazed at the undying with a blank expression.

Mara watched as he approached her. He began to unsheathe his sword.

"What are you doing?" Mara asked. But her words fell on deaf ears.

She tried to stand, but the intense pain returned to her left leg. Mara looked down to find her knee mangled. She struggled to her feet, but could barely walk.

Commander White approached her with the Hand of Kratés, intending to kill her. Having no choice, Mara held her Silver Thorn straight sword out in front of her. In a swift motion, he lifted his sword and dashed at her. He brought the sword down. Mara raised her blade to meet his, but his strength took her by surprise. She needed to use both of her hands to block him.

Mara pushed him away, but the pain in her leg was a distraction. She could not focus on fighting him, but she was dead if she didn't fight. Commander White stepped back and swung at her again. Mara blocked his back-swing. Even after being turned into a mindless slave, the commander remained a threat. He wore her down with each blow. Mara could not keep this up.

He eyed her injured leg and delivered a swift kick. The pain paralyzed Mara's mind as the blow knocked her down. Seeing her sword by her side, the undying tried to reach for it, but the commander stepped on her arm, pinning her down. She could only watch as Commander White lifted his sword.

"No... Stop..." she pleaded, but it was futile.

He plunged the Hand of Kratés into her chest and through her heart. The black ooze surged up her throat and poured out of her mouth. He stared at her with a blank expression. Placing his boot on her chest, he pulled the blade out. Death came swiftly. Mara's vision turned dark as she watched him return to Anna's side.

Chapter Nineteen

Friends and Allies

The tingling sensation returned to Mara's body. Her fingers twitched as every nerve came alive. The tingle became a burning sensation, causing her eyes to fly open. As she bolted up, the pain left as quickly as it came. Mara glanced around, finding herself in a different place. It looked like a laboratory.

"How did I get here?" Mara asked herself.

"The Watcher insisted that we save you."

Searching for the voice's owner, she found a man in a white lab coat. She recognized his blond hair and glasses. Dr. Moen worked at his desk, looking through a microscope.

"You were here all night," he told her. "Took a while to heal, given the damage you sustained. But I'm glad you're okay."

The Watcher was also there, staring at her in silence. Mara sighed, swinging her legs around and facing him.

"I wouldn't say I'm okay," she replied in a sombre tone. At least she did not use one of her two healing stones. It would have been a stone wasted.

"No? Well, at least you have your mind. It was very stupid of you to fight Anna." Dr. Moen lifted his gaze to her. "Why did you go there?"

"Anna abducted Commander White. His father asked me to save him."

"Oh, is that so?" Dr. Moen peered back into his microscope. "I hear he's now without his mind."

She stared at him. "I made a deal with his father. He promised to help me gain passage to Thoron if I rescue his son."

The doctor glanced up at her again, this time with a raised eyebrow. "If you bring him back in that state, what do you think will happen?" Dr. Moen questioned sharply. "Can that priestess mend his mind? Will the Faith honour their end of the bargain?"

Mara had no answer. Seeing Commander White like that—he would never be the same. The doctor frowned at her and rose from his desk. He walked to a black box sitting on a pedestal in the middle of the room.

"I can help you, but you must help me," he told her.

Mara watched him cautiously. "What must I do?"

Dr. Moen opened the black box, revealing a syringe filled with a glowing blue substance.

"I need a test subject for this experimental drug," Dr. Moen said. "Commander White will do." Then he explained, "Anna's diet consists of brain fluid. She injects her victims with a neurotoxin, rendering them helpless as she feeds. While feeding, she releases other toxins, causing the zombie-like state and enslavement. She can also make her victims feel intense pain or pleasure."

His words went over Mara's head, but more or less, it explained what Anna did to the commander.

The doctor gestured to the syringe. "After some experimenting, I created this drug. Not only should it neutralize the toxin, but also restore the brain to its original state."

She eyed the antidote. "How did you make this?"

"That is a secret," he replied, giving a wink. "However, I've been to Thoron some years ago."

Mara looked at him with intrigue. "How were you able to get there?"

"I had my ways," said the doctor. "Learned many things during my stay."

"Like what?"

"It's certainly not a hellish land ruled by demons as the Faith claimed. Thoron is more advanced. One of the most iconic places is a prestigious college for the intellectually gifted." His tone became sombre. "But the college had a darker side. It was a research hall run by a group called the Seekers, who experimented with students. About ten years ago, one of their experiments turned on them, exposing the faculty's true nature." He shook his head. "Was not pretty. Even though the Seekers were no more, others used their research to make medicine and technology none would imagine." He gestured to the drug again. "Things like this serum and the Watcher were the results of me obtaining that research."

Mara stared at the serum. "And now you want me to fetch you a test subject?"

Dr. Moen smirked at her. "It'll be dangerous. I suppose you haven't seen the way she feeds."

"Yes, I have," she replied.

"Okay, but have you seen the other way?"

"What?" Mara asked, confused by his question.

Dr. Moen led her to another room, which contained a small black box adorned with a green gemstone. Touching the bauble, Dr. Moen activated it.

A holographic image appeared, showing Anna's transformation. Her face sprouted tentacles, which she used to grab a man by his head. A sharp proboscis extended out. With enough force, she penetrated the man's skull and dove into his brain. He screamed in agony as she began to suck out his grey matter. Within seconds, the victim's screams died down. His eyes rolled back into his head as his face turned pale. After Anna finished, she released the man's corpse. A gaping hole was visible in his hollow skull.

Mara stared at the footage in shock.

Dr. Moen looked at her and explained, "The Watcher captured this footage, for studying Anna, and making sure she does not escape the Black Tower. The Silver Thorns watched over her, but they are no more. It's now our task, but someone or something tampered with the seal."

Mara gawked at the image of Anna, still stunned by her appearance. "What is she?"

"She is a darkling. A rare and strange creature."

She looked at Dr. Moen in confusion. "What's a darkling?"

"In Thoron, they are called godlings, believed to be akin to the divines," Dr. Moen explained. "The Seven Divines are named Aazalith, Cenobia, Mantos, Pharos, Nocturna, Aldin, and Ulrika. Thoron worships them and Nymera, the Mother of Gods. Coming into contact with magic will turn one into a monster. The darkling happens to be one of the resulting creatures. It's causing a debate among scholars on whether or not the divines were once regular creatures. There's a theory that a human can become a god." Then he switched the subject. "Regardless of what she is…" He walked up to the hologram and gazed back at Mara with a stern look. "If she gets you with this, there is a good chance you will not recover."

"But I—"

Dr. Moen lifted his hand to stop her from speaking. "Look, I know you can return to life, but I never said you would die from this. Chances are, you will become a mindless vegetable for all eternity."

Mara sulked at him. "So, all I have to do is not get caught by that?"

The doctor stared at her in disbelief. "You're still willing to go back there?"

"I have to," she replied.

Dr. Moen smirked. "Might as well go all out, swords flailing." He walked out. "Come, we're going to get you ready for your rematch."

"How so?" Mara asked.

He looked back at her. "I'm going to create another Watcher."

She stared at him in shock. "What?"

"Don't get too excited. I'll inject the serum used to make the Watcher, but I cannot guarantee you will get psychic powers overnight." He gestured to his creation. "The human test subject, who became the Watcher, already exhibited latent abilities. At the very least, it'll block Anna from reading your mind. Her psychic powers allowed her to anticipate your moves. That's why you lost."

Recalling her fight with Anna, Mara was unable to land a hit on her.

"This should give you an advantage," the doctor told her. "Any other powers manifesting will be a side-effect." He led her to a metal table.

As Mara lay down, Dr. Moen looked at her with an odd expression. "Aren't you going to remove your hood?"

Mara shook her head. "I can't... my face. I'm not..."

Dr. Moen shrugged. "Ah, it's okay," he murmured. "Just lie down."

As she lay down, Dr. Moen placed a strange device on her head, exposing her forehead. It appeared to be a type of mount. Without warning, metal straps held her wrists and ankles.

"What is this?" Mara asked, feeling distressed.

The doctor gazed at her. "I'm sorry, but this is a necessary precaution." Dr. Moen prepared a needle containing a glowing blue liquid.

Mara stared up at the ceiling. It was the only thing she could do. "This won't hurt, will it?"

"Try not to move too much." He began to insert the needle through the threading in the device on her forehead.

She gasped, feeling a sharp pain as the needle dove into her brain. Her entire body began to seize up while her heart raced. The doctor was as careful as he could be and began to inject the liquid. She felt the foreign fluid enter her brain. Her vision blurred. The intense pain made her pass out.

* * *

A bell's chime pulled her from her sleep. Mara didn't know how long she was unconscious. She no longer felt any pain. Her eyes scanned the room. The room was dark, and all the lights were off. Dr. Moen and the Watcher were gone. Where did they go? No longer strapped to the table, Mara began to move. Getting up, she noticed a white light shining on her. She looked up to see a glowing white figure standing before her. A veiled woman wore a white dress and a hood. Mara tried to see her face, only to be blinded by the light. The ghostly figure began to approach her. Mara felt a hand on her shoulder.

"Are you okay? Can you hear me?"

Mara heard Dr. Moen calling her. She gazed back at him, seeing his concerned face. The Watcher was also looking at her. She stared at him for a while, then looked back to where the woman in white stood.

Mara grew baffled. "Where is she?"

Dr. Moen looked concerned. "What are you talking about?"

"There was a woman here, wearing a white dress and a hood." Mara looked around again. "Didn't you see her?" She looked back at them.

Dr. Moen and the Watcher exchanged glances. Judging by the looks on their faces, Mara reckoned they never saw the ghostly woman.

"No one else was present during the procedure," the Watcher stated.

The doctor rubbed his chin. "Could be a hallucination?"

Mara stared at him in horror and anger. She did not sign up for this.

He saw her expression. "Never seen such a side-effect before," he said. "You are the first."

"Is this permanent?" Mara demanded.

Dr. Moen looked back at her with sympathy. "Hey, no need to get worried. I will make sure it doesn't get worse." He stood up. "Can you stand?"

She rose to her feet despite feeling upset.

He nodded. "Okay, that's good. Can you walk to that desk?"

She looked at the desk and approached it with no problems. Mara turned around and looked at him. "Why do I need to do this?"

"Wanted to make sure you're still functional," he admitted. "I've never actually attempted this on anyone since the Watcher."

Her eyes widened. "What?"

Dr. Moen lifted a finger. "Hey, at least you turned out okay despite a little side-effect. Though I better take a blood sample to observe any changes."

He left to get a syringe. Upon his return, Mara removed her glove. After the doctor extracted a sample, he put it away as she placed her glove back on.

"Why are we doing this?" Dr. Moen asked as if to remind her.

"To defeat Anna," Mara sighed.

"Great! Now come over here."

He beckoned Mara to an enlarged golden clock face with a hollow centre. The outer ring had runes etched on. She also noticed more of those staves near the device, but the gems were not glowing.

"What is this?" Mara asked.

"This is the Gateway, a teleportation machine," he said proudly. "While being in Thoron, I got to look upon one of the greatest pieces of technology ever created—a time-travel machine! However, the Thoron Sages forbade its use, claiming it was dangerous. I got limited information, yet enough to reverse engineer and create this. The technology is also in the Watcher's armour, and she can use it at will. It's limited to teleporting to a different place in the present time, and only in Ardana. But it is still effective for a one-way trip." The doctor pointed to the staff-like objects. "To use the Gateway, we use these staves to mark the locations. I placed some around Ardana with the Watcher's help. We'll send you back to the Black Tower."

Mara gazed at the machine with uncertainty. "Is this safe?"

"Don't worry," Dr. Moen reassured. "We've used this many times before. It works perfectly."

He then turned to a lever and pulled on it. The lights began to flicker in the laboratory. The machine hummed as its runes gleamed in blue hues. The doctor approached a pedestal and began to push on some tiles on the dial. An image appeared in the hollow centre. It looked like the entrance to the Black Tower.

Mara stared in awe. "It's a portal," she murmured, taking a few steps towards it. Before entering, Mara looked back at the two. "Anything else I need to do?"

"Find Commander White, and the Watcher will do the rest," the doctor instructed. "I'll also have the Watcher help. If Anna tries to get you with her tail, the Watcher can attack her mind."

Mara looked impressed. "She sounds pretty powerful."

The doctor nodded. "Even I don't know the extent of her powers, but I know her body is fragile." He looked at the Watcher. "Even with the armour, one strong hit will critically injure her."

"Oh," Mara murmured.

She turned around and approached the portal. In a flash of light, she found herself standing before the Black Tower.

* * *

Wandering the tower, Mara returned to the room where she last died. She heard the hissing sound again and peered into the darkness. Anna emerged from the shadows. Mara stared at her, resting her hand on the hilt of her sword. The shadows pulled back to reveal Commander White. He was kneeling before Anna, kissing her hand. Anna's eyes widened as she gave a wicked smile.

Opening his eyes, the commander pulled away and stood up. He turned to face Mara with a blank expression while drawing his sword. Anna slithered around, grinning from ear to ear. Mara ignored her and gazed at him. In silence, the commander dashed at her. Mara reached for her sword.

"Do not draw your blade," came the Watcher's disembodied voice. "I will deal with this."

Mara became still, watching Commander White. As he was about to strike, the Watcher suddenly appeared between them and touched him. They both disappeared in a flash of blue light, blinding Mara.

"We have him," the Watcher said into her mind.

With the commander out of the way, Mara could deal with Anna. While Mara's vision cleared, she heard a low hiss from behind. She turned around and saw Anna transforming into a hideous creature. The darkling grabbed her head with her tentacles. She extended her sharp proboscis, poised to plunge into her head. Mara grabbed it in time, although it dug into her skin and drew blood. She struggled to push the feeding tube away. With a free hand, she grabbed her sword and swiped it in front of Anna's face. Anna screeched as the severed proboscis fell to the ground. She released Mara while blood sprayed everywhere. Mara struggled to her feet, but the tail appendage grabbed her head. Anna began to pump the paralyzing substance into her.

Mara convulsed violently as several images assailed her brain. She found herself set ablaze, her skin charred as the flames ate her body away. She had no time to scream. Another image flashed into her mind. No longer was she on fire, but lying on her bed. Mara saw herself as a small toddler. A fever gripped her, sapping her strength. Mom took her to several doctors, but none could diagnose her ailment. Everyone decided to give up on her.

However, Dad refused to let his daughter die. He went away to return with a possible cure. Dad appeared before her with the moonstone necklace.

"Put this on, sweetie," he said softly. "It's magical. It will help you get better."

Upon donning the necklace, Mara's illness vanished as if she were never sick in the first place. An older woman approached her.

"This is Alkina," Dad introduced, "the shaman from my home village."

Mara remembered the kind shaman, who came to perform a rite that would aid in Mara's recovery while keeping evil away.

The Stone Mages surrounded her, dancing and chanting in an unknown language while the shaman approached. The pounding drums produced a roaring sound. Dipping a finger inside a bowl, Alkina painted on Mara's face. Her fingers drifted over her eyelids, the edges of her cheekbones, and the sides of her face. Then the shaman brought the bowl closer.

"Drink," she instructed calmly.

Mara drank the liquid. It tasted awful as if it were copper. After drinking the entire contents of the bowl, the painted marks on her face began to darken.

"Fight poison with poison," said the shaman.

The undying felt a powerful tingling sensation on the base of her neck. A blue glow caught her eye. With her right hand tightening into a fist, Mara became filled with an intense rage.

A bright blue flash blasted Anna back. Her tail detached from Mara's head. The visions and the paralysis wore off. Mara opened her eyes to see the blue light beneath her cloak. A round object, sitting at the base of her neck, remained quivering until it stopped. Once the glow faded, Mara gazed back at Anna with glowing eyes.

"I think it's time for you to die," she hissed in a low tone.

It was more than enough to frighten Anna. The darkling's plan to stop her failed. Mara noticed her tail and swung her sword at it. She slashed it in half.

Anna screamed and writhed away from her. The other half of her tail flopped around before withering and dying. The darkling crawled away from Mara. Her tail writhed and wiggled, spraying blood everywhere. The loss of blood made her weaker. Mara approached her with glowing eyes. Anna became less mobile from her blood loss. Taking her sword, Mara plunged it into Anna's heart. A loud gasp escaped the darkling's lips as her body turned to dust. She gazed at Mara, uttering some parting words.

"Aazalith is... coming..." Anna said just above a whisper.

Mara watched as Anna's remains dissipated into the air. The yellow glow in her eyes faded. In Anna's place was another healing stone. She picked it up and decided to save it. Mara turned around and walked away.

Anna's parting words sank into the deepest corners of her mind. Dr. Moen mentioned Aazalith, one of the Seven Divines. What did Anna mean about Aazalith's return? Maybe Harold knew? Still, there were other things to deal with, and she could not return to Greyward Hold just yet.

The Watcher appeared before her, ready to take her to the doctor's laboratory.

Mara looked at her and said, "Thanks for helping me back there."

The doctor's creation tilted her head in confusion. "Excuse me?"

"You know, for helping me," Mara replied.

"What are you talking about?" The Watcher was clueless, which was contrary. Mara furrowed her eyebrows. "You helped me defeat Anna, right?"

The Watcher shook her head. "No, I did not."

Mara gazed back in confusion. "What do you mean you didn't help me?"

She thought about what happened and recalled the strange tingling sensation at the base of her neck. Looking down her cloak, Mara found a choker. The choker was nothing special, just a dull gold and black piece of jewellery with some lace and embroidery. Underneath was a black cord attached to golden beads and two round sapphire crystals. Reaching for the larger gemstone, Mara recalled the gift Dad gave her when she was a toddler. She got it around the time of her illness. He claimed the necklace was magical and would cure her. While this jewellery seemed to cure her, it did not do anything else. Still, it was beautiful, and she rarely took it off. Now, Mara wondered if she was wrong about Dad's gift. Harold mentioned moonstones and how they could neutralize magic. Now that she thought about it, the necklace had moonstone.

Then she thought back to the time she got ill. After Dad gave her the necklace, he invited the shaman from his home village. They did a strange ritual and made her drink that awful soup. Thinking about its coppery taste, Mara realized it was not soup. It was blood. Why did they make her drink blood? She also recalled the shaman's words.

"Fight poison with poison."

What did that mean? Dad had some explaining to do.

Mara looked up at the Watcher, who offered her hand. As soon as Mara took it, they teleported back to Dr. Moen's lab.

* * *

Mara arrived at the laboratory with the Watcher. She saw Commander White strapped to a chair, his head convulsing. The doctor stood over him. He gazed back at them and waved.

"Hey, glad to see you back. Dealt with Anna?"

"Yeah, she's dead. How are things on your end?" Mara looked at the commander.

Dr. Moen also glanced back at him. "We're about to find out."

Four knocks on the door grabbed their attention. The doctor went to answer, only to have the Faith's followers and the Holy Blades flooding in. Mara was surprised, seeing so many people in the laboratory. She looked at Dr. Moen, noting his dismay towards all these people crowding his lab.

"What's the meaning of this?" Dr. Moen demanded.

A priest in gold and ivory robes stepped forward and gazed at them dismissively. "We have come for Commander White. Now, release him!"

Mara looked surprised. She glanced back at the doctor, who expressed a similar reaction. Looking back at the crowd, she saw Mr. White. He spotted the commander strapped to the chair and having a seizure. The father looked horrified to see his son in that state.

"Karl!" Mr. White ran to him.

The priest also approached him, looking disturbed. "By the Goddess…" He then glared at the doctor. "What are you doing to him?"

"We're saving him," Dr. Moen explained. "He fell victim to Anna."

Mr. White gazed at Mara in horror. "You brought him here?"

"I needed their help," Mara replied, gesturing to the doctor and his creation.

The doctor nodded. "And she was right to come to us," he said in a stern tone. "After what Anna did to him, I doubt your priestess can mend his mind."

Mara glanced over at Commander White, whose seizure had ceased. His eyes fluttered open as he began to groan.

Mr. White took notice. "Karl!"

Commander White gazed at his father in confusion. He also noticed the congregation, the doctor and the Watcher, and Mara. He looked at Mr. White again.

"Arthur?" Commander White asked. His softened voice garnered mixed reactions. He was not his usual self.

Mr. White looked stunned and confused.

The priest scowled at Dr. Moen again. "What is this devilry? What did you do to Commander White?"

"Please, Father Vernon," Mr. White addressed the priest. "Let's give him some air." He turned to his son. "Do you know who you are?"

"My name is Karl White," he replied with a soft and quiet voice. "But I was adopted after losing my father. I was only five."

Mr. White nodded. "Good… Do you know where you are?"

The commander glanced around. "I… I don't know." Gazing down at his uniform, the commander grew more confused.

Even the doctor took notice.

"Seems he's suffering from partial amnesia," Dr. Moen said. "He should go home and rest."

Mr. White looked at the doctor. "Yes, I think it'll be best."

Dr. Moen walked up to them. "Here, let me undo these straps."

He released Commander White from the chair. Dr. Moen and Mr. White helped him to his feet. The commander was wobbly, almost falling on his first attempt at standing.

"Okay," said the doctor, "his motor skills may need some time, but I'm sure he will be fine."

Father Vernon approached them. "He should return to the Temple of Kallisto. The High Priestess sensed this would happen. And she shall mend him."

Mr. White glanced back at him, looking less than keen with the idea. "I believe he will benefit more from a few days of bed rest."

Father Vernon frowned at him. "Please, I insist. We shall take him to Golden Mountain."

"I don't think he is well for travelling," Mr. White argued.

"She is the only one who can help him," the priest persisted.

"Why don't you let the commander decide?" Mara butted in, shaking her head.

It was then the huntress noted everyone's stares upon her. Even the commander was gazing at her. She looked back at him and noticed his soft facial expression. Ever since he awoke, Commander White never once glared at her. Instead, the followers of Kallikratés were scowling at her.

"What do you know?" Father Vernon hissed.

"I think it's a great idea," said Mr. White. He looked at his son. "What do you think? Do you want to go home to rest? Or the temple to heal?"

The commander gazed at his father. After staring at him for a while, he looked away and closed his eyes. "I'm so tired and confused," he said barely above a whisper.

Mr. White watched him. "Very well." He looked at everyone. "I shall take him home and make sure he's gained enough rest."

Dr. Moen nodded. "Good idea. Any doctor would say the same as well."

Mara looked at Father Vernon, who was glaring at Mr. White. The Holy Blades and the disciples eventually left. She looked over to Mr. White. He released a sigh, then looked back at Mara. He approached her.

"Thank you for saving Karl." The older man held out his hand for a handshake. "You did the right thing, bringing him here."

She shook his hand. "It wasn't easy to save him. Did you send my request?"

The older man's face fell into a frown. "I did, but she refused. I'm sorry." He pulled out his wallet. "But I shall not leave you empty-handed. How does two thousand gold sound?"

Mara shrugged. "I guess it is better than nothing."

Mr. White began to count out the gold coins owed to her. The commander approached them, placing his hand over his father's. They looked at him.

"Karl?" Mr. White asked.

Commander White looked at Mara, then reached into one of his pockets. He pulled out his wallet and began to count out some gold coins.

"I should pay her," Commander White said.

Mara frowned underneath her mask. "You don't have to. Your father asked for my help."

"She is right, Karl," Mr. White said. "You don't have to pay."

"But it's my fault," the commander argued.

Mara gaped at Commander White. He became a completely different person. She glanced back at Mr. White, who didn't seem too upset at the drastic change in his son.

"Maybe you should accept the money?" Mr. White suggested. "I don't think he will take no for an answer."

Mara sighed, "Fine…"

She accepted the money from Commander White. Mara looked at his face, still stunned at his transformation. The commander looked back at her with bright green eyes.

"I'm sorry," he murmured.

She kept gawking at him.

Mr. White dug into his wallet to retrieve a bunch of gold coins. "Here, I shall also give some gold. I am a man of my word." He handed her the gold.

She stared at her reward, now worth four thousand gold.

"I know it is more than expected, but I do believe we are grateful," said the nobleman. "Once again, thank you for helping us."

Commander White looked back at her with sad eyes. "I'm sorry," he repeated.

Mr. White guided him out.

Mara sighed as she watched them leave.

"Nice," Dr. Moen said.

Mara gazed back at him. "I guess I owe you." She held out her hand to offer some gold.

Dr. Moen shook his head. "Keep the gold. You deserve it."

She stared at him. "What happened to him?"

Dr. Moen shrugged. "The serum worked as it should."

"But his personality is different!"

"According to my research, it was supposed to restore the brain to its original state." The doctor shrugged. "Then again, this appears to be a better version of him. Perhaps he'll be a nicer guy for now on?" With that, he laughed.

Mara could not believe he said that, but he brought up a good point. Any future encounters with the commander might be better from here on out. The next thing on her mind was the next undying. After that, she planned on seeing her parents. As Mara walked away, she heard the doctor call out to her.

"Hey, wait up."

Mara stopped and looked back at him. "What is it?"

"Had a look at your blood and noticed something very unusual—did you get attacked by a werewolf in the last few days?"

She recalled the previous job. "Some wandered south. Chancellor Davis asked me to slay them, but their alpha attacked me." Mara paused briefly. "I didn't get infected again?"

"No, it's nothing like that. According to the readings, you are immune to lycanthropy thanks to the cure." Dr. Moen approached her. "When Lady Isabella died, the cure was lost. However, with your blood, I can recreate it. You are one of the very few individuals to have a sample. I doubt I'll get one from Commander White."

If true, then there was no harm in helping him.

"Okay…" She rolled up her sleeve to expose some skin.

Thrilled, the doctor went to get a syringe and returned to her. He pierced the exposed skin and drew some blood. "You're doing a great thing."

"I hope so," she murmured.

Dr. Moen looked back at her and smiled. "I think you are." Upon the needle's removal, her wound healed. "That's so neat!"

Mara grew amused by the middle-aged man. For a very brilliant scientist and inventor, he acted like a big kid. He reminded her of the friends she made in her college years. She met the twin brothers, Allen and James Moen. Both were very smart—Allen was energetic and eccentric, while James was calm and quiet.

Looking at the doctor, Mara realized his last name matched the twin brothers'. He even looked similar to Allen. She remembered hearing how much he resembled his father.

She thought it wouldn't hurt to ask. "Do you have two sons?"

The doctor looked at her strangely. "No, I don't have any kids. Not even married."

Mara looked at him, surprised by his response. "Oh, I'm sorry." She felt a little foolish.

"It's okay, people make mistakes," he responded softly.

"It's just, you look like someone I met in college," Mara explained.

"You attended the College of Ardana?" Dr. Moen asked.

"Yes, I was twenty-one," she replied. "Graduated a few years ago."

"Oh, is that so? For me, it's been thirty-two years. Things sure have changed. Once, I was an instructor there, encouraging students to think for themselves." He sighed. "Unfortunately, I was asked to leave."

"Why?"

"The Faith controls the college, and I don't exactly see eye to eye with them. I've been an advocate of education being unbiased and not clouded by one's perspective."

"So, truth?" Mara asked.

"I'd be careful with that word," Dr. Moen warned. "The truth is a matter of perspectives. Don't believe everything you hear." Then, "Oh, and they also banned Stone Mages from attending the college."

Mara was surprised.

Dr. Moen noted her reaction. "Yeah, I was shocked too. I knew a friend who attended the college—a Stone Mage. She was a bit of a she-wolf, but she was very sharp and a quick learner. Sadly, she was the subject of racism and others pressured her to drop out. She didn't even have the lowest grades. I helped her raise her grades, but the other students accused her of cheating."

"I'm sorry to hear that," Mara said sombrely. "That also happened to me."

The doctor sighed. "I think Kallikratés wants to portray them as uneducated savages. On the contrary, they are intelligent and civil. I think my friend proved the Faith wrong." Dr. Moen smiled. "I should get back to work. Maybe I'll see you again the next time you get into major trouble."

"Okay, but I hope it's nothing too serious," Mara replied.

Leaving the lab and the city, Mara returned to Greyward Hold.

Chapter Twenty

The Marionette

Mara returned to Greyward Hold after a long and uneventful ride. First, she had to retrieve the little lady, which remained near Medulla. Then they had to travel the snowy trail on Grey Mountain. At least the mare got used to travelling this road.

The huntress arrived around the afternoon on November 30. Many thoughts ran through her head. Despite having to tell Harold about Anna, finding the next undying put Mara's mind on other things. She hoped to see her family and friends and tell them what happened. Mom and Dad had to be worried sick about her.

"Ah, you have returned," the former master greeted. "I suppose Anna is dead?"

She sighed. "Guess it's too late to say I regret it. I thought it would bring me one step closer to lifting my curse, but Alena refused my request. Now I'm back to square one."

"True, but all is not lost," Harold said. "Before long, your true form will be restored."

Mara nodded in agreement, though his words caught her attention. What did he mean by that? He was probably talking about her regaining her human form again. Thinking of other things, her final encounter with Anna lingered in her thoughts.

"Anna mentioned Aazalith," Mara said.

Harold stared at her, appearing surprised. "She spoke to you? What else did she say?"

"Nothing else," she replied, shaking her head.

"I see," the former master murmured. "Anna was a brilliant scholar and a truth seeker. She was also very critical of the gods and questioned their legitimacy."

"What happened to her?"

"She discovered the name, Aazalith, and began to ask questions. Her curiosity drew the attention of the gods, who ordered her execution. The Faith burned all of her research along with her."

Mara wondered about the images the darkling planted in her head—the one where she was being burned alive. She reckoned it was a common form of execution long ago.

"If Anna told you this, then you deserve to know the truth," he confessed. "The Dark One is Aazalith."

Mara's jaw dropped. "The Dark One is a god?"

"Yes," the former master answered. "Thousands of years ago, Ardana declared war on Thoron to seek their magic. The Thoronites called upon their gods for aid. Dragon Goddess Aazalith answered by sending forth her children, the great dragons. But after losing many of her children, Aazalith unleashed her wrath indiscriminately, viewing humans as a blight. Ardana and Thoron united to defeat her after the loss of innumerable souls. Stripped of her deity status, she became the Dark One. Entombed deep in the Dark Labyrinth, underneath Ghost Mountain, she is the source of the magic blight."

Mara remained silent. No wonder why people feared this creature. After learning of the Dark One's identity, a question crossed her mind. "Was I wrong to kill Anna?"

"She would have posed a great threat if kept alive. The Faith would have stormed the Black Tower to save the commander. However, she also possessed a seal. Now three remain."

"Yet, you showed little concern about the seals breaking."

"Yes, there is the prophecy," he hesitated. "The gods shall return to vanquish the Dark One and usher in a new Golden Age."

"You think it'll happen?" Mara questioned.

"I believe they shall return," he replied, "but defeating the Dark One is the real question. The gods were arrogant and underestimated the power of the divine. Kratés died as a result." Looking at Mara, he took a step forward. "That is why I turned down your offer to kill the Dark One. Even though you have this curse, you need to be aware of the limits of your power."

"Okay," Mara said. "Speaking of which, what about the next undying?"

"I figured you would ask." The old master reached into his robes and gave her a work order.

"The next undying!" Mara took the work order and gazed at it. "The Marionette?"

"This was someone I knew quite well," Harold revealed. "A herbalist, who often came to our aid with healing supplies and medication. However, a rumour painted her as a witch and the source of the plague ravaging the nearby village. A follower from Kallikratés spread the rumour, claiming her herbs caused hallucinations. Haranta Village believed burning her would stop the plague. But she was the only one keeping them alive. After they burned her and her herbs, the illness claimed the whole village. We even lost a few of our own. Kallikratés denied any responsibility." Harold looked at her. "After you kill her, I need you to return to me."

Nodding, Mara turned from the former master. Studying the contract in her hand, she discovered that Chancellor Davis had issued the work order.

"The Marionette lives in an old house, outside Lupine Woods and the abandoned Haranta Village," Mara read out loud. "This might be the last undying."

She gathered her things and headed out to Haranta Village.

* * *

Her horse trotted along the road, heading towards the abandoned village. Getting there was straight forward. Haranta was near the foot of Grey Mountain, sitting near the border of Lupine Woods. She spotted a merchant on the side of the road. The old female merchant appeared to be asleep, so Mara rode past her. Within minutes, she stood before the quiet and empty village. There were no signs of the Holy Blades and no one to interfere. Scanning the area, she spotted an old abandoned house near the woods. Mara reckoned this dilapidated abode belonged to the undying. Dismounting from her horse, Mara walked towards the house. The sun began to set.

"Guess this is the place," she murmured to herself.

"Excuse me!"

Mara turned around. The old merchant, who was asleep on the roadside, ran up to her. She stopped in front of Mara, trying to catch her breath. The older woman glanced up at her. The lantern she held illuminated her wrinkled face.

"If you value your life, stay away from this place," the merchant warned. "The Marionette lives there."

The huntress watched the older woman. The merchant's attire was nothing but rags, possibly a homeless vendor. Despite her raggedy appearance, she appeared to know quite a bit about the undying. Mara decided to obtain more information.

"What do you know about her?"

"It is a doll possessed by a spirit, giving it life and the power to steal the souls of others."

Mara folded her arms. "So, this thing claimed many victims?"

"The Marionette cursed Haranta Village, making it abandoned," according to the merchant. "Once, a strange and lonely girl lived in that house. The villagers believed she was a witch, so they burned her. Her spirit took residence in a doll fashioned to look like her. Out of revenge, she unleashed a plague and claimed their lives."

Mara looked confused, for this was a different tale from the one Harold told her. She glanced back at the old derelict house.

"Well, I came here to kill it…" With that, she began to walk towards it.
"Wait!"

Mara looked back at the older woman again.

"It'll be dark soon," said the merchant. "You may want to buy a lantern. I'll give you one for a thousand gold."

Mara raised an eyebrow. "A thousand gold for a lantern?"

"I'm offering the better deal," the old merchant claimed. "A general goods store will have you paying more for the same thing." She noticed the flask on Mara's belt and pondered something else. "Hmm, since you're unwilling to pay for a lantern, I can offer Moon Water." She held up a large flask of glowing blue liquid. "For the price of five hundred gold."

Mara shook her head. "Never heard of this."

"It's just as effective. You can put it in your flask and use it as a makeshift lantern."

She paid the merchant five hundred gold. "Where did you get this stuff?"

"Can't tell you, it's a secret." She poured some liquid into Mara's flask. "Shake the flask and the light will grow stronger for a while."

Mara tried it out. The blue liquid grew brighter after being shaken a few times.

"Thanks," Mara said to the merchant, and then ventured towards the house.

* * *

Mara entered the dark house. The glowing water in her flask offered a decent amount of light. The old furniture was in varying states of decay. A life-sized doll sat on a chair, next to the grand fireplace. Mara noticed a picture on the small table. Picking it up, she wiped away the dust.

"So, you're just like me," Mara murmured underneath her mask.

The woman in the picture looked identical to Mara. She appeared very pretty, like a doll. She wore a black lace dress, while her dark hair formed a tight bun. Her face showed a joyful expression on the verge of tears. While placing the picture back, she heard the floorboards creaking from the hall. As she looked away, the life-sized figure rose to its feet. Sensing a presence behind her, she turned around to see the doll grab her neck, trying to strangle her. Mara immediately realized it was not a doll, but the reanimated remains of a man. His face was rotten beyond recognition. Due to advanced decay, she was able to pry him off and threw him to the ground. As soon as he hit the floor, he exploded into dust. She stared at the broken remains while feeling her neck. While unharmed, the attack stunned her. Mara had to find the Marionette and defeat her. She dashed to the hallway.

All of a sudden, a gust of wind rushed towards her. Dust flew into her eyes, forcing Mara to close them. Opening them again, she found herself surrounded by a blur of colours and lights. No longer was she in the Witch's House, but in the banquet hall at the College of Ardana, on the night of her graduation. Students and professors surrounded her, dancing in circles.

"Will you forgive me?"

Recognizing his voice, Mara turned around to see his vibrant green eyes and shiny brown hair. His face was clean-shaven, save for the stubble on the chin.

"What is this?" Mara asked. "How did I get here?"

He took another step towards her, holding his hands behind his back. The young man gazed at her, appearing unaware of what she just said.

"I'm sorry," he said in a formal tone. "I never meant to hurt you."

She looked back at him, recalling this scenario. She never had any intention of going because it meant encountering him. Unfortunately, Mom bought her a dress made of blue satin. Dad persuaded her to go, at least to make her mother happy. Mara looked down to find herself wearing that dress. She even appeared human. Looking up, Mara saw everyone gazing at her.

He held out his hand, desiring a dance. It was the least he could do to apologize for all the hell he put her through. Mara looked back at him, unsure about taking his hand. At the corner of her eye, Mara saw a woman in a black dress. The gothic style of the dress looked out of place among the fancy ballroom dresses. Everyone began to dance. Mara stuck out like a sore thumb. She looked for the woman again, but she vanished from her sight. A terrible stench filled the air, like rotting flesh. Looking around, Mara saw not the other graduates dancing but reanimated corpses. Strings guided their movements, like puppets. A pair of hands wrapped around her waist, holding her close. Mara looked to the one who grabbed her. He gazed back with dead eyes. With cold hands, he took her face and guided her gaze to his own.

"Dance with me," he said.

His eyes sank into the back of his head. His skin cracked and chipped, like paint coming off of wood. Ball joints replaced his wrists and elbows. His movements grew more twitchy and shaky. Mara stared in horror, for the man she was dancing with was not human! She tried to pull away, but he held on tightly. Looking into his eyeless sockets, Mara became paralyzed. A blue glow emanated from his eye sockets. She began to feel weak as a faint light connected their eyes. Mara tried to pull away, but her strength was fading fast.

All of a sudden, she was pulled from the creature's embrace. The Hand of Kratés impaled the chest of the monster, stopping it from killing her. Turning around, Mara saw shiny golden plates cascading down a left arm.

"Get her out of here," Commander White barked to another. "If we lose her, we're all dead!"

She fell into the arms of another. The other man said something, but she could not understand. Mara watched as Commander White turned to face the Marionette alone. Then she lost consciousness.

* * *

"Hey, wake up. Wake up!"

A male voice jarred Mara awake. Opening her eyes, she found herself in the cellar with another man. The short black hair identified him as Boyd. She saw a gash above his left eye and blood trickling down his face. Mara got up, staring at him in bewilderment.

The young man shrugged while sitting across from her.

"Did you have a nice sleep?" Boyd asked sarcastically.

With her hand on her forehead, Mara shook her head. Her mind reeled from the illusion. Looking around, Mara discovered that she remained trapped in the Witch's House. This time with Boyd.

She sulked at him. "What are you doing here?"

"I was seeking Commander White on behalf of the Faith," he revealed. "He was looking for you and followed you here. We tried to leave, but this house is bound to the Marionette's curse. So, it's a great thing you, the neighbourhood undying, showed up. You almost died, so we had to save you. We've been trapped here for two days."

She stared back at him and lowered her hand. Mara was surprised to know Commander White and Boyd saved her but realized their motives. She was the only one who could kill the Marionette. If she died, they were also as good as dead. Mara looked at Boyd and noticed the commander's absence.

"Where's Commander White?"

"He's probably getting his soul sucked out as we speak. How about you help me save him and maybe we can all leave this place?" Boyd suggested. "As far as I'm concerned, he has not fully recovered."

The two escaped and began their search for Commander White. After dealing with the reanimated corpses, they finally found him with the Marionette. Kneeling before the living doll, he gazed at her with adoration.

"I love you," he said.

The Marionette just stared at him in silence, sitting in a chair. She lifted her right arm, and Commander White took it. He leaned over and kissed her hand.

The commander looked into her hollow sockets. "I want to spend the rest of my life with you."

Boyd and Mara watched their romantic exchange.

"Damn, he's been hypnotized by that thing!" Boyd exclaimed.

Mara stared at the two. The Marionette caused Commander White to see her as a different person, just like she did to her. After taking his face into her hands, the creature made him look into her eyes. He became paralyzed as a faint blue light wave connected their eyes. Mara recognized this scenario.

"She's taking his soul!" Boyd cried.

Mara ran at them and pushed the Marionette off of him. The undying released her hold, allowing the commander to crumple to the ground. His wide eyes stared up at the ceiling.

Mara lifted him to his feet and shoved him into Boyd.

"Get him out of here!"

Taking a very stunned commander, Boyd scrambled out of the room. Mara watched as they fled, then looked at the undying. The Marionette shuffled towards her. Watching her with glowing eyes, Mara removed her mask.

"None of your tricks are going to work this time," Mara hissed.

The Marionette dashed towards Mara, attempting to grab her. Unsheathing her sword, Mara stabbed the undying in the chest. She kicked the creature off of her sword. The Marionette fell to the ground, where she lay there for a few seconds. Then the living doll shuddered while rising as if strings were pulling her up. Mara stared in horror.

Even with a gaping hole in her chest, the Marionette remained unfazed. Still, she kept fighting. Mara took off an arm and a leg. The Marionette fell to the ground. The living doll lost both legs and could only drag herself using one arm. Grabbing the undying by her hair, Mara sliced the head off. The Marionette was now out of commission.

Mara walked over to the front door and tried to open it. But the door would not budge, for the curse remained. She gazed back at the Marionette, realizing she didn't absorb her soul yet. To her convenience, the soul rose out of the doll. She walked up to the orb of light. Mara was about to claim it, but the soul flew away and went upstairs. She was stunned to see this happen but was not about to let it escape.

Mara chased it to the master bedroom, where she found a body lying on the bed. The corpse was in a similar dress to the Marionette but disfigured from massive burns. Her face was barely recognizable, while the fire claimed her dark hair. The corpse jolted to life and took a sharp breath of air. The soul had returned to its owner, bringing her back to life. With her original body damaged and burnt, she somehow placed her soul inside the doll.

The corpse looked at Mara with her left eye. The right eye was gone. Her muscles wasted away from being bedridden. She was unable to walk, let alone get out of bed. The living corpse made a raspy breathing sound. Mara approached her, gripping the sword in both hands. She lifted the blade above her head, ready to strike the undying down. A weak and pathetic moan escaped from the charred and decayed lips.

Mara stopped and stared at the face of the living corpse. A single tear fell from the undying's eye as her breathing grew more uneven. She tried to speak, but her vocal cords were useless. She appeared to be in extreme pain and anguish. It would be better to put her out of her misery, but something was amiss. It looked like she was trying to tell Mara something. The living corpse lifted her left arm and pointed to the door. In confusion, Mara looked at the doorway. No one was there. She turned her attention back onto the undying. She stared into the dead teary eye of the Marionette. She removed her hood and revealed her face.

"I am also cursed," Mara murmured. "You are not the first undying I've killed. Harold sent me. He said you were once a herbalist and a victim of wrongful accusation."

Looking at the undying, it seemed the creature understood her. The former herbalist tried to talk, only to make raspy moans.

Mara lifted her sword again. "I'll make it quick."

She pointed the blade to the Marionette's head. The huntress kept her promise. The undying's hand fell limp on the bed. The Marionette was no more. An orb of light rose from the charred remains. Mara watched the soul before absorbing it. Her body trembled violently. She collapsed to the ground in agony. Mara was always unprepared to endure the intense pain. She remained on the floor, having a fit.

* * *

Mara didn't know how long she was unconscious, but she finished her task. She was unsure if Commander White and Boyd left the house, nor did she care. Upon opening her eyes, tears began to form.

"Madeline," she uttered.

The herbalist's name surfaced in her mind. She absorbed the third undying soul, restoring her humanity. With her task done, it was time to return to Harold. And maybe she could finally see her parents. She wanted them to know she was okay. It was painful getting up, but it meant she was alive. Mara gazed at the Marionette, seeing how peaceful she looked despite being burnt. A single tear fell from her closed eye. Then Mara saw a dried flower in her hand. Something in the back of her mind told her to take it, so she did. Mara gave one last look at the undying before exiting the house. She had put another victim to rest.

Chapter Twenty-One

Vivid Memories

The sun began to set as Mara left the house. Upon emerging, she spotted several Holy Blades, who arrived in three carriages. They seemed to be searching for something or someone.

Mr. White was among them. He noticed her and approached. "Ah, there you are," the older man addressed her. "I see you have defeated the Marionette."

Mara looked at him and nodded. "Yes, I have." She glanced back at the Holy Blades, who were still searching. "What's going on?"

Boyd approached them, shaking his head. "He took off."

The two looked at him.

"Who?" Mara asked.

Mr. White frowned. "It's Karl." He glanced at the Holy Blades. "The Faith has been pestering me for days, demanding his return." He gazed back at Mara. "He has not made a full recovery and needs more rest, but now he's run off somewhere."

Mara folded her arms. "Now you want me to search for him?"

Mr. White nodded. "I would appreciate it. Besides, he wanted to see you. He was heading to Greyward Hold, but saw you enter the Witch's House and followed you inside."

"I've heard," Mara said. She looked at Boyd. "Where should I look?"

Boyd pointed to Lupine Woods. "Thought I saw him go over there." He gestured to her. "Come on, follow me."

He ran ahead. Mara followed him to the edge of the woods.

"This is where he entered," Boyd told her. He looked at her and gestured to go on ahead.

Mara raised an eyebrow. "You expect me to go alone?"

He shrugged. "I tried to follow, but Commander White demanded to be left alone. Besides, he wanted to see you."

Mara looked ahead. "That makes no sense."

"Look, he hasn't been the same since Anna messed up his brain. Everyone in the Faith took notice. Even the High Priestess is demanding his return, claiming he needs help. Only she can mend his mind and restore him to his old self." Boyd shrugged again. "He's changed. He is no longer the commander we knew."

"Fine, I'll look for him."

She went to search for Commander White.

* * *

Mara wandered into Lupine Woods, following the commander's footprints in the snow. Eventually, she found him sitting on a tree stump with a liquor flask in his right hand. The commander stared at an unfrozen pond, taking a swig. Her boots tread across the snow, making a soft crunching sound.

"What do you want?" Commander White asked. His words sounded as cold as the air around them.

Mara stopped seven feet away from him.

"They're looking for you," she replied softly.

The commander looked at her with glazed eyes, hinting to his drunken state. He took another swig. "Why should I care?"

"Your father asked me to find you." She changed the topic. "Heard you were looking for me and followed me into the Witch's House."

He kept staring at her. "You heard wrong." The commander turned his gaze back onto the pond. "And you can tell my father I'm fine. I'll come home on my own."

She could not believe his denial. How else could one explain why he followed her into that house?

"Really?" Mara rolled her eyes. "Must have great navigational skills when drunk."

Her words earned her another glare from the commander.

"What do you know?" He rose from the stump to face her. With every step, he told her, "The expectations I must meet, the pressure I face, and the scrutiny I receive. All my life, I've been treated differently, for I was born a commoner. I have been constantly reminded of my origins, how I do not deserve to be where I am. Every move I make has been judged and criticized."

Unfazed by his words, Mara shook her head. "Well, maybe half of your problems will go away if you stopped drinking!" She snatched the flask out of his hand. "You shouldn't even be drinking. Probably killing off the last of your brain cells!"

"Give it back!" Commander White shouted in anger.

He lunged at her, trying to grab the flask out of her hands. Mara stepped to the side, causing him to fall into a snowdrift. Seeing his snow-covered face, Mara began to snicker underneath her mask.

He glared at her. "How dare you mock me?" Commander White hissed, brushing the snow off of himself.

"Yeah, how dare I mock the Great Commander of the Holy Blades," Mara jested.

He kept glaring at her. All of a sudden, he grabbed a handful of snow and threw it into her face. Caught off guard, she pulled her mask away, trying to get the snow out of her hood. In her distraction, Mara got tackled to the ground. Looking up, she saw Commander White on top of her.

"Aha!" he shouted, wrestling the container from her grasp. The commander triumphantly got his precious flask back. He looked down at her, realizing their positions. He had pinned her down with his thighs, straddling her hips. He blushed in embarrassment, then got up.

Mara also felt uncomfortable by the exchange. She slowly rose to her feet and took a few steps away from him.

"I did what your father asked. I should take my leave." She began to walk away from him. Upon taking a few steps, something grabbed her left arm. Turning around, Mara saw Commander White grasping it.

The commander's eyes focused on her face. With a free hand, he reached for her hood and pushed it back. Long dark hair fell to the middle of her back. While gazing at her face, the commander's mouth dropped open.

"Your face," he murmured.

Why the surprise? He saw her face before and after killing the undying. But the way he observed her felt awkward and strange. She wanted to look away, but his gaze demanded attention.

"I saw you kill the Marionette," he admitted.

Mara was surprised. No wonder why the former herbalist was pointing at the door. He was probably watching them, and the undying noticed.

She shook her head. "So?"

"Did she talk?" Commander White asked.

"No, she couldn't," she replied. "It was better to put her out of her misery."

The commander kept watching her. "How much of your memory have you retrieved?"

She stared at him in confusion but decided to answer. "Got most of them back, but I still don't know how I became cursed."

His face softened. Mara looked up at him, still unable to look away. His bright green eyes drew her in.

"Do you remember me?"

Mara grew perplexed. "What are you talking about?"

"We met in college," he answered.

She looked at him and began to remember her college years and the night of her graduation. Her eyes widened. "You?"

Mara now knew who the commander was. The so-called nice boy, as Mom described. The popular one, who all the girls fawned over. The same guy who singled her out in History and even pressured her to drop out. And the jerk who also accused her of cheating when she worked hard to raise her grades. She now remembered his face as he stood before her.

He released her arm and fell to his knees. The commander gazed up at her face.

"Please, forgive me."

Mara's eyes remained on him. The snow fell around them. He seemed different from the guy she knew from college. Should she forgive him?

"Karl," called a familiar older man.

Mara and the commander turned around, realizing they were not alone. Mr. White was watching the two while accompanied by the Holy Blades. Mara did not know how long they were watching. She saw Mr. White looking back at her.

The commander rose to his feet and scowled at his subordinates. "Must you pester me?"

One of the Holy Blades stepped forward. "Sir, you must return to the temple."

Commander White sulked at him. "I made myself clear. I've no intentions yet."

The Holy Blade nodded. "We understand," he said. "However, High Priestess Alena requests your presence at once."

Mr. White looked at Mara. "And we would like you to accompany us."

"What?" Mara asked. "Why?"

The Holy Blade gazed at her. "After rescuing the Commander of the Holy Blades once again, the High Priestess can no longer ignore this."

Mr. White smiled. "It shall be a wondrous opportunity."

Mara grew baffled. "Didn't she refuse my request?"

"She has changed her mind," said the older man.

Mara looked around. It seemed like a great idea, but a thought crossed her mind. "Harold asked me to return to him, and I don't know how many undying are left."

"It shall not take long," Mr. White insisted. "You can see him later."

Mara pondered her choices. If she could get to Thoron, she would be one step closer to being free of her curse. "Fine, I'll go."

The commander looked at her. "Is this what you want?"

She looked back at him, perplexed by his question. "What do you mean?"

Looking into his eyes, Mara could see tears beginning to form. His face twisted in a variety of emotions, such as regret and dread.

"Do not mind him," Mr. White reassured. "He remains unwell." Then, "We should take our leave. It's getting late."

"But, Arthur…" Commander White protested.

"Your father is right," the Holy Blade agreed. "We should ride back now."

Commander White regained his composure. "Very well."

Mara donned her hood, then pulled her mask back up as they returned to the carriages, and began their journey to Golden Mountain. Much to her surprise, the commander and his father allowed her to ride with them. The Holy Blade also accompanied them. Once everyone was in place, the carriages began to move.

* * *

Mara sat beside Commander White. Mr. White and the Holy Blade took the opposite seats. It felt weird to sit beside the commander. The last time she rode in a carriage with him, she was bound and restrained like some beast. Gazing out the window, she felt a hand resting over her own. Looking back, she saw Commander White reach over and pull her mask down. Then he pushed her hood back. His eyes took in her visage.

"Commander White," Mara began, confused by his actions.

His face softened. "Please, call me Karl."

Closing his eyes, Karl leaned in and pressed his lips against her own. Mara froze, her eyes widened as her heart fluttered.

A memory surfaced within Mara's mind. Since graduation, they continued to have more encounters. He often visited Mara in her home, and sometimes her father's workshop. He took her to various places, even to the White Manor. People often stopped and stared, but Karl proudly walked around with her on his arm.

He took her to the gardens at the mansion. The manor's servants prepared lunch, serving the most excellent food and wine. She reckoned it was something nobles enjoy, although it seemed weird to serve alcohol this early. Flowers bloomed on a hot spring day. Mara remembered having a great time before being caught by his kiss under a torrent of blossoms.

Eventually, he pulled away. Karl opened his eyes and looked at her. Mara glanced around to see that they were back in the carriage. The vivid memory faded away.

He began to blush. "I'm sorry."

She looked at him in shock. Her face was also red. Mara never expected him to do that. She glanced over at Mr. White, noticing his reaction. Even the Holy Blade took notice and frowned at them. They were surprised by his actions. Looking back at the commander, Mara found him to be a far cry from what he used to be. They looked into each other's eyes.

"I'll do anything to help you," he told her.

Mara nodded in agreement.

Karl wrapped his arm around her and held her close.

Mara rested her head on his chest, listening to his beating heart. The carriage took her further away from Grey Mountain. She looked out the window. The snow continued to fall as the sun was setting. It never looked more beautiful, especially now that she was with her prince. It would have been a perfect moment if not for the scrutinizing gaze of the Holy Blade and the shocked reaction of Mr. White. She hoped to have more of these special moments, once freed of her curse.

* * *

Later that night, the carriages arrived at Golden Mountain. Karl and the Holy Blade were the first to leave. Mara left after Mr. White. Her eyes followed a snow-covered trail up to the Temple of Kallisto, lit up with gold and ivory pillars of fire.

She followed them up the trail to the temple. Some of the Holy Blades held up lanterns to light the way. The ivory sculpture of the goddess, Kallisto, stood before the entrance. Seeing the statue made Mara uneasy, but she shrugged it off. Holy Blades guarded the main doors. They held their spears over the door, barring anyone from entering the temple. They stood before the guards, who took notice of Karl.

"Commander White, we've been expecting your return," said one of the guards. They withdrew their weapons and opened the doors. They walked down an ivory hallway. At the end was another door with another pair of Holy Blades guarding it.

Karl looked back at Mr. White. "Wait with her while I speak with Her Eminence."

With that, Karl left them. The guards allowed him entry. They closed the doors behind him, leaving Mr. White and Mara to each other.

Mara glanced over at Mr. White and began to observe him. She had seen him before—he was the professor in History, which she took with Allen. With more of her memories returning, Mara also recalled the older man as a family friend. She kept gazing at him. So far, he did not notice her gawking. As soon as he glanced back at her, Mara stopped her observation.

"What did Karl tell you?" Mr. White asked.

Mara was puzzled. "What do you mean?"

"My son spoke to you, did he not?"

"He asked about my memory. I know who he is; we met in college. My mom tried to introduce me to him."

"So, you remember?" Mr. White asked, looking away. Then he gazed back at her. "Do you remember me?"

"You were my professor in History," Mara said softly. "You kept apologizing for the way Karl acted." She stared at him. "You know who I am?"

Mr. White nodded. "I have known for some time," he hesitated. "Been trying to figure out how to talk to you."

The older man glanced around, appearing nervous of prying eyes.

"I knew your parents for quite some time," he continued. "I planned with Daniella to introduce the two of you. But things did not go as planned."

"Is that because I reminded him of his wife?"

Mr. White nodded. "I tried to help him get over his loss and move on, and that's where you come in, Mara Ashwood. You two met again in college.

Eventually, you did grow close." He frowned at her. "I must ask—do you remember the day Karl asked for your hand in marriage?"

Mara gawked at him, her mind reeling from the revelation. She shook her head.

"Well, he proposed to you. And you accepted. Before the wedding, we travelled to the Temple of Kallisto for a ceremony—a custom of the Faith. We summoned the Goddess. However..." the older man sighed, "I wish I could go back in time."

"How did I die?" Mara asked.

Mr. White's face turned pale. He refused to answer her question.

Karl emerged from the throne room. He gazed at the two while approaching them.

"The High Priestess will see you now." Karl stared at her briefly before turning around and leading them into the next room.

They entered the throne room. Alena, veiled in white gauzy fabric, sat on a golden throne high atop a flight of stairs. Two pillars of gold and ivory stood on both sides of the throne, lit with flames. Dark red drapes cascaded behind her. Walking into the room, Mara felt very uneasy. This room was familiar, but the details remained elusive. Mara felt annoyed with her amnesia. Something was not right, but she brushed it off. Getting here for an audience won over that nagging feeling. Both Mr. White and Karl bent the knee before the priestess. Mara took notice and followed suit.

High Priestess Alena gazed at Mara. "So, you rescued my valuable commander many times?"

Mara glanced up at the priestess' veiled face. "Yes, I have."

"And you are the one who turned him against me?" Alena asked, her voice becoming harsh.

Mara never expected to hear these words from the older woman. She looked at the father and son. Karl glanced back at her, expressing surprise as well. Mr. White, on the other hand, gazed at her with eyes full of sorrow and guilt.

Mara looked back at the priestess. "What are you talking about?"

"I know what you are," Alena hissed. "The depraved slave girl who desired Lord Kratés and Queen Kallisto's throne. The one who awoke the Dark One and allowed it to destroy the world. Now you have returned to lead my commander astray."

Mara's mouth dropped open, for the mad woman's claims left her baffled. Glancing around, she noticed the ominous stares of Kallikratés' followers. She felt uncomfortable. Mara glanced back at her.

"All the undying are fragments of the one who awoke the Dark One. You, who broke three seals, are one of them." Alena pointed at her. "You, Mara Ashwood, are the Cursed Herald!"

Mara was shocked. They knew her name.

"Your name is very appropriate," the priestess remarked, "for an incomplete fragment."

Karl rose to join Mara. He took her hand and held on as if to never let go. Mara gazed up at him, seeing sorrow and guilt in his eyes.

"Commander White," Alena addressed. "Turn away from her and look upon me."

Karl closed his eyes. "No, I will not."

"You are the reincarnation of Lord Kratés," Alena told him. "It is your destiny to join the Goddess."

Mara stared at the older woman in shock, and then to Karl. He kept his eyes closed as he shook his head. The priestess rose from her seat and descended the stairs.

"You choose her over me? The one responsible for the death of your progenitor?" Alena's voice began to change. No longer did she sound like an old crone but a younger woman. "Now, I see how unwell you are." She looked at Mara. "She has poisoned your mind against me."

Mara glared at the veiled priestess. She wanted to say something but was interrupted.

"I am free," Karl murmured.

Mara looked at him, confused by his words.

Alena stared at them while reaching for her cover. "Look at me and love me!"

Upon removing her veil, the priestess unleashed a flash of light that blinded everyone.

Once the light faded, Mara finally saw the woman behind the veil. The woman was beyond beautiful with flawless pale skin and long blond hair. Her thin lips and nose sat on a heart-shaped face, which looked identical to the ivory sculpture. It was the goddess, Kallisto! High Priestess Alena was only a disguise.

The goddess cast her golden gaze onto her followers. Everyone, except Mara, sank to their knees. Falling under her spell, no man was safe from her beauty. Even Mr. White fell under her thrall.

Mara looked at her, but only felt dread. One could claim she was jealous, yet seeing the goddess resurrected a profound memory—the day she died. She looked at Karl, who also became bewitched. He released Mara's hand and fell to his knees.

"Karl," Mara called, but could not reach him. She glanced around, only to find everyone completely enthralled. Mara turned around to see Kallisto approaching Karl with fluid and grace.

The goddess reached out, stroking the side of his face. Karl closed his eyes as his head followed the motion of her divine hand.

"Come," Kallisto ordered.

Karl rose to his feet and walked to the goddess.

Mara saw this and lifted her hand.

"Karl, no…" Mara reached over to grab his right arm, but he suddenly jerked it away. Mara stared at him, stunned by his cold demeanour. She felt hurt but knew this was not him. He was falling under a spell.

Kallisto's intoxicating beauty drugged his senses. She caressed his face and gazed into his eyes, hypnotizing him and drawing out his desires. She leaned in and pressed her lips to his own.

Mara grew horrified. This scenario was worse than the time she saw him with Morgan. Karl was not pulling away. Instead, he deepened in the kiss while holding Kallisto. Seeing them together caused her mind to drift back to the day she died.

Her former fiancé and his father persuaded her into coming to the temple, unbeknownst to her family and friends. They claimed it was a custom, a test to prove Karl loved her more than Kallisto. If he resisted, their marriage would be blessed. Mara hoped he would pass, for she believed in him. Unfortunately, that never happened. She remembered trying to save him, only to lose her life in the process.

Eventually, Kallisto slipped from Karl's embrace and looked at Mara in triumph. "Thirty years ago, I had slain you because you stood in the way of our love!"

Mara froze. "Thirty years?" She shook her head. "No, it can't be."

She looked back to see the disciples' evil stares. Even Mr. White and Karl appeared more cruel and malicious.

"No," Mara murmured. It was like a nightmare, but she could not wake up.

"Yes, it has been thirty years!" Kallisto hissed. "Just like that pitiful creature I punished, you tried to take away my beloved and awaken the Dark One!"

Mara's mind continued to reel. Thirty years was a long time. Were her parents still alive? Would her friends recognize her? She glanced at Karl and removed her hood and mask. Hopefully, seeing her face would make him realize he was under a spell. Instead, he looked away in disgust.

"Karl, please," she pleaded.

Instead, he glared at her. "Glad I didn't have to marry you."

Mara felt numb. She then saw Kallisto lifting her left hand to reveal a silver ring on her finger. It was the engagement ring Karl gave to Mara. After seeing Kallisto, he demanded the ring back and gave it to his new love. Kallisto gazed up and kissed Karl. Mara shook as tears blinded her view.

"We shall soon marry and rule the world as gods! But first…" Kallisto looked at Mara and approached her. In one quick motion, the goddess struck her across the face.

Mara fell to the ground, her face stinging from the hard hit. It would surely leave a mark.

Kallisto stared down at her. "I shall deal with this enemy of mine!"

Mara remained silent while getting up. She looked at no one, knowing she had no allies here. Everyone looked on in silence, anticipating the defeat of their greatest enemy—this so-called Cursed Herald. The goddess lifted her hand, poised to strike her down.

"You—" Mara was cut off. It felt like a fireball had hit her. The burning sensation sent her into shock as she flew through the air briefly. Upon hitting the ground, every bone felt broken. All her strength waned away. Mara was going to die, and all of her efforts undone. As the life left her, Mara watched her murderer hold Karl in her embrace, kissing him.

"No," Mara hissed.

She refused to let it end this way. The rage glowed brightly in her heart, like embers from a flame. The fire rushed through her veins as the hatred seeped deep into her bones. Her left hand twitched, then tightened into a fist. Her eyes began to glow while watching the two. She planted her left hand onto the floor. A dark aura exuded from her as she tried to lift her broken body. She lifted her head to show her undead and scar-riddled visage. Her bones shifted and cracked, causing her to groan.

Kallisto and Karl pulled away from each other and watched her get up. Everyone was surprised to see her swift resurrection.

Kallisto glared at Mara. "What is this? How are you still alive?"

Mara scowled back at Kallisto. Loud cracking sounds could be heard from her body as her bones reset. Her dark aura strengthened, scaring the followers. None had witnessed the power of an undying, especially within a sacred place. Focusing on her target, Mara reached for her sword.

"You will pay," Mara hissed, unsheathing her blade. She bared her teeth as her fangs grew.

The goddess glared at her, showing no fear. "How dare you produce a blade upon a deity?"

Mara dashed at her, wanting to kill her.

Kallisto lifted her hand to strike her down again. A blue glow emanated from within the undying's cloak. The moonstone activated, neutralizing the magic of the goddess. In a blind rage, Mara dashed straight for her. Despite wanting revenge, Mara did not think this through.

Intense pain stopped her in her tracks. She gazed down to see a sword impaling her through the abdomen. Recognizing the Hand of Kratés, her eyes drifted up to the face of the one who stabbed her. Commander White dashed in between Mara and Kallisto, to protect his beloved queen.

The yellow glow in Mara's eyes faded. Blood seeped from her mouth. Tears welled up in her eyes as she broke down. "How could you?"

The commander just glared at her, disgusted at her undead appearance. With no intention of explaining himself, he pulled his sword out.

Mara hit the ground with a thud. Her body writhed in pain. Looking up at the commander, she lifted her hand to reach him. She thought about the moments they had. All the times they spent together, and the first kiss they shared. All those happy memories shattered before her eyes. Tears streamed down her face.

"Karl, please," Mara cried.

Commander White stared at her for a while. Enraptured by Kallisto's beauty, none of her words reached him. No longer did he see Mara, but a low creature who tried to harm his goddess. He walked away from her.

She tried to reach him again. "Karl…"

He ignored her and returned to his goddess. The commander approached Kallisto and embraced her. Kallisto caressed his face and leaned in to kiss him.

Mara tried to get up again, only to be flanked by the Holy Blades. They stabbed her to death with their weapons, and her blood drained onto the cold floor. Her vision of Kallisto and Karl became blurry and bloody. Everything faded to black.

Chapter Twenty-Two

Hope's Chime

Here she was again, lying in the darkness. Within the silence, Mara could hear herself crying. The image of Kallisto kissing Karl bored deep into her mind. The goddess took her prince away, turning him against her. She could not save Karl. She felt useless. Mara wished she had the strength to defeat a god.

A lone bell chimed within the darkness. Mara heard the bell before, making such a delicate sound. It was a call of desperation, pulling her from her death-like slumber. The bell rang again, seemingly so close, but was nowhere in sight. The soft ring came from the other side, calling out to Mara.

"You already have it." The mask of the Watcher appeared before her face. Seven blue eyes glowed in the darkness. "Mara, wake up!"

The tingling sensation returned one more time. It was like little embers dancing in the darkness. Soon they touched every nerve in her body and caught fire. The burning sensation rushed through her, jolting her awake.

Mara's eyes flew open. Looking around, she saw only darkness. There was no sign of the Watcher. She was alone. Mara tried to move, only to find herself confined within a tight space. The lid would not budge. Mara began to hit it, trying to force it open. She bashed her fists repeatedly until her knuckles began to bleed. The smell of blood added to the stench of her blood-soaked clothing. A large crack formed, and a faint light poured in. She kept at it, and the lid eventually broke open.

She took a deep breath before sitting up and looking around. She was inside a black and gold coffin. Looking at her surroundings, Mara saw torches adorning the brick hallway. She was back in the Dark Labyrinth, assuming Kallisto had her tossed down here again. To make matters worse, she lost all her weapons and valuables. Only her necklace, the keepsakes, a brass key, and the flask filled with Moon Water remained. Seemingly useless trinkets they allowed her to keep. But with the brass key, Mara still had a chance of escaping.

Upon getting out of the coffin, she heard a familiar growl. The guttural sounds bounced off the walls, echoing all around her. Mara had to get out of here. She chose a path and began to follow it, hoping it would lead her out.

Mara could not see anything within this dark path. Remembering the Moon Water, she took her flask and began to shake it. The glowing particles in the water grew brighter, but she still could not recall her surroundings.

As Mara searched for a way out, her mind continued to reel from all that happened. She could not believe someone would want her dead. Why should Mara be judged for the actions of a predecessor? There had to be more to this.

While being deep in her thoughts, a creature ran at her and grabbed her head. Mara felt a sharp pain in her neck as it broke. Everything went black.

* * *

After some time, she awoke to the fire rushing in her veins. Opening her eyes, Mara saw the monster towering over her. She recognized the bird-like head and the four bulging white eyes. The Dark Dweller made a creepy guttural growl. The smell of her blood attracted the creature. It had no problem finding her in the dark.

Mara saw this creature before. It happened thirty years ago, after being struck down by Kallisto. She resurrected and sought a way out of the Dark Labyrinth, but encountered this creature. It killed her before. She returned to life again, only to find the monster tearing into her abdomen and ripping out her uterus, thus solving the mystery of the ugly scar. The massive blood loss killed her. Not only was it disturbing, but the way it gazed at Mara showed its intentions to do this. Afterwards, it pretty much left her alone, unless they crossed paths again. She did not know why it mutilated her like that.

The monster stared back at her and began to cry. Mara was baffled. What brought on this strange behaviour? The cries sounded like a man overwhelmed by grief. The creature walked away but never went too far. It crouched down and continued to weep. Mara recalled a similar sound the last time she escaped from the Dark Labyrinth. Trying not to make any quick movements, she slowly rose to her feet. The creature whipped its head around and stared at her.

Mara ran for dear life, her heart pounding like a drum. The monster chased her, making a low growl. After a moment of running, she stopped. The creature was no longer pursuing her. She wandered into a large dark room filled with corpses. The stench of death invaded her nostrils and made her cringe. Not wanting to stick around, Mara left the room.

Where was the exit? Wandering the maze, she could hear the creature. Its growls echoed throughout the hallways. Finally, she found the gate to her freedom, but someone locked it again.

"Damn it," Mara hissed, shaking the bars.

She remembered the key, but the rattling of the bars echoed in the hallways. The creature responded with a guttural growl. Turning around, Mara saw it dashing towards her. Despite having no weapon, Mara refused to let it kill her again. As the monster came close, she fought back. The two struggled to the ground. The creature rolled on top of her, trying to grasp at her head and pulled the mask off. Managing to wrap its dirty hands around her neck, it strangled the life out of her. At the last possible moment, her eyes flew open. She saw her fist plunging into its torso. Bright red blood gushed out of the creature. It fell off of her and slumped to her right. Mara stared at the monster as her heart pulsated. She lifted her hand to her face and wiped the blood away.

After being killed and mutilated many years ago, she finally got her revenge. Still stunned at what happened, she scrambled away from the creature. It was still alive. The Dark Dweller looked up at her, trying to reach out. It made gurgling sounds once again as if it was trying to form words.

"Ah... Amara..."

Mara was mystified. Did the creature try to call her by name? The Dark Dweller began to transform. In its place was an emaciated man with brown skin and short black hair. He had some resemblance to her, yet she did not recognize him. Tears spilled from his dark brown eyes.

"Amara, I'm so sorry," the man pleaded. "Please, forgive me."

Mara shook her head. "I'm not Amara. Who are you?"

He looked at her in bewilderment. "Oh, you are one of them? So was my daughter..."

She shrugged, unsure what he meant.

"He wanted to buy her, but I refused his gold," the man continued in a feeble tone. "That evil king sought to defile her. I would not allow his seed to grow. He threw me out and took her away..."

Mara stared at him. Now she knew why he mutilated her.

"They hurt her, lied about her... I confronted them. That vile witch tried to fool me, but I knew the truth. They trapped me down here, so I would never tell anyone. I remember now. My daughter is bound to Aazalith. The divine's soul must return to its rightful place."

Mara stood frozen before the mysterious man. She recalled Harold's words about a certain monk, who was missing for a thousand years. According to Lady Isabella, he also had a daughter.

"Are you Khan?" Mara asked.

The man nodded feebly. "I beseech thee," he spoke. "Save my daughter. End her suffering." His body began to crumble away into dust. "I failed to protect her from evil..."

Mara watched as Khan faded away. In his place was a healing stone. After claiming her prize, it was time to escape the Dark Labyrinth. She took the brass key out and looked at the gate. Mara unlocked it and left. Why no one took the key away was beyond her.

* * *

As Mara headed for the exit, she heard voices in the distance. Her escape from the Dark Labyrinth was too good to be true. Two men came her way. There was nowhere for her to hide. At the end of the pathway, she saw two Holy Blades wielding gold and silver swords. They took notice and dashed towards her. She suspected they came to prevent her escape. Mara needed to fight. There was no going back.

One of the men lunged at her with his sword. She stepped back and dodged him. When he came at her again, she grabbed his sword hand and pushed his blade back onto him. The sword sliced through his face and neck. He died before he fell to the ground. Mara grabbed his sword and armed herself. Then she turned her attention to the other. In her blind rage, she stormed over to him with the intent to kill. He backed away and lifted his hands.

"Wait! Let's talk this over!"

Mara stared at him in confusion. Since when did a Holy Blade want to talk? Then it dawned on her. She recognized that voice. The short black hair and smug face were also familiar. She grabbed Boyd by the collar and scowled at him.

"I should have known," Mara hissed. "You have a lot of nerve showing your face here."

"Well, just hold on a minute," he pleaded. "I know I've done you wrong. I didn't mean it. I'm sorry."

"Sorry? You're sorry?" Mara shook her head. "That is not going to undo all the shit I went through!"

Mara lifted the sword, ready to stab him in the face. He squeezed his eyes shut.

"The commander did it!" Boyd spat out some words to save himself. It worked.

Mara gazed at him in confusion and lowered her sword. "What are you talking about?"

Boyd opened his eyes and looked at her. He took a deep breath and lowered his hands.

"Commander White killed Saskia," he said candidly. "She knew what you were and intended to take you to Greyward Hold. The commander found out, broke into her home, and fatally stabbed her with a moonstone weapon. We conspired to frame you for murder."

She gaped at him for a while, then lifted her sword again.

"You knew?" Mara grew furious. "That village executed me!"

"You were a prisoner!" Boyd claimed. "It was the only way to recapture you."

She began to tremble. "I was innocent!"

Mara had every reason not to trust him, but Boyd had more to reveal.

"Wait! The deaths of the other possessors are also Kallikratés' doing!"

She looked confused. "Hema's ruler was responsible for the deaths of Saskia and Heru. I had to save Karl from Isabella and Anna!"

"That's what the Faith wants everyone to think," Boyd confessed. "The commander was never glamoured into writing that letter. He did it of his own free will, to make Heru and you kill each other! With Lady Isabella and Anna, Karl placed himself in danger and had his old man beg you for help. He knew Hema's queen planned to hold them hostage. And he had the seal on the Black Tower tampered with, so the darkling's powers could reach out. The commander knew you'd save him and used you to avoid suspicion to themselves."

She stared at Boyd with surprise and softened her grip on his collar. She released him and backed away after hearing this new revelation. The aggression faded from her face as she grew calmer, though curiosity remained.

"Who are you?" Mara asked.

"Boyd Masterson, Church Spy," he revealed. "The exit is guarded by four Holy Blades."

"Why are you helping me?" Mara questioned.

"I'm helping myself. I've been trying to pay off a debt to the Faith for a minor infraction they took offence to."

"What did you do?"

"Nothing too serious," Boyd said. "But they still don't trust me. They have even kept me on a tight leash. Well, I have a few choice words for them—praying has never put food in my mouth nor anyone else's! Kallikratés doesn't care for the common or poor folk. It relies on nobles and their money, like your Prince Charming."

Mara shook her head, feeling embarrassed to know another was aware of her attraction to Commander White.

"I was a petty thief and got caught," he spoke. "They gave me a choice—serve the Faith or end up in the Dark Labyrinth."

She folded her arms. "Now, you want me to help with your great escape from the Faith?"

"I'll never cross paths with you again," Boyd promised. "You have my word."

She raised an eyebrow. What kind of promise was that? Then again, if she never saw his face again, she would not miss him.

"Fine, I suppose I can help you," she sighed.

Boyd nodded. "Good, now let's get out of here!" He walked ahead of her. "This place makes me feel sick."

"What do you mean?"

"Don't you feel it? There's a strange power in this mountain. It feels dark, almost wicked. I don't even know why anyone would want to build a temple or a palace."

Mara looked at him. She never expected to hear those words from his mouth. Following Boyd to the exit, she heard voices.

"Oh, that's them," Boyd said.

She unsheathed her sword, ready to fight them.

Boyd held his hand out in front of her. "Wait! I have an idea."

She gazed in confusion while he walked out. He began to limp, holding his right arm. The Holy Blades noticed him.

"What are you doing out here, Masterson?"

Boyd appeared shaken up. "My partner is dead."

"What of the prisoner?"

"We couldn't contain her. She is coming this way!"

Boyd then gestured to Mara. The Holy Blades took notice and approached her with their swords drawn.

Whatever Boyd's plan was, it was not a good one. Then again, Mara had to fight them. As she got ready for battle, Boyd pulled a blade on one of the Holy Blades and stabbed him in the back. The Holy Blade cried out before falling to the ground dead. The others turned and looked at Boyd. They were not going to tolerate his betrayal. Mara took the opportunity to kill another Holy Blade before they realized their mistake of ignoring her. With their unexpected teamwork, Mara and Boyd turned the tables on their opponents. However, one of them escaped.

"Damn it!" Boyd exclaimed. "One got away!"

She looked back at him and shrugged. "So?"

He shot a glare at her. "So? So? In case you haven't realized, one of them survived! He'll report to the Faith and the Holy Blades. They will turn every village, town, and city upside down to find us! We're now wanted fugitives."

He turned his attention onto the dead and began to search the bodies. After robbing the corpses, Boyd tossed a bag worth five hundred gold to Mara.

"Here, we're going to need this to buy some equipment or provisions. Don't feel too bad. The gold was likely yours before being captured."

Mara gazed at Boyd for a while and then turned around. She began to walk down the same mountain path, towards Ozin Village. He looked at her in bewilderment.

"Where do you think you're going?" Boyd demanded.

She stopped and stared down at the path. "I'm going to find my parents. I need to make sure they are okay."

She began to walk again, but Boyd ran in front of her.

"Maybe you misunderstood me? You are a wanted fugitive! Once the Faith learns about your escape, there will be nowhere for you to hide!" Boyd then gave a sombre look. "Besides, your parents are probably dead."

"What did you say?" Mara glared at him.

Boyd gazed at her. "I saw everything. If it's true and thirty years have passed for you, then your parents might be gone. It may not be worth going to Mirahyll."

She stared at him.

"Thanks for caring," she murmured in a cold tone, walking past him.

Boyd gazed at her and shook his head.

"Don't say I didn't warn you," he said calmly, and then went the other way.

It was the last time Mara saw him.

* * *

Mara wandered the forest. She was here before, except all the leaves had fallen as snow covered the ground. The birds were absent, and it was dead quiet. She eventually saw Ozin, where she first met Saskia. It was also the place of her execution. The village was crawling with Holy Blades. If they were not looking for her now, they would in due time. She needed to keep a distance, for no allies would be found there. Mara felt alone, but that was not true.

There was Harold, given he remained alive. If the Faith were responsible for the seals failing, then the last two were targets. And the former guild master might know about the undying bound to the Dark One.

There was also Talon. The old blacksmith had been a valuable ally. She needed to find him and see if he could forge a new weapon for her. Mara missed her straight sword.

Thinking of Dr. Moen and the Watcher, she had to see them. Thanks to them, she got most of her memories back. Her mind began to wonder about Dr. Moen. The last time she saw Allen and James, they were around her age at twenty-five years. Today, they would both be in their mid-fifties. Thinking about the doctor's bright blue eyes, Mara began to realize who he was.

Despite knowing what became of her friends, another thing bothered her. Karl, or Commander White, who remained the same. If thirty years had passed, he should have aged with the rest of them. But he stayed the same, just like Mara. Many thoughts ran through her head, like Morgan discussing Karl's special status. There was also that thing Dr. Moen mentioned—that a human could become a god. But if he were so powerful, he should have been able to resist Kallisto, which led to another thing.

Mara had to find a way to save him. After seeing what happened to Karl, she could not leave him like that. She needed to find a way to defeat Kallisto. It seemed crazy taking on a god, but Kallisto was the reason why Mara became cursed. If the Faith did this to her, could they be responsible for the others? Kallisto and her followers had to pay, but for now, Mara needed to find her family.

It would be difficult explaining to her parents what happened. Not only was she inhuman, but she also became an enemy of the Faith. But she could no longer hold this secret another day. Mara wondered if she should have contacted them sooner. Would it even make a difference? Either way, she needed to reach Mirahyll.

Mara looked around. Being on the trail was a bad idea. Getting off the road, she disappeared into the forest. Her cape fluttered as she dashed past the trees. Delving deeper into the woods, the huntress wondered about her current state. She could have given up, stay trapped in the coffin, and rotted away until the end of time. Instead, she broke free and fled from her oppressors. She planned to find her family and friends, who cared for her deeply. Mom and Dad never gave up on her, so why should she? Now that she thought about it, Mara was more human than monster. And no longer was she the lost and cursed, as long as hope remained.

About the Author

Rina S. Mamoon started writing ever since she could pick up a pencil. Currently living in the City of Edmonton, Alberta, she got into fiction writing at the age of fifteen. Among her favourite stories are Hans Christian Andersen's *The Snow Queen*, and H. Rider Haggard's *She*. Rina is also a fan of fantasy movies like *The Lord of the Rings*, *The Hobbit*, and *The Mummy*, and video games such as *Demon's Souls*, *Baten Kaitos*, and *Bloodborne*. In addition to writing, she is also a digital artist.

www.ingramcontent.com/pod-product-compliance
Lightning Source LLC
Chambersburg PA
CBHW061222170626
46809CB00007B/2550